PENGUIN BOOKS

THE MANDARIN ROSE

Aishwariyaa Ramakanthan's writing is a fusion of flavours. It is reflective of the multi-cultural ethos of her birthplace, Singapore; of the languid grace of Malaysia where she was raised; of the eclectic lifestyles of the United States where she now lives; and of the rich cultural heritage of India, where she engages in her other passion, Indian Classical music. Ramakanthan is a graduate of the National University of Singapore and the University of San Diego, California. She travels to Singapore frequently to reconnect with family and friends and to energize her bond with the city. Typically a night owl, Aishwariyaa writes best when the rest of the world is asleep. Her first novel, *Beyond the Shores of Home*, is available on Amazon.

T0096229

The Mandarin Rose

Aishwariyaa Ramakanthan

PENGUIN BOOKS

An imprint of Penguin Random House

PENGUIN BOOKS

USA | Canada | UK | Ireland | Australia
New Zealand | India | South Africa | China | Southeast Asia

Penguin Books is part of the Penguin Random House group of companies
whose addresses can be found at global.penguinrandomhouse.com

Published by Penguin Random House SEA Pte Ltd
9, Changi South Street 3, Level 08-01,
Singapore 486361

First published in Penguin Books by Penguin Random House SEA 2023
Copyright © Aishwariyaa Ramakanthan 2023

ISBN 9789815058857

Typeset in Adobe Caslon Pro by MAP Systems, Bengaluru, India

www.penguin.sg

For my mother, the strongest woman I have ever known.

Contents

Prologue

The hands that held the *chim* bucket were surprisingly unlined and still very delicate, like they were unaccustomed to hard work, much like the woman whose hands they were. Carrying herself with the grace and dignity of one who cared about her appearance; she did not look her eighty years. Her face still bore traces of the beauty she must have enjoyed in her best years. The ambient air where she stood was infused with a faint and curious but very pleasant scent—a mix of rose, lavender and lemon. Well-dressed in a salmon-pink silk blouse and black trousers and artfully made-up, complete with bright pink lipstick, she stood in stark contrast to the companion who stood by her side, a younger, grim-faced woman in white and black, who looked like she had long forgotten the virtues of a smile. The companion stood watching as she held on to the older woman's cane and handbag. Her mouth drooped at the ends, perhaps dragged down by unrealized dreams. Her hands, like her face, were worn and lined by the unending toil they had felt for years.

The presence of the dour-faced companion with lined hands was easily eclipsed by the older woman with her gentle smile, her still-attractive face, and an unabashed display of brilliant gems on her ears and her hands. Diamonds and emeralds sparkled on her ears and on most of the fingers of her hands. Perhaps the most eye-catching piece of jewellery that she wore was the bangle on her now-thin wrist. It was a circle of gold encrusted with diamonds, held together by a clasp at the top, which was fashioned like a dragon with a jade ball in its mouth. The dragon head sparkled with emeralds and rubies. It was her favourite piece of jewellery, and she considered it her lucky charm. She always wore it to the temple so that she could present her most fortunate self to the goddess Gun Yam, who would then give her the best answer to her question through the bamboo sticks, the *chim*.

Looking up reverently at the goddess, she held up the *chim* bucket and swirled it around in the smoke that curled out of the incense burner, to cleanse the *chim* bucket of any evil forces before she shook it. Then, with her eyes fixed on the deity, she muttered her question slowly and clearly, leaving little opportunity for doubt in the goddess's mind. Next, she shook the bucket and held it just so to ensure that only one stick fell out. If too many sticks fell out, she would have to perform the ritual again. Her question was always the same, about the same person. And the goddess smiled down at her benevolently like she knew what the woman had in mind. After all, she had been coming to the temple for years now—much like a weekly pilgrimage, asking the same questions about only one person, her daughter, who was hers and yet not hers, and through whom she derived the greatest of joys and then, at times, the deepest of sorrows.

The Players

Chapter One

Linda would have been reduced to tears by now if Ma had been listening, thought Simon, glancing at his mother a tad nervously. Linda was the relatively new senior marketing manager, whose hire Rose had not endorsed. Ethan, one of Rose's twin sons, had insisted on hiring her, and Simon had supported his brother, much to their mother's annoyance. Linda was typical of the kind of young woman that his mother disliked—smart but overtly aggressive and too self-assured. 'This is the type that is impatient and unwilling to learn the right way. They will learn by making mistakes that could cost the company. She has no finesse even in the way she interacts with the staff. She always sounds like she is whining, and she does not display any leadership. How can she lead a campaign?' she had often told Simon after Linda was hired about six months ago. Simon was now worried that Linda was quickly digging her own grave with a presentation that was low on facts but high on ambition.

Thankfully, other than Simon, no one else guessed that Rose Lee, the much-admired self-made millionaire Chairman and CEO of Lee Constructions, one of the largest construction companies in Asia, was restless and had absolutely no interest in the presentation about one of her company's most expensive ventures. Lately, it was becoming increasingly difficult for her to focus on the business. Her eyes, her most beautiful feature because of their perfect almond shape, looked a little glazed, red-rimmed and sleep-deprived. The lines that had just recently begun to appear around them looked deeper because of the time and length of the day. The light brown of her eyes, not exactly common for a Chinese, hinted at a hidden story that had intrigued her as a teenager. Much to her chagrin then, her earnest queries had been dismissed by her parents with a laugh. 'Sometimes these things happen. Don't worry, we didn't pick you up from somewhere,' they had said good-humouredly. 'Maybe we have some long-forgotten *Ang Moh* ancestor.' As the years passed, the mystery had ceased to be of great concern to her. But she had certainly enjoyed the attention that those beautiful brown eyes, coupled with her flawless alabaster skin and shiny straight black hair, had attracted.

Even now, if not for those lines around her eyes and the strands of grey that showed in her black hair, Rose's appearance defied her sixty years. With her dignified good looks, her always stylishly coiffured hair, and her impeccable sense of style, she still made heads turn when she walked into any room. Her still clear and luminescent skin was a cause for envy among women much younger. 'Surgery for sure,' her younger staff tittered. 'How can a sixty-year-old not have a single line?' was often the focus of their lunchtime conversation. 'Good genes!' would be the rejoinder from the disapproving older staff who happened to be around. 'Her mother is just like that, the same porcelain skin. Still so beautiful at eighty,' they would continue, looking at each other and nodding in agreement among themselves. 'If you are a good person, it shows on your face,' was their rebuke to the cringing youngsters.

Rose flicked a glance at her watch as she absently felt her mother-of-pearl and diamond earrings and shifted in her seat, leaning back and tapping ever so gently on the armrest of her leather chair. She uncrossed her legs and then crossed them again, flicking an imaginary speck of dust off her ink-blue dress. The Rose of five months ago would have been sitting upright, her ramrod straight back not once touching the back of the chair, taking notes and shooting questions at the presenter. Making a presentation to 'the boss' was the acid test that made or broke a new manager in the company, and even her seasoned managers dreaded it. While she could be generous with the bonuses that came with the praise when a job was well done, Rose was known to be ruthless with slackers or those who did not deliver what she expected of them.

Much to Simon's sorrow, most of the staff—except for a few old-timers who had stayed on over the years—only knew this side of her and not the real Rose, who was warm, vulnerable and kind. Shy and private by nature, the Rose Lee that most people now saw rarely smiled and merely nodded when she approved. Even the charities to which Rose donated thousands of dollars every year never saw her at their galas. It was always Simon, or one of the twins or Peter, when he had been alive, who went in her place. 'You are unrealistic in your demands, Ma. And you have alienated yourself even from the boys,' Simon would often say. 'The boys' were Rose's twin sons from her marriage with her second husband, Peter, who was now dead. Growing up, they had rarely seen their mother, who at that time was in a great rush to grow the business or 'make money'. This was a sore point that Rose's mother, Sylvia, was fond of scoffing.

'Now your sons don't know you,' Sylvia chided, to which Rose retorted, 'Did I have a choice, Ma?'

To be fair, Rose made no excuses for the time she had invested into what began as a humble real estate and construction business. She had set it up using borrowed capital from her mother's embroidery business while living in her parents' two-bedroom Housing Development Board apartment in the Commonwealth area. The business was now Lee Constructions, an empire that operated out of its own steel and glass building in the centre of the island city with offices in several major cities around the world. 'Would you have preferred that we remained poor, Ma?' Rose would continue, doing her best to keep the edge out of her tone.

'Well, Rosie, as your father used to say, nothing comes for free. This is the price for the money you made,' was Sylvia's calm rejoinder laced with the cynicism that did not escape Rose.

Sadly, even those who dearly loved Rose, like Simon, felt that over the years she had become hard to like—always demanding perfection, and completely and implacably intolerant of fools. And, yet, they could not deny that Rose's journey had not been easy. They had watched her grow from a helpless young widow with a young son and a mountain of debt left by a compulsive gambler first husband into the perspicacious success that she was now.

'Mrs Lee?'

Snapped back into the present and suddenly aware of all the eyes in the room looking at her, Rose stared at Linda, completely at a loss for words.

'We were talking about the new development in Kuala Lumpur. Would you agree that we need to increase the budget for its marketing? Especially with the competitors' new developments cropping up there too?' said Linda.

Simon cleared his throat uncomfortably, as if preparing to speak on his mother's behalf. Ethan, who was sitting directly across from him, first looked at his mother from above his glasses and then shifted his gaze to his brother with a raised eyebrow. Simon shook his head subtly and opened his mouth to speak but fell silent when his mother stood up abruptly. 'Well, this is the time to use all the training we have given you here, Linda. You make that decision and let's see where that takes us,' she said crisply, as she shut the folder in front of her with a snap and walked out briskly. As was usual these days, her face was inscrutable, even to her sons. No one in the room could tell if 'the boss' was serious, or if she was so displeased that she was telling Linda off for the shoddy work that was apparent to some of the senior staff.

The heavy glass door of the conference room closed quietly as staff members watched the tall, regal figure in stilettos walk away with her back straight and head held high, as always. While some looked surprised, some actually had their mouths open in wonder. This had never happened before. The boss had never walked away without having the final say on meetings. Simon reddened when his eyes caught Linda, who was gathering up her papers and looking like she was about to either burst into tears or explode in anger. He stood up quickly and walked to her. Gently patting her on the shoulder, he asked her to take a seat so they could finish the meeting. He smiled at his audience as he made apologies for his mother's strange behaviour. 'She did mention that she wasn't feeling very well. And, I think she has quite a bit of confidence in you, Linda. So, as she said, go ahead, set the direction for this project. Just keep us posted.' He sounded hollow even to himself but there wasn't really any other way to save the situation. Linda lowered her eyes and thus hid the maleficence that glinted in them. As she shuffled busily through her papers she thought to herself, *The bitch! If it wasn't for what's at stake, I have a good mind to just slam through that fucking door of hers and tell her what a hag she is.* As the others left the room, Simon caught Ethan's eye and nodded towards his cabin, which was next to the conference room.

Rose walked back to her office at the far end of the floor. She obviously had the most desired suite in the company, with a spectacular view of the island and the sea. Unlike the glass cubicles of all the other senior executives, Rose's room had solid walls that shielded her from prying eyes. Much like the person, everything in the office, from the solid black oak desk to the light grey Berber carpet, to the grey Boca Do Lobo sofa which sat against the wall, was minimalist and reflected Rose's impatience with fuss and small talk. The furniture, the books, the fountain pens, and the leather folders that Maryanne, her personal assistant, placed every morning on her desk with papers for her to look at and sign, all sat neatly in their place, unobtrusive but distinguished by quality and good taste. A single large painting by Liu Wei adorned one wall and potted foliage in a corner provided the only colour, but lush colour, to the otherwise sober and subdued room. The colour was more surprising than refreshing, much like the occupant of the room. There were rare moments when people close to 'the boss' were pleasantly surprised when the old light-hearted Rose re-emerged.

Rose flung the folder she had been carrying on her desk. Some of the papers it contained spilt out and scattered on the desk. She merely glanced at the mess of paper and walked towards the large window that framed the perfect picture of the sea glinting reddish-gold under the setting sun. The swanky city-state, which had been bathed by the brilliant sun all day long, now welcomed twilight with lights that gradually appeared as little dots everywhere. Rose stood staring out at the sea. Her fatigue, her anger and her helplessness at being unable to change anything that had happened overwhelmed her. Her frustration at having to hire someone for whom she had no respect was entangled in all of this. She had to say nothing for the sake of pleasing Ethan, her son, whom she was not sure she even liked at this point because of his father. It had been almost a year since Peter, her husband, had died, but she still went over her relationship with him at all hours of the day. Little things triggered memories that painfully peeled away the scab and revealed the raw wound beneath. Linda's presentation was bad, but the idea of another project in Malaysia was worse because it had been Peter's.

They had already completed six high-end luxury apartment projects all over the country when Peter had suggested one more, and she had been reluctant. She had been ambitious and wanted the company's fame and quality to be known in countries like China, Australia, and even the US; so, concentrating all their resources in Malaysia for the seventh time felt limiting. She had had an unavailing argument with Peter, who had been very insistent, and she had finally given in to keep the peace. 'And now look at the incompetent handling of the whole job by a *dud*! To hell with it. Let it all go to hell. I'm sick of it,' she whispered harshly through clenched teeth that seemed to be the only barrier to her exploding fury. Breathing heavily, she stood staring at the wide expanse of water that lay in the distance, with a deep frown etched on her otherwise smooth forehead and her usually calm brown eyes now steely with unspent anger. The tranquillity of the sea that stretched out beneath her had soothed her in the past but did nothing for her today. The race that she had been running for twenty-five years seemed to be coming to an ignominious end in a manner that she had never dreamt of. She could clearly remember, but not feel, the pride that had filled her when she had bought this building, because now Peter's stench was everywhere. And that was mostly the reason why it had lost its lustre.

A gentle knock on the door distracted her, and she glanced up. The heavy door opened slowly as 'Aunty', the tea-lady, shuffled in painfully on her arthritic legs, pushing a small tea trolley with a cup of steaming Teh-C kosong, black tea with Carnation milk and no sugar, Rose's favourite beverage, sitting on it. The wizened old woman, whose fingers were bent, carefully, and almost reverently, placed the cup and saucer on Rose's polished desk.

The clinking china broke the heavy stillness in the room, and the deep frown on Rose's forehead vanished as she chuckled resignedly and said in Hokkien, 'I have told you not to do this, Aunty. Make the tea and tell Maryanne. She will bring it in for me.'

'I will not let anyone else do this one little thing that I do for you,' replied the old woman without looking at Rose, in a raspy voice that suggested a personality that brooked no nonsense, even from the boss. A hint of a smile played on Rose's lips as she shook her head and watched the old woman slowly push her cart out of the room.

The anger that she had felt minutes ago had quietened, the steel in her eyes had softened, and the tightness in her jawline had relaxed somewhat. As soon as the doors closed noiselessly, Rose sighed and glanced down at her watch. She had a dinner date with Nalini and Penny, her two closest friends from school. But before that—she grimaced as she thought of 'the damn daily evening debrief with Simon'. Almost as soon as she thought of the meeting, she firmly resolved to skip it, before turning back to the window again.

Chapter Two

Peter, Rose's dead husband, had been the sort of man who could either help you or embarrass you. You would hang around him if you wanted to be introduced to someone who could do something for you. But otherwise, most people cringed, or at least stared aghast, as soon as he walked into a room, because everything about Peter—the thick gold chain around his neck, an equally thick gold bracelet on one wrist and a large gold Rolex watch on the other—hit people between the eyes and forced them to acknowledge that he was rich. In addition to all this gold, he was also never seen without his large gold ring set with an enormous green jade, which he claimed he had been given by a Taoist priest just a few months before he had met Rose. 'I met my lucky goddess after I got this jade,' he would say to anyone who asked and, after a few drinks, to everyone around him at the bar, even if they didn't ask. When his friends had teased him about the amount of jewellery he wore, his light-hearted response had been, 'I earned it, and I'm not ashamed to show it off.' He had had the same response the day Rose had been aghast when he had driven home in a brand new, gleaming, gold-coloured Mercedes Benz. He was not remotely awkward or embarrassed about having all eyes on him. 'In retrospect,' Rose scoffed, 'He lived for the drama and an audience around him. Which is why even his death and funeral were a spectacle.'

So, it had been a surprise to everyone who knew Rose, whose idea of accessories was rarely more than earrings and a watch, when she decided to marry Peter, about eleven years after her first husband, Stanley, had died. Sylvia, Rose's mother, in particular, had been flabbergasted. 'He is so crude, Rosie. What on earth do you see in him?' she had exclaimed after having dinner with her daughter and Peter. Rose had just told her mother about her marriage plans. Rose's response had been impatient and sharp. 'We're not exactly royalty, mum. He is a good man.' And that, he generally was. He enjoyed a good laugh, and he was generous with his money, particularly when inebriated. He was very good to Simon. He treated him exactly the same, if not better, than his own sons, and that eventually won Sylvia's heart. When Simon started working for the business, Peter, like Rose, trusted Simon's judgement implicitly. For Simon, whose own father was often missing while he lived, having Peter in his life as he entered adolescence reassured him. He had watched his mother sob uncontrollably after his father's death, fearful for the future. Peter gave him and his mother stability, and he was thankful for it. Simon even took to calling Peter 'baba' very soon after he entered their lives.

Even though he was loud and obnoxious when drunk, Peter was actually easier to like than Rose. He made friends easily, laughed aloud quite a bit, and put people at ease because they thought he was an open book, at least until the day he died. When Rose first met Peter, he was the owner of a small construction and interior decoration firm that she used as a realtor. She then started to work on small projects with him before their relationship grew into a more personal one. After their marriage, her acumen in the real estate business and his skill and experience in construction and interior decoration laid the foundation for Lee Constructions, which, over the years came to be known internationally for its elegant and high-quality buildings. While Peter had undoubtedly been the people-person who had brought in the business, it was Rose's focus and foresight that had turned the company into a phenomenal success. Peter would proudly and constantly refer to his wife as the 'mastermind behind the business'. He would laughingly and frequently declare, 'I would be a nobody if not for Rosie. She made me who I am.' Despite her discomfiture about Peter's open admiration of her, Rose couldn't help but glow in private when he spoke proudly about her.

While she was married to Peter, her life was perfect by most people's standards. She had a good husband, three wonderful sons, and a thriving business, with which she gained entry into the most elite circles of Singapore. 'One of Singapore's Most Successful Women' was the endorsement she got when she made it to the cover of *Style Singapore*, a luxury lifestyle publication. This was indeed more than she had ever imagined when she was struggling to make ends meet with a young son, soon after the death of her first husband. The problems that ensued, coupled with the sudden death of her father, who had supported her in her dark years, had put suicidal thoughts in her head, and it was about that time when she had met Peter. If Peter had seen Rose as his lucky goddess, Rose had seen him as a sort of saviour when she first got to know him.

Peter's devil-may-care personality, loud can-do attitude, and ability to live with panache even when money was not exactly plentiful were all new to Rose who had been nurtured by conservative and cash-strapped parents. Peter had never allowed a lack of money to encumber his flamboyance. Somehow, he would always find a way to dress well, eat well, and drink a lot. 'You should never let the world know that you don't have much in your pocket. You'll be sunk. Live like you have plenty and you will,' he would say when she worried about money, and it was this recklessness that Rose had found strangely exciting and rejuvenating, even though he sometimes embarrassed her with his flashiness. He never let anything or anyone dampen his spirits. Everything was possible in Peter's world, and restraint was not something that he took seriously.

Although Rose did not stop to think about whether she loved Peter, she knew from the first day she met him that she found him immensely invigorating—a refreshing change from the drabness of her life at that time. Even before her marriage to Stanley, money had been barely enough for her middle-class family to live with dignity and without debt. Her father ran a noodle stall at a hawker centre, and her mother was a seamstress. It had been Rose's excellence at school that had won her a scholarship to the Annenberg School for Communications and Journalism at the University of Southern California. Brimming with passion and hope for the future, Rose returned to Singapore confident that her life and that of her parents would be a little more affluent. Soon after she returned, she found herself a job that she liked in a boutique PR firm as a junior executive, with the promise of greater things in the future. By this time, her mother had become a well-known seamstress specializing in custom-made clothing for clients as far as Europe. Everything looked very rosy and hopeful, but unfortunately for Rose, Stanley, an old junior college crush and his yen for gambling and get-rich-quick schemes, came along.

Stanley had kept his gambling habit a secret until the debts became too huge for him to pay by himself on his sales executive salary. By the time Rose found out about the gravity of the problem, Simon was four years old. After that, her marital life became troubled, and she had to rely heavily on her parents for emotional, and sometimes financial, support. In addition to that, the stress of her tumultuous personal life proved to be too much for her demanding job in the PR firm, and she was forced to quit. About the time when the situation was worsening, with debt collectors banging on her door and Stanley disappearing for days, Rose received news in the wee hours of one morning that her husband was seriously ill and had been admitted to the Singapore General Hospital. Other than his gambling, something else that Stanley had kept hidden were his serious drinking problem and cirrhosis. 'I didn't even know that he drank so much, Ma,' Rose had cried to her mother. Her world had quickly withered with Stanley's death when Simon had been just about seven or eight.

But when Peter came along, loud and boisterous, about two years later, a whole new colourful world blossomed for her. Everything was beyond anything that she had ever imagined until it came to a screeching end when Peter died in a head-on collision with a tour bus while returning from one of his business trips to Malaysia. He had been making his fortnightly visit to the ceramic factory that he owned in the state of Pahang. It may very well have been his characteristic disdain for caution that caused his death.

The shock and grief that Rose suffered because of his sudden and horrific death very quickly turned to perplexity and mortification at the very public revelation of Peter's other family, a wife and a fifteen-year-old daughter in Malaysia. The woman claimed that she had been married to Peter for almost fifteen years. Some days after Peter's other life unravelled, and when Rose was calmer, it struck her that the relationship with that woman would have started about the time their business had begun to flourish and her life had begun to reach dizzying heights. Their business was growing internationally, beyond Asia. Rose had laughed at that time, with a bit of irritation, at Peter's insistence on holding on to his tiny ceramic factory in Kuantan and his need to visit the factory twice every month. 'Sell it off, Pete. It doesn't really make much money, and you are better off being here and focusing on the business here.' The appearance of 'that woman' at his funeral revealed the real reason behind Peter's inconvenient and frequent trips to Malaysia.

'That woman', who would remain 'that woman' in Rose's mind for a long time, was nothing like Rose, and that chafed her raw nerves all the more. Rose had an excellent sense of dress, even in the early days when money had been short. Her friends admired her sense of style and colour and the immaculate taste that made her stand out wherever she went. On the other hand, 'that woman's' clothes, shoes, and her whole appearance were inexpensive and poorly put together, to say the least. She was short, with short hair that had suffered a poor perm and skin that was marked with acne from her youth. The contrast between Rose and the woman was so stark that she was sure that everyone was talking about it. Why would Peter have an affair with a woman so inferior to his wife in so many obvious ways? The possible answers that must have been whispered made Rose feel the burn of her humiliation more severely.

To her credit, 'that woman' did not attempt to project herself in any way as Peter's wife. In fact, they may have never known if the woman had not stood by the coffin, weeping silently for longer than would be natural for a colleague, member of staff, or even a friend or acquaintance. It was only when Sylvia approached her that the family discovered that she was Peter's other wife. Her fifteen-year-old daughter had stood by her, gently consoling, while curiously following Rose and her sons with her eyes. Simon and Sylvia had a hard time trying to contain the anger of the twins, especially Ean—the older of the two. Rose, who had been silently grieving until that point, had, for the first time in their lives, been at a complete loss for words or any kind of action. Her initial disbelief had turned into anger as the reality of the situation had dawned on her.

Her grief and shock at her husband's untimely death turned to silent fury at his treachery. She refused to stay at the funeral, and Sylvia had a hard time convincing her to change her mind. 'It'll be more embarrassing and obvious if you're not here, Rosie. Everyone will talk about you and your absence. He's gone, thank goodness. You can now live your life with more dignity.' Rose had stared numbly at her mother, who had happily declared just two weeks before his death, 'You were right, Rosie. Peter is a good man. Despite his gaudy manners and appearance, he's been good for you.' While Rose's love for her mother was profound, at that moment, the eighty-year-old's voice grated on her nerves, and she could barely stop herself from snapping at her.

Peter's other family stayed through the funeral, much to the embarrassment of Sylvia and the boys. Rose had simply allowed Simon to take charge, while Sylvia struggled to get her to speak to the people who tried to approach her to offer their condolences. 'It looks really bad, Rosie, especially since almost everyone here is here for your sake. You are letting that woman take over the life you shared with Peter—' Sylvia had stopped short in response to the way Rose glared back at her. Sylvia felt a wave of compassion for her daughter. The woman who stood by Peter's coffin had taken over her daughter's life with her husband fifteen years ago, and the look in Rose's eyes said it all. People who attempted to approach and offer their condolences to her made a hasty retreat when their eyes met Rose's smouldering gaze that froze them.

Most of all, Rose avoided even glancing at the other family, especially the girl, Peter's daughter, the searing reminder of his binding union with a woman other than herself. Finally, when the funeral was over, she had let Simon handle everything concerning them, and he had gone about dealing with the matter as Rose would have, at a calmer and less emotionally draining time, as business that needed to be dealt with through lawyers. Simon later informed his mother that he had paid the woman enough to cover her living expenses for the rest of her life. He had also paid her for the girl's education.

The woman had no real claims on anything in Singapore as she had not been legally married to Peter, but she had lived like a wife to Peter for fifteen years and borne him a daughter. 'And so she deserves to live well for the rest of her life with my money?' said Rose, interrupting Simon, who had been patiently reporting an itemized list of what he had done for 'that woman'. Simon merely glanced at his mother silently. They could have just ignored 'the woman' and not paid her a cent, but Simon felt that it would be best to settle with her financially in case there were claims, accusations and lawsuits in the future. He felt his mother's humiliation, but there was little that he could do to ease her pain.

There were so many things about his mother that changed in a very short time since the funeral. She looked tired and drawn and seemed to not care about anything at all. As much as his mother had been a hard worker, she had also been a stickler for health and healthy habits. As far back as he could remember, this was the woman who used to say, 'Alcohol makes the brain fuzzy and your judgement gets messed up,' if her sons drank too much. 'Look at you, with your eyes all puffy. The whole world will know that you had too much last night,' Simon had heard his mother scold Peter. And, yet, these days he caught her drinking in the afternoon.

Most importantly, though, her zest and enthusiasm for the business, which Simon knew was his mother's lifeblood, was waning fast. It was obvious in everything she did and said. She seemed to almost detest the work. Whenever she came into the office, she seemed to want to get out as quickly as she could—the opposite of what she had always done. And this was clear to everyone around her. Rose's passion for the business had been doused just as suddenly as Peter's other life had been revealed. These days, she rarely came in before ten thirty in the morning and then almost always left by two in the afternoon, even cancelling the evening meetings that she had always had with Simon. She would never do that in the past because that was the time she would run ideas by him and keep her finger on the pulse of the day-to-day affairs of the business. In the days before Peter's death, Rose had even maintained a small suite behind her office, for her to stay in if she had to work all night, which was quite often.

Simon worried about his mother and the future of the business that she had built. Over the years, Rose had worked at grooming her sons and her directors to manage the business after her. She had carefully selected her team, and Simon was sure that the business would continue very well on its course. But he was gripped with sadness at the thought of his mother retiring completely from it. As much as he and his step-brothers knew the ropes well and could manage without her, she was the soul of this company, and he simply couldn't imagine a time when she would no longer be there. But that time seemed to be racing towards him now.

And then there was the issue with his brothers, who these days saw him more as their mother's son and less as their brother. It was a change that had occurred so gradually that it hadn't been, and still wasn't immediately obvious, but he could feel the change in the way they spoke with him, or in the way they conducted themselves during meetings. While they were growing up, Simon, who was a good ten years older, was the one they turned to for everything, mostly because their parents were always busy. After Simon, it would be Sylvia, who was the perfect indulgent grandma. But as the years went by and they started working in the company, the change began, especially when they observed that he had as much say in everything as Rose. The staff looked up to him and, more than that, liked him immensely and were therefore willing to go beyond the call of duty for him, even more than for Rose sometimes.

The twins didn't get the same trust from their mother or the same affection from the staff. This irked Ean, especially because he too was the boss's son, and he actually felt more entitled because Peter, who was also the boss, was his father. But it wasn't that clear cut for Ethan, who was torn between his fondness for Simon, his loyalty towards his twin, his insecurities about his capabilities at work, and his lack of clarity. He wasn't even sure if he liked being in the business, but he didn't know what else he could do and was too afraid of his mother to question her. No one had ever thought that it was necessary to discuss career options for the sons of the family. Ean, who loved being in the business, took to it like a fish to water, while Ethan simply followed with trepidation buried in his heart. Now and then, when he expressed his concerns to Ean, to whom he was closest, he would get a slap on the back and some light-hearted counsel, 'Don't think too much about it. You need to work somewhere, so why not for us?' Ethan, who couldn't argue with that, remained an unhappy, reluctant, and often irritable accomplice to Ean, who only stoked his diffidence.

Simon suspected that his mother knew what was happening but just never said anything. Despite his sadness about the widening chasm in his relationship with his step-brothers, Simon did what he did for his mother. And he was right.

Rose was aware of the rift, but she had little choice other than to place her hopes on Simon. She didn't trust the twins yet and wondered if she could ever trust them. Ean had certainly inherited her love for success and power and maybe her shrewdness and acumen too, but he appeared to have missed out on her patience and willingness to work hard. She also had a small but niggling fear about his integrity. She hated to admit it because he was her son, but she could never be sure that he would do the right thing. He had his father's love for expensive things but had missed out on his easy and unassuming manner with people. And Ethan exasperated her. He stammered when she spoke with him and seemed to take his time getting into his job. So yes, she needed Simon at the helm. She worried that, left entirely to the twins, the empire that had taken more than twenty years to build would disappear in half that time. Every once in a while, just as she was falling asleep at night, a tiny feeling of guilt would nag at her. Was she using Simon and his deep affection for her to keep what she had worked so hard to build alive against his wishes? When this happened, she would shake her head and sigh impatiently before switching off the lights and turning over to sleep.

Chapter Three

Darkness that was stealthily casting its mantle over the island found Rose still staring in the direction of the water that framed the island as the evening traffic bustled below. She was clutching the side of the window so tightly that the white of her knuckles showed. She glanced at her phone as it buzzed insistently. Sighing, she walked over to her table and picked it up. 'Yes, Maryanne.'

A husky voice with a lilting Filipina accent responded, 'Ms Rose, I'm leaving for the day. Do you need me for anything?'

Maryanne had arrived in Rose's home as the house help. But when Rose had discovered that she had a college degree and spoke and wrote really well, she had supported her through a skills training programme in the evenings, where Maryanne had trained to be an executive assistant. Rose had promptly hired her as her own personal assistant after she was done. Hence, the gratitude that Maryanne felt for Rose was immense, and her conviction that her family in the Philippines lived and ate well and that her brothers and sisters were on their way to obtaining college degrees because of Rose's generosity was unshakeable.

Rose continued to look out of the window as she replied, 'No, Maryanne. Have a good evening. Thank you.'

'Uh . . . Ms Rose, Mr Simon is here for your evening meeting with him.' Rose scowled briefly, and Maryanne thought she heard an impatient sigh before she heard, 'Yes, okay, send him in.'

Rose had barely responded to Maryanne, when she heard the door to her room open. She sighed wearily and turned around to see her eldest son walking up to her desk, slapping some files against his thigh with a frown lightly etched on his brow and his lips pursed. It was clear that he was perturbed. The fatigue that she had felt a minute before felt heavier on Rose's shoulders when she took a swift glance at her son. Nothing ever fazed Simon unless it was a matter that concerned her or his twin brothers. She sensed what was coming and hastened her escape.

'That was unfair, Ma,' said Simon as soon as he sank heavily into the chair across from her. Rose looked up briefly and irritably shook her head before continuing to put her personal belongings back into her purse. She had told him a thousand times not to flop into chairs. 'You're in the office, Simon. People observe you. You are going to head this organization someday. It won't do if you sink into chairs like a sack of potatoes,' was her constant reminder to him.

She glanced at him sharply again and shut her bag before responding impatiently, 'What? What are you talking about?'

'You shouldn't have insulted Linda that way. You should not have walked out of that presentation,' Simon persisted, ignoring his mother's look and tone. Rose silently continued to put away her folders and pens, in readiness to leave.

The phone buzzed again, and Simon and Rose glanced sharply at it, both a tad peeved by the interruption, but for different reasons. Rose wanted to leave, while Simon was anxious to speak to his mother whom he only saw very briefly these days.

'Uh ... Ms Rose ... there's a Scott Wilson on the line. He says you know him well,' said Maryanne. A frisson of an indescribable emotion shot down to her stomach when she heard a name she hadn't heard in a while. The tautness of her jaw relaxed a little, but her heart began to beat faster.

Scott, dear Scott, she thought to herself. *Always coming back at the right time. Even after so many years.* Scott Wilson was an old boyfriend from her days at USC. The last time he had called, she was just about to marry Peter.

'Ms Rose, are you there?' repeated Maryanne. 'Would you like me to take a message?'

Rose frowned a little and drew a sharp breath before she said, 'Y . . . yes . . . um . . . take a message.' Almost instantly changing her mind, she called out, 'Uh . . . Maryanne . . .' but she heard a click and stopped. Aware of Simon's eyes on her, she held back from appearing too anxious on returning Maryanne's call. Simon studied his mother with a slight hint of a quizzical smile, wondering about the faintest of blushes that he observed on her face, but said nothing. Rose glanced at her son, a little embarrassed by the fluttering that she felt. She busied herself with gathering her things and getting ready to leave as her mind snapped back to the conversation she was having with her son. She cleared her throat. 'The woman was full of nonsense, as she was right from the start. Just an empty vessel with a loud voice and lots of ambition. You know that. She had no solid figures and no real plan. She is talking about us investing thousands of dollars in an advertising campaign to advertise a name that is already established in Malaysia. Yes, we have competition, but we are known as quality builders catering to a certain class of clients. You tell me how an advertising campaign of that magnitude is going to help,' said Rose picking up her keys. She picked up the phone without waiting for Simon to respond. 'Uh . . . Maryanne . . . about the message . . .'

'Yes . . . Ms Rose?'

'Um . . . hold on to it. I will pick it up on my way out.' Rose hung up without waiting for Maryanne to respond. She picked up the rest of her things.

'Where are you going, Ma? We have a meeting,' grumbled Simon. His mother ignored his question, making it quite clear to Simon that Linda was not worth a sit-down discussion.

'So you were listening. Then why did you ask Linda to proceed?' persisted Simon, suddenly feeling silly about belabouring an issue that his mother seemed to have no interest in.

'Well, you and your brothers selected her as our Senior Marketing Manager and persuaded me to sign her appointment letter despite my misgivings. It's time for you to ensure that she does what you promised she would do. Step in, and guide her. Sometimes duds do blossom with some help,' responded Rose dismissively and began to walk out. 'Also, Simon, I'm cancelling our evening meeting. I have to be somewhere else. But think about my proposal,' she said over her shoulder.

'What proposal, Ma?' asked Simon, looking perplexed as he turned back to look at his mother walking to the door.

'About you taking over . . . at least for a while,' Rose replied without looking back.

'But Ma, we talked about that. I wish you would stay in the office a little bit more and not run off at odd times! You never used to do that. Are you leaving because of that phone call? There are so many things to discuss and so many matters to settle. Everything is slowing down because you're never here. And right or wrong, we still need your approval for so many things,' grumbled Simon, standing up clumsily as if attempting to catch up with his mother, who was already reaching for the doorknob.

'That's the problem. It shouldn't be that way any more. You should be deciding these things. Or, the twins should be. I'm clear about wanting to get out,' said Rose decisively, as she shut the door in Simon's face.

Exasperated, Simon watched the heavy wooden door shut just as he was about to ask his mother where she was going and if he could at least ride with her so that they could talk in the car. He sat down heavily on the black leather couch next to the door, stretched out his legs, and folded his arms over his slightly protuberant stomach. He couldn't believe his mother's flippancy. This was just not like her. 'What does she think of this whole business! Like it is the noodle stall that grandpa had?' he asked himself crossly. A memory of the old man walking slowly towards the hawker centre every morning at five with his large basket of produce crossed his mind, and his face softened immediately. His grandfather was always up before anyone else and awake until everyone else had gone to bed, preparing the items for his stall for the next day. He never once wavered in his support of his daughter and her son, no matter how difficult times were.

Simon closed his eyes and leant his head back. As much as he loved his mother, he was drained—tired of pretending to want this position in the office, tired of managing his step-brothers' suspicions of him, and tired of managing his mother's relationship with them. In short, he was just fed up with holding everything together. Already, he had had to grow up so quickly after his father's death when his mother began to depend on him emotionally. He remembered sitting outside his father's hospital room, holding his mother's hand as she wept through the night. He hadn't quite understood what was happening, but he had had an idea that his father was ill—very ill. Simon had loved his fun-loving father, who made up for his irresponsibility as a parent and husband with the gregariousness and benevolence of his personality.

Even when he used to disappear every few weeks, leaving his wife frantic with worry, he would return home with armloads of presents for his son and kisses and embraces for his wife. The Rose of those days would fret and fume with her parents every time he disappeared and vow to present him with divorce papers when he came back, but would melt at the sight and feel of her handsome husband, much to the frustration of her anxious parents and much to her embarrassment! For a week or so after he returned, everything would go back to normal; they would be a happy family of husband, wife, and young son. They would go out as a family, laugh, play and love until he disappeared again a few weeks later. What Rose and Simon did not know then was that they were enjoying those halcyon days as a happy family on some loan shark's money.

As Simon and his mother sat outside the ICU of the hospital on that fateful day, he had, in his innocence as a ten-year-old, believed that that day too would miraculously turn out okay.

He believed that like those other times, this time too, his father would return after a couple of days, grinning and reeking of alcohol. Unfortunately, there were no more miracles left for Stanley and his family. The doctors told Rose that they couldn't save him, since his cirrhosis was too advanced. Gripping his mother's hand tightly, Simon had watched her cry in bewilderment. His sadness was more for his mother, who was sobbing uncontrollably. Simon was used to his father's absence, but the sadness he had felt then stayed with him through his adolescence. There was always a piece of lead that weighed down on his heart, a heaviness that would not go away, even on the rare occasions when he laughed. But he could never quite understand if it was fear or sadness, fear of losing his one parent, or sadness at the struggles of that one parent. He had grown up being anxious about his mother's well-being, always watching, always worrying.

And then there had been something else buried deep within him—his confusion and his shame through his teenage years. He couldn't understand it initially, but it began to make sense when the girls didn't catch his eye. He hated himself for that warm sensation that spread through him when he had stolen glances at the head prefect, who was the most popular boy in the school— good looking, a bright student, and a great sportsman. Once when he had found himself sitting next to this boy, he had relished and yet hated the raging emotions that spread like fire within him. Lying in bed that night and thinking about the boy in school, his shame had heightened when he felt a sudden gush of heat between his legs. As tears had flowed freely down his face, he had prayed fervently that these shameful thoughts would disappear and that he would wake up 'normal' in the morning. He grew out of his attraction for the head prefect of the school but became aware of other young men, all clandestinely.

Thankfully, as he had grown older, he had learnt that he was not alone and that other men were drawn to him, who had felt for him as he for them. He grew to accept himself but still secretly. He still didn't have the courage to share it with anyone at home. He knew that Sylvia had no clue because she kept asking him if he had a girlfriend, and why he was not bringing any girl to see her. She wanted him to marry so that she could see her great-grandchildren before she passed on. 'You need to get out of the office a little more and get yourself a girlfriend,' Sylvia would lament. Simon had been tempted to reveal his true inclinations at least to Sylvia many times, but had held back for fear of how she would react. She was from an era that strongly believed in the idea that men married women and had children.

Rose never said anything, and neither did she ask about a girlfriend. He didn't know if she knew. He sometimes felt that his mother and his brothers had guessed, but no one ever spoke about it. Once when Peter had been alive, he had asked Simon in his usual loud, brash manner, 'Eh! Why don't you have a girlfriend? What's wrong with you?' Simon had blushed inadvertently and prepared to reveal his real inclinations, but Rose had quickly stepped in and skilfully brushed the question aside. 'He knows how to handle his life. All in good time.' Simon took such pains to keep his private life completely hidden that he preferred to have love interests outside of Singapore, hence his enthusiasm to travel at every little opportunity, especially to Italy now, where Luis, his partner, lived. Luis and he had numerous conversations about making their relationship permanent and travelling the world to take beautiful pictures before they were both too old. Simon brushed a hand over his red-rimmed eyes and sighed deeply. 'I need to get out soon,' he said to himself while reaching for the files that he had unsuccessfully tried to discuss with his mother. The deeply furrowed brow and the droop at the ends of his mouth were telling of the frustration that he felt.

Rose quickly walked out of the office, snatching the small piece of paper from Maryanne's hand as she walked past. She hurried out of the building while reading the message: *Scott Wilson - staying at the Hyatt. Will be in his room till 8 p.m.* A telephone number and a room number were written in Maryanne's neat handwriting at the bottom of the page. Rose felt a surge of excitement coupled with trepidation at the thought of seeing Scott again. The memories of her days with Scott at different periods in her life flitted through her mind in quick succession. She wasn't sure what she wanted out of this meeting with him, but at least it would be a break from the dreariness that was her life now. She wondered if he was still married and quickly chided herself for hoping that he wouldn't be any more, just for her sake. *Perhaps he has children. Just like I have children. Why shouldn't he? But why is he calling me after all this time? Has he heard about Peter?* She suddenly felt hot and bothered. *Has he heard about everything else? How could he have when he doesn't even live here?* But a nagging fear played in her mind as she thought about the gossip magazines that had run articles about philandering husbands, and their wives making shocking discoveries about the 'other families' of their spouses' soon after Peter's death, without specifically referring to Rose or her family. She was well-known in many circles, and gossip and speculation about her life were always circulating in those. Rose quickly sneered at her fears and even laughed softly to herself at the thought of Scott, a reputed journalist who covered the Iraq war and the fight against the Taliban, reading a gossip magazine.

Rose hesitated. Should she return the call, or should she just pretend that she never got the message? Her chauffeur of ten years, Maniam, drove up and attempted to step out of the car to open the door for her, but she waved him back and glided into the plush backseat of her Porsche. If there was one thing that Rose had never bothered to learn, it was to drive. Even in the US, she had either taken the bus or the train, or ridden in Scott's beat-up old Chevy. The skill did not interest her, and she had always told herself that until she could afford to have a chauffeur, she would either ride the bus or take a taxi.

Rose looked down at her watch. It was seven in the evening. A light rain had started, and it had slowed down the vehicles while sending pedestrians scurrying for cover. With her thoughts fixed on the little piece of paper that bore Scott's message, she stared out of her window as the car whizzed past a blur of evening traffic, people and brightly lit buildings. Biting her lower lip, Rose fished out her cell phone from her purse and made the call, thankful for the thick glass that separated her from Maniam. She could feel herself subconsciously holding her breath as the phone rang. She hung up suddenly, wondering if she was doing the right thing, and lay back against the seat. A slight hint of a smile appeared at the corners of her mouth. She was suddenly embarrassed by her excitement. *Such silliness! And, at my age. He is probably just passing through. He must have had a free moment. I really don't think I should return that call.*

Rose leant forward and knocked on the glass. Maniam looked at her through his rear-view mirror before the glass slid open. 'You can drop me off at the restaurant. I will have Penny drop me at my mother's house later, Maniam. Pick me up in the morning at ten,' she said, and Maniam nodded before the glass slid shut again. She would spend the night at Sylvia's Peranakan-style home on Tank Road. It had been a long time since she had visited her mother.

Chapter Four

Like an empress she sat, in her courtyard in the middle of her house, bathed in the bright morning light. As always, Sylvia was immaculately dressed, complete with bright pink lipstick, her favourite colour, even if she was just sitting at home playing Mahjong with herself. The jade and diamond earrings, the numerous emerald and diamond rings, and her favourite gold bangle, which was fashioned like a dragon with a jade ball in its mouth, sparkled in the light. The fact that Sylvia would meticulously dress, complete with makeup and jewellery, every morning after her shower—which was always early in the day, even if she was not stepping out anywhere—never failed to amaze Rose. 'I dress to make myself happy, not for some fellow on the street. When I look in the mirror, I need to feel like I'm alive,' Sylvia would declare. Ling Ling, the bright-red and turquoise-blue parrot that Simon had bought as a present for Sylvia for her last birthday, sat swinging on his perch, pecking on and off at the red apple that he had half-finished. The open courtyard in which Sylvia sat was filled with lush green ferns and foliage in Chinese ceramic pots. In one corner sat a hibiscus plant in full bloom, with splotches of red flowers.

Situated right in the middle of the house, the courtyard was open and exposed to the elements, even when it rained. On a fine day like this though, it was drenched in sunlight, which helped light up the hallways that surrounded it. The circulating fans that

surrounded the courtyard kept Sylvia cool, as did the sunshade
above the swing on which she sat. Sylvia's house was one of several
Peranakan-style houses in a row on Tank Road. When Rose and
Peter had bought a penthouse overlooking the Kallang River,
Sylvia had stubbornly continued living in the old apartment her
husband had bought for her. 'He bought this for me, and this is
where I will live for the rest of my life,' she had insisted, despite
numerous entreaties from Rose, Peter, and the boys to move in
with them. For a year or two, Sylvia continued her sewing business
with Ming, her helper, and lived in the old apartment. But one day,
Rose came by and picked her up, telling her that they were going
to look at a house that she was interested in buying.

Despite its terrible state of disrepair, it had taken Sylvia's breath
away. It was a replica of the home of her childhood in Malacca.
The owner of this house had been an old widower who had lived
there all his life without doing very much in terms of maintenance.
After his death, his children, all of whom lived abroad, had wanted
the place sold. Sylvia had stood looking around her in the grungy
courtyard, her hands crossed on her chest. Everything about the
house was unprepossessing, broken, dirty and badly in need of
paint. But to Sylvia, everything about the house—the sunlit open-
air courtyard where the family dined on a stone table with matching
stools if it was a fine day, the covered hallways surrounding it where
visitors could sit, the chipped tile on the floor, the dark rooms; the
stairway with its peeling bannisters that led to the upstairs, and the
rusty protective railings that ran all around the second floor just
above the courtyard—brought back a flood of memories.

Sylvia saw herself running after her eleven-year-old brother,
who was laughing and darting here and there as he threw
mischievous glances at her, holding a doll above his head so that
she couldn't get it. It was around August of 1942. She was known
as Hui Fen in those days. No more than eight or nine, she could
see herself running behind him, yelling, pleading with him to
return the doll and not to break it, as it was her only one. All her

other toys had been lost when they had run helter-skelter to save themselves as the Japanese had arrived in Perak, which is where her family had once lived and where her father and his brother had jointly owned a tin-mining business. Sylvia could see her sister sitting on the floor in the courtyard cleaning fish, throwing longing sidelong glances and laughing when the boy dodged the little girl, who was desperately trying to grab his arm. Her sister was just two years older than her brother but Sylvia's mother felt that she was old enough to spend her time responsibly working on household chores like gutting fish with a sharp knife and no longer young enough to fritter it away by playing with her younger siblings.

Sylvia could see her mother yelling at the two children to stop getting in the way as she tried to go about her tasks, her face, once beautiful and serene, now lined and taut with worry and fear. Her husband and his brother had been accused of funding the Malayan People's Anti-Japanese Army, the MPLA. Their business premises had been burnt. Sylvia's father had been dragged, in full view of their horror-struck neighbours, to what was believed to be an interrogation camp. Since he was never heard from again, it was assumed that he was dead. His brother's head had been cut off with a single stroke of a long samurai sword because he had protested when they had tried to drag him away as well. The head had been stuck on a stick and planted in the ground in the middle of their little mining town, as an example of what happened to people who did not submit to Japanese rule.

Distraught and terrified, the womenfolk of the family, Sylvia's father's mother and younger sister, her mother, and Wang Shu, the wife of the dead uncle, had scrambled to gather the children and a few belongings and fled with the help of one of their workers on a truck that was southbound towards Singapore. Before they reached Malacca, the matriarch, Sylvia's father's mother, had succumbed to grief from the devastating loss and sheer fatigue from the journey. She had just slumped dead on Sylvia's mother's shoulder as the lorry made its way into inky darkness. What was left of the miserable family got off in Malacca, so that they could give the old woman a decent burial since they couldn't possibly travel with a dead body. With the help of some old contacts that their husbands had had in happier and wealthier times, the womenfolk managed to find a Peranakan house abandoned by the owners fleeing for their lives. And that was home for a few years, and that was where young Sylvia—oblivious to the turmoil around her—enjoyed the happiest days of her childhood.

Sylvia continued to stand in the light that streamed into the courtyard of the house that Rose was considering buying, with her eyes closed as scenes from her childhood flashed randomly into her mind. Here, she saw her mother drying out the family's laundry, there she saw her father's sister chopping vegetables. This sister had been betrothed to the scion of another tin miner before the family's world had been turned upside down. They never heard from her fiancé or his family again. Perhaps it was just as well because the same young lady lay dead at the bottom of the stairs of their home one morning. Sylvia could still see her white face with her mouth slightly open. No one knew why she'd died. All they knew was that she had complained of pains in her abdomen now and then. During those desperate war years, pains like those were soothed with herbal concoctions and foul-smelling liniments. Then, Sylvia saw that same house that they lived in go up in flames because of a carelessly left stove. Her mother and her older sister, who was that lovely young girl cleaning fish, had perished in that fire because they had been in the kitchen. Sylvia and her brother had been saved by Wang Shu, the only remaining adult, who had escaped the fire with the children because she had been outside the house while the four younger children played, two of her own and Sylvia and her brother.

Aunty Wang Shu, the wife of the slain uncle, had a son and daughter of her own, but from that day, she had treated Sylvia and her brother as her own. With the help of neighbours and strangers—and there were many strangers who willingly helped during the war years—she had found another abandoned house for herself and her brood. This time, it was a kampong house with a thatched roof. Aunty Wang Shu took on several jobs doing laundry, tapping rubber—just about anything she could find to feed herself and the children. The aunt that Sylvia knew as a little chubby, with a constant smile on her face, had gradually become gaunt and tired, going from one job to another throughout the day. The smile would still appear occasionally, but it became rare, to the point that it became more of an attempt to smile than an actual smile. Thankfully, the odd, sad family survived the Japanese occupation.

It was only when the Japanese left in 1945, and the British came back, and life for Malayans slowly returned to some form of normality, that the family began to see some stability. The children went back to school into grades that were either too high or too low because of the few lost years in between, but at least it was some education. Their aunt, who had in happier and wealthier times been a good seamstress, slowly started a sewing business. Anxious about the well-being of her brood, she watched the two girls, Hui Fen and her own daughter, Hui Ming, growing up too beautiful for their own good. Although she looked at them both with pride, it was a pride laced with a generous amount of trepidation and anxiety. She was proud that they were beautiful but fearful that she would not be able to marry them off respectably because they already attracted too much attention, even as teenagers. She stopped them from going to school and kept them indoors as much as she could, teaching them how to sew and embroider.

She had a different concern when it came to her son and Sylvia's brother. As a woman, there was only so much she could do to discipline them, especially as they became young men. While they were respectful towards her and appeared responsible, there was something shifty about their activities; they would often disappear in the evenings and return late at night. When she questioned them, they told her something about friends and meetings. When she pushed them for clear answers, they frowned and told her that she wouldn't understand. As rumours about communists recruiting young people floated around, a gnawing dread festered within her. She knew that some of her neighbours had sons in the Malayan National Liberation Army (MNLA), the communists. They were proud of them because they were 'serving the country' they claimed. 'Stupid!' spat Aunty Wang Shu. 'We lost everything, our whole lives, because of those people. You boys be careful. Don't go anywhere near those people,' she declared emphatically. But there was fear in her eyes. She knew that the boys nodded because they respected her and not because they agreed with her. The fear gnawed away at her insides.

Some months later, a neighbour lamented the disappearance of her son. Apparently, he had just left a letter on a table and disappeared during the wee hours of the morning when everyone was asleep. A few days later, British soldiers arrived with guns barking orders, and Aunty Wang Shu relived everything from which she had fled. The only difference was that the soldiers were barking in English, and not Japanese. They installed barbed wire fences around the village and warned the villagers that if they did not cut off their connections with the MNLA, the consequences would be dire. There was some alarm among the villagers, but there was also defiance. Aunty Wang Shu was able to see that many of the villagers were not going to comply with the orders. After all, the British masters had proven that they were not all-powerful. They had been defeated by the Japanese just a few years ago. Nocturnal activities where food and money exchanged hands continued.

One day, the soldiers arrived again and took away several young men from the village. They took away the two remaining men from Hui Fen's family with Aunty Wang Shu pleading, crying, scrambling, and screaming behind them. Sylvia still woke up on some nights because of nightmares of that fateful morning when soldiers had banged on their door. The boys, Sylvia's brother Hui Cheng and Aunty Wang Shu's son Hui Beng, tried to flee through the back door but were captured and made to get into an army truck along with several other young men. Aunty Wang Shu's piteous pleas and cries were met with stony stares and deaf ears. The soldiers had guns that they would have readily used. The captured young men from the village cast farewell looks at their families as the truck drove away.

Some days later, Aunty Wang Shu received news that Sylvia's brother, Hui Cheng, had died of cholera in prison. The family never got to see the body because of the highly contagious nature of the disease, or so they were told. Her own son, Hui Beng, remained in prison, apparently under a rehabilitation programme. He spent about a year in prison before he came back to the family, a gaunt and quiet shadow of the robust and happy teenager who had teased the girls mercilessly in play. By this time, the string of misfortunes and years of hardship had caught up with Aunty Wang Shu, who slowly but surely whittled away, and what was left was a shrunken old woman who struggled to keep the girls, Hui Ming and Hui Fen, safe from prowling eyes. In fact, Hui Fen had forgotten that the hunched and scrawny old woman before her had once been the laughing, cherubic woman who would reach into her samfoo pocket and pull out a treat for the children. Even Hui Ming, Aunty Wang Shu's daughter, didn't remember this.

Meanwhile, everyone was talking about better opportunities down south, in Singapore. There was also talk that Singapore was going to separate from the rest of Malaya, and this churned up a general fear and anxiety that going to the island after the separation would become difficult. Rumours about how life would change drastically floated around and uncertainties about livelihoods drove people to places that they thought would improve their lot. Hui Beng, the one remaining male member in the shattered family, now an odd-job labourer, wanted to move because there was not much of a livelihood for him in Malacca. He did this and that and brought in a few dollars, while the girls sewed. But the income wasn't enough, especially with Aunty Wang Shu being sick. Everyone was talking about how there was more money to be made in Singapore because there was more work. So, one morning, with hearts filled with hope, the odd little family moved with their meagre belongings, the treasured sewing machine taking pride of place in the middle of the truck, to Singapore. Strangely, the same hope for a better and brighter future that burnt in the hearts of the girls led each one into completely diverse journeys. Hui Ming allowed the hope to mingle with envy, sloth, greed and competitiveness, and was led into a life full of missed opportunities. Sylvia, on the other hand, used hope as a beacon that strengthened her to work hard and generously give off herself to those in need even if they had wronged her in the past. Despite the trials and tests that challenged her initially, she was rewarded with Rose, the daughter who took pains to fill her mother's life with a calm that she enjoyed till her last breath, even if Rose's own life was devoid of it for the most part.

Sylvia glanced at Rose from above her glasses and chuckled as she caught her grimace. Rose hated porridge but that was all there was for breakfast. 'You should have called before you came last night. Ming had to go to Melaka yesterday. She left a few hours before you arrived. Said something about an old friend being sick and needing some help. And you know I don't cook. She cooked everything that I would need for my meals before she left.' Rose smiled as she swallowed the porridge. She knew very well. Sylvia didn't cook even when Rose was growing up. Sylvia focused on sewing and her tailoring business, while her husband cooked and cleaned after he came back in the afternoon from his noodle stall.

Even as a child and then a teenager, Sylvia had preferred sewing and embroidering to housework or cooking. And because she was so skilled as a seamstress even then, and customers would often come looking for her, Aunty Wang Shu let her spend all her time doing just that. 'Don't spoil your hands. Save them for the finer things. Hui Ming and I will take care of the work.' The greater load of cooking and cleaning fell to Hui Ming because Aunty Wang Shu was old and weak. Hui Ming silently worked in the kitchen and cleaned most of the day, and when she was done, she helped Sylvia with the tasks that required less skill than the actual cutting and embroidering of the garments. Although Aunty Wang Shu loved Hui Ming dearly, she didn't notice that while Sylvia's hands remained soft and white, Hui Ming's hands were slowly becoming rough and lined. But Hui Ming noticed. She would sometimes hold her hands up to the sun and examine them closely and then steal looks at Sylvia's delicate and fair hands.

Later, as a wife and mother, Sylvia spent most of her time at her tailoring business, leaving around ten in the morning and returning at about eight in the evening. Rose remembered that when her mother was home, she preferred to embroider quietly while listening to Cantonese musical programmes by Rediffusion on the radio to doing household chores. She sometimes sang along, and that crystal clear voice and amazing ability to hit the really high notes remained etched in Rose's memory.

Sylvia still hummed those songs as she played Solitaire on quiet afternoons, and those were Rose's favourite afternoons. They felt like nothing had ever changed in her life. They reminded her of a simpler life when it had been just the three of them, Sylvia, her father and herself, in the sparsely furnished two-bedroom Housing Development Board apartment. This peaceful scene that she held close to her heart was easy to visualize right here in Sylvia's home. There, she saw her father going about his chores in the kitchen, cooking the evening meal or mopping the floor; there was a younger Sylvia, softly singing along with a Cantonese pop singer on the radio while her fingers worked with a needle at lightning speed. And then Rose saw herself, sitting at the dining table, working on schoolwork or reading a book. 'If there is such a thing as a mismatch made in heaven, Ma and Baba were it,' Rose often thought to herself. But they had shared a strange, quiet relationship that endured for forty years. The only time Sylvia had ever sobbed was at her husband's cremation. There had been a calm and warmth in her parents' simple, sparse home that seemed to be missing in her own stylish apartment with its expensive custom-made furniture.

Sylvia rarely spoke about her past or childhood. She claimed
that she had no living relatives, and Rose believed her. 'Most of
them died during the war. I had an old aunt who raised me, but
she died before you were born,' was all that she would share with
Rose. When Rose had been about thirteen, she discovered some
old photographs while rummaging through a trunk looking for
family photos for a school project. The stack of photographs
bound together with a rubber band showed some women laughing
merrily. There were four of them, all with beehive hairstyles and
painted faces. She had looked at the photographs curiously and
closely, intrigued by the fact that one of them looked so familiar,
strangely like her mother. Yes, it was her mother, laughing, in a
sarong kebaya, holding the arm of another woman, who was
looking at her and laughing. The other two women were laughing
as well as they looked at her mother. They were standing beneath
a neon-lit arch with the words 'The New World' engraved on it.

'Who are these women? And why are you standing outside the
New World? You've never taken me there,' she said to Sylvia, staring
at the picture. 'Are these your friends?' Sylvia's eyes widened. For
a brief second, she looked furtive like she had been caught doing
something wrong before she forced a loud laugh and snatched the
photo from Rose.

'Where did you find this, Rosie?' she asked. 'Taxi Girls, all
of us,' she laughed, moving like she was dancing the twist. Rose
stared at her in wonder.

'What do you mean "taxi girls"?' Rose persisted.

'Dancing girls. We danced for a living. There were many like
us in the New World in those days,' Sylvia smiled, looking closely
at the photograph. Brushing it lightly with her fingers, her laugh
now reduced to a wistful smile.

'And where are they now?' asked Rose.

'Hmm . . . I don't know. We lost touch. This was a long time
ago, in the fifties. You weren't born then. We went our separate ways
when we all got married. We never contacted each other again.'

'Why were you called taxi girls? Was that a bad name?' Rose persevered, suddenly anxious about what her mother might have been in the past.

'No!' Sylvia responded sharply. 'We danced with anyone who had a coupon. Dancing—that's all we had to do,' Sylvia snapped while shooting Rose a warning look.

The photograph was returned to its stack at the bottom of the trunk, and the matter was never brought up again. But not before Rose noticed that there were several other photos, and in one or two of them, Sylvia had her arm looped with a white man in an army uniform. Her thirteen-year-old mind fantasized about a lover that her mother might have had before she had met her father. Rose opened her mouth to ask but closed it again, partly because she knew when not to cross the line with her mother and also because Sylvia had switched her attention to the embroidery on which she was working. Rose forgot about it in time, and the subject never came up again.

A few months after Rose's father's death, Ming came to live with them as Sylvia's helper. Sylvia didn't seem to think it was necessary to introduce her to Rose as anything other than a long-lost relative. Until that day Ming arrived at their home, Rose was only aware of an 'Uncle Beng', her mother's cousin, who had lived in Melaka and made rare and brief appearances in their home once in a while. Rose remembered having seen him only three or four times in all her life when her mother entertained him in the sitting room for an hour at most and sent him on his way. Rose did not know of any other relatives on her mother's side, so she was reasonably surprised by the appearance of Ming. Sylvia had not bothered to explain the details of their relationship and simply brushed aside Rose's queries with a wave of her hand. 'Haiya, Rosie! Just some old auntie's daughter. I don't even remember how we're related. I don't even remember if she's from my side of the family. In fact, I found the address while clearing some of your father's things.' The explanation sounded dubious, but Rose was at that

time too engrossed in settling her dead husband's debts, managing
a fledgling real estate business, and caring for young Simon to take
an interest in the details. She was just thankful that there was now
someone in the house who could cook and clean, something she
and her mother could not do.

A few years after Ming had settled in Sylvia's house, her
background ceased to be of importance to Rose. During this time,
Rose married Peter and had the twins, and moved into a condo that
was across the island from the little apartment that belonged to
her mother. A now-ageing Sylvia needed a companion, and Ming
served that purpose. Speaking little, constantly busy cleaning or
cooking, and always dressed in a pair of loose black pants and a
brilliantly clean white top, Ming reminded Rose of an ant that
never stopped. Her almost-permanent morose expression and her
lacklustre eyes hinted at some sad past, and her rare smile was
always a half-smile. Rose and Ming hardly ever exchanged a word.
As soon as Rose entered the room, Ming would withdraw into the
kitchen or somewhere else. Sometimes Rose wondered if Ming
disliked her, and she even joked about it with Sylvia. But Sylvia
dismissed her doubts with the usual wave of her hand, '*Haiya!*
Rosie! Why do you want to talk to her? She is just here to do the
work.' And Rose didn't bother to pursue the matter. There was
nothing endearing or even welcoming about Ming.

Chapter Five

Rose ate a few more spoonsful of the distasteful porridge and laid her bowl on the lacquer table beside her. 'How long is Ming going to be away?' she asked her mother as she stretched out her legs on the silken cushions of the sofa.

'Oh! She should be back today. She never stays longer than that. She hates staying anywhere else but here,' responded Sylvia, still engrossed in her game of Mahjong, which she played on her laptop.

A quietness ensued, and the only sounds heard were the hum of the traffic, the clicking of the keys on Sylvia's keyboard, and Ling Ling's quiet chatter. Rose closed her eyes like she was in repose. Sylvia glanced at her and thought it was a good time to broach the subject that had perturbed Simon. But she knew her daughter well enough to tread carefully. 'How have you been?' she asked slowly, without looking away from her screen. Rose had always been reserved and quiet, very unlike her mother, but these days she was more withdrawn, even with her. 'Simon was here yesterday. He is very concerned about you,' continued Sylvia. 'He is worried that you may be drinking too much. Are you?' she asked matter-of-factly, still clicking away at her game. If Simon had been present, rolling his eyes he would have said to himself, 'I might as well have asked her myself.'

Rose, who kept her eyes closed, laughed softly and mirthlessly. 'Simon's always worried about one thing or another. He needs to be with people his own age a little more,' she said.

'Well, he can't since you have given him such a huge responsibility,' said Sylvia, looking up from her game of Mahjong and looking directly at her daughter. 'Even more so now, since you're hardly ever in the office. It's almost been a year, Rosie . . . and you're still so angry and indifferent.' Sylvia sighed, sitting back in her chair finally and frowning at her daughter, whose reticence was beginning to frustrate her.

'Well, it's time for him to take over,' responded Rose frowning slightly and without looking at her mother. 'I'm more than a little tired of the office, the business, the people involved. I think it really is time for Simon to hold the reins now.'

'But you do have two other sons. What about them? Why not them?' grumbled Sylvia before turning back to look at her game. This last statement, too, had been part of Simon's request. 'Try to persuade Ma,' he had said, sinking his teeth into the Char Siew Pau that his 'Popo' had bought especially for him from her trip to Waterloo Street that afternoon.

At this point, Rose swung her feet to the floor and sat on the sofa facing her mother calmly. 'Did Simon put you up to this? Did he ask you to talk me into drawing the boys in instead?' she asked her mother, smiling stiffly. 'No, not quite. But I know it's on his mind. Simon is not exactly the type who enjoys being at the helm, Rosie. And, you've known that all along. He's there because you are there. He'll leave the minute you leave the business. You know that he is not half as agg— I mean driven, as you are,' said Sylvia, quickly correcting herself.

'Did you mean to say aggressive, Ma,' laughed Rose finally relaxing. She was used to her mother's disapproval of her inexorable drive.

'Oh! Rosa,' exclaimed Sylvia, who could switch effortlessly between calling her daughter Rosie or Rosa. She called her Rosie when she was affectionate or cajoling or soothing and Rosa when she was exasperated. Rose could always guess where a conversation with her mother was going just by what she was calling her. 'You know what I meant. There is nothing wrong with being aggressive. That's what made you successful anyway, and I'm very proud of you. But Simon is a little different. The twins are more like you but...' Sylvia tapered off before Rose finished her sentence for her.

'... but they are not as level-headed. That is why I need Simon, to ensure that everything I have built over these years does not sink,' said Rose decisively. 'And, don't lie. I know you don't care for my "aggression",' she laughed making quotation marks in the air with her fingers.

Sylvia was silent for a while as her daughter leant back against the sofa and closed her eyes again. 'Have you heard anything at all about the other family?' resumed Sylvia cautiously. She knew the subject irritated her daughter and so was extra careful. Rose didn't reply. 'Have all the matters been settled?' Sylvia tried again.

'Simon dealt with it, and I think he settled everything. I don't know, I have not asked him and I don't intend to,' said Rose decisively, and rose from the sofa, clearly tired of the small talk with her mother. 'I'm going to drop into the office before going home.'

Sylvia glanced at her daughter and shook her head before resuming her game. It was so unlike her daughter to not go to work early in the morning. It was almost ten in the morning, but Sylvia knew better than to ask. *She has to get out of this ... somehow.* Then, she turned back to her screen.

A little after Rose left that morning, Sylvia shut down her Mahjong game and made her way slowly, and with some difficulty, to her room, mumbling to herself about a hope that Ming would get back soon. She needed to rest. She didn't feel quite so well. When Rose was not around, Sylvia let her guard down about the difficulties she faced in moving around. Her years of smoking were finally catching up with her. Despite the reassurances that the doctor had given her, Sylvia knew in her heart that all was not right these days. Her breathing was more laboured, and she found it more and more difficult to get out of bed in the mornings. But she didn't talk about it even with Rose because she was Sylvia— always strong, always uncomplaining about herself. Moreover, if Rose knew, it would be the end of Sylvia's independence. Rose would insist that Sylvia move in with her, and if she resisted, Rose would move into Sylvia's home, just to show her displeasure, and that would be inconvenient all around. Sylvia loved Rose fiercely but couldn't imagine living in the same home with her any more. 'She is such a nag,' she laughed to herself, shaking her head.

Sylvia loved Rose fiercely but there were things about her daughter that scared her—like her inclination to never give a person another chance once she had decided that she didn't like them, her dislike for shades of grey, everything had to be black or white, and her insistence on never forgetting a hurt. Over the years, try as she did, Sylvia had never managed to make Rose see her point of view that sometimes people did what they did because of their circumstances and not because they were bad. 'There is no such thing, Ma. If your head is in the right place, you will do the right thing no matter what the circumstances. Values are either right or wrong.' Sylvia was glad that she had succeeded with Simon. 'Or perhaps he is naturally a gentler person, and less "scary",' she chuckled. 'The twins, too, were good boys when they were young . . . I think their father was too much of an influence. But that's her fault. She was never there when they were growing up,' she said sighing, as she slowly and carefully got into bed, holding the sides for support.

After Stanley's death, Sylvia had worried about what Rose would do all alone with a young son. Then Peter had come along. Although she hadn't quite understood Rose's choice, she had accepted him. When Peter died, she couldn't help conjecturing about what might have gone wrong. *He wasn't a really bad fellow. Sometimes I wonder if my Rosie was a little too preoccupied with the business and money-making, and that's why she drove him*

away. Perhaps my Rose has become too difficult to like or even know.
Her thoughts then turned to the twins. Simon had mentioned
that Ethan had a girlfriend who worked for them. They had both
agreed that it was best not to say anything to Rose. *But she is just
too sharp to miss anything. Wonder why she doesn't say anything.* Sylvia
was thankful for Simon. 'He will be there for her after I'm gone.
Not sure about the twins, but my Simon boy will be there,' was her
oft-repeated reassurance to herself, and today too, she repeated it
to herself as she dozed off, lulled by the creaking fan that swirled
lazily above.

It was hot outside as Maniam drove Rose to the office.
Despite her conversation with Sylvia, which had agitated her a
little, she felt a tingling within, as if a light feather was floating
through her and touching her here and there ever so gently and
spreading a soft warmth that she hadn't felt in a long time. A
smile tugged at the corners of her mouth and she gave in, just a
little, even humming softly. Out of the blue, without any warning
at all, it started to rain a little against a curious backdrop of
bright sunlight. Rose was reminded of an Indian myth that her
friend Nalini had once told her when they were pre-university
students. 'When it rains like this with the sun shining brightly,
it means the birds are getting married,' Nalini had said laughing
and frowning at the same time at having to run for cover. The
smile that played on Rose's lips broadened slightly when she
saw rainbow colours that danced when the light from the sun
shone through the drops of rain. Maniam glanced at his boss in
the rear-view mirror. It had been a long time since he had seen
her smile. The last time had been about a year ago, while on a
drive like this to the office. Rose had casually said, 'By the way
Maniam, I have asked Maryanne to include Anita's university
fees in your pay cheque. And don't worry, she has a job in our
company when she graduates if she wants it.' He had looked at
his boss through the rear-view mirror and nodded in gratitude.
And she had smiled at him then.

It was quiet where her office was when she arrived at about eleven that morning, but she could hear voices in the bullpen further down the hallway. Rose glanced at Maryanne's empty desk as she walked into her room. She had probably stepped out for something. Only Maryanne was aware of Rose's comings and goings since the suite of rooms that she shared with the boss was tucked in a corner. In the past, Rose had considered moving closer to the rest of the staff, so that she was more reachable by everyone, and Simon had encouraged the move—but lately, she was thankful for the distance. She liked that she didn't have to meet and engage in conversation with anyone as she walked in and out. She communicated mainly through Simon and Maryanne, and met the staff only if it was business and unavoidable. Even her twin sons complained that she was inaccessible, especially when they needed her to sign off on something.

Today, she was thankful that even Maryanne was not around when she entered the office. What Maryanne didn't know was that today was different. Rose hadn't felt this way for many months, especially after Peter's death. Looking radiant in her lime green dress and brilliant peridot and diamond earrings, she relished the quickening of her heartbeat and the flutter in her stomach. She was considering meeting Scott. She even wore her diamond tennis bracelet that sparkled on her slim wrist, a rare accessory for her unless she was headed to an evening engagement. Her skin had regained some of its lustre and looked less sallow than it had for a while. The subtle makeup artfully covered the lingering but faint signs of her sadness.

Rose had looked at herself critically as she was dressing in Sylvia's home. She wondered if Scott would still see the old Rose in her but had scoffed at her own thoughts. *I'm sixty. There's no running away from that. And he's sixty too. He's probably bald and paunchy!* She laughed at this last thought as she brushed her hair. Unlike Sylvia, whose hair was coloured jet black, Rose loved the silver strands that only enhanced her perfectly styled coiffure.

'You think you look dignified. You look old! You're too young to have grey hair,' Sylvia would repeatedly grumble. 'So Ma, when will I be old enough to have grey hair?' Rose would quip, stroking her mother's jet-black hair as she walked past. '*Haiya* Rosa,' Sylvia would exclaim with an impatient wave of her hand.

Like dawn that cools a sultry night, Scott's call had brought a rush of fresh air into her life. Sylvia had not seen Rose leave the house that morning. If she had, she might have been surprised by her daughter's slightly cheerier demeanour, which softened the grimness that seemed to have settled permanently on her mouth and in her eyes. The balmy warmth within her even tempered her feelings about Linda and enabled her to be a little bit more generous. *Perhaps Simon was right. Maybe I was a little too hard on the girl. I'm going to have Maryanne pull up Linda's presentation. Maybe there is something there . . . some guidance might help.*

However, Maryanne didn't need to be told. She had laid Linda's presentation folder on top of all the other files and folders that needed Rose's attention. Rose smiled when she saw the presentation folder right where she needed it. *That woman knows me a little too well.* Maryanne had heard about what had happened in the conference room. So when Simon came to see Rose almost immediately, Maryanne knew that it must have been about Linda. After this, Maryanne had guessed that the boss would want to take a second look at Linda's work. Over the years, she had learnt that even if Rose didn't openly admit it, she trusted Simon's judgement completely.

By the time Maryanne returned to her desk, Rose had made the necessary ticks and comments with a pencil. 'Have Simon come in to see me, please,' she said to Maryanne. 'Sure, Ms Rose. By the way, Scott Wilson called again this morning.' Rose took a sharp but quiet breath at the mention of Scott's name. Refusing to look up immediately from her reading for fear that Maryanne would see the colour that had rushed to her face, she continued to look at the document in front of her, pretending to be absorbed by it. 'Ms Rose,' repeated Maryanne. 'Mr Scott called again.' Rose looked up over her glasses, her lips drawn thin, and sighed.

'All right, give me the number. I will call him now. Please hand this to Simon and have him deal with it. I will speak to him in the evening if necessary.' She handed Linda's folder to Maryanne. As soon as the door closed behind Maryanne, Rose took off her glasses and closed her eyes with her palms pressed on the top of her desk. She took in a deep breath and braced herself for the questions that he was bound to ask. Yes, it would be humiliating to admit that she had lost and that the choice she had made was wrong, but at least she would have Scott back in her life.

Their relationship, hers and Scott's, had been sweet and warm while in USC, but it had ended when she had chosen to return to Singapore, while he had gone on to become a journalist. There had been no promise of a long-term relationship as neither one could make a commitment. Rose had to return to Singapore because she had parents who had wanted her back, and Scott had had dreams of hitting the headlines as a journalist with CNN. The distance and completely divergent lives had made memories of their relationship fade into the background. Neither one had attempted to initiate a connection again until after Stanley's death when Scott had called. He had by then become a senior correspondent.

They had briefly rekindled their relationship when he had surprised her on her birthday in Singapore. The ten days that had followed had been perfect, like their days in college, but perhaps it had been the niggling reassurance at the back of their minds that it was once again temporary that had made their reunion warm and sweet. Scott had talked about his work most of the time, and the fire in his eyes when he spoke had made it clear to Rose that a commitment was not on his mind. Rose, on the other hand, had been a little embarrassed by the turn that her life and career had taken and the fact that she had moved so far away from the girl that Scott had known in college. By that time, she had lost her job at the boutique PR agency, and her old fire about being successful in a premier PR agency, someday working with the 'best' in New York, had completely died. While he spoke about meetings with presidents and prime ministers, she worried about debt and debt collectors while raising her son alone.

But the ten days had done wonders because they had taken her mind off of her dreary life. Scott had been kind and attentive, as he would have been to someone he cared about deeply. At the airport, neither one had met the other's eyes for fear of, perhaps, revealing what might have been on their minds. Rose had fleetingly wondered about a life with Scott, but he was already busy studying his schedule of meetings and appointments that he had set up for the next few days. And she had been too proud to ask anyway. After that, they had kept in touch sporadically and met whenever he came to Singapore. It was all warm and loving, but there was never any talk of a permanent relationship.

Then, when Peter came into her life and asked her to marry him, Scott's image had come into her mind, ever so briefly, but she had quickly dispelled the thought. 'There will never be anything there, Rose,' she had told herself sternly. Two weeks after her wedding, Scott had called, and she had found herself faking excitement that she disconcertingly had not quite felt about her marriage when she heard Scott's voice. She had always wondered if it was sadness at having lost Scott or a desire to make him jealous that had fuelled her excitement about marrying the 'best match' for her. She had also wondered what Scott would have thought about her choice. A brief pause had followed, and then he said, 'I wish you all the best, Rose. You know, I always will.' About a year later, she had received a brief note from him informing her that he had married a fellow journalist and that they both lived in Iran. The heaviness in her heart was one that she had never felt before, not even when Stanley died. It felt like some inner light had died, and that was the last time she had heard from him, until today.

The crisp and friendly voice of a Hyatt receptionist came on the line. Rose found herself breathing a little harder as she waited for the connection to be made. The phone rang a few times before she heard Scott's voice, strong and reassuring as always, melting in that minute the years that they were apart and reigniting the closeness they had always shared. 'Rose? What took you so long, girl?' he asked with a little laugh.

Rose cleared her throat before she responded, 'I was busy in meetings yesterday. When did you come in?'

'Oh! Just yesterday in the afternoon. I plan to be here for a week for a little vacation before I return to Indonesia, which is where I live now.'

'Are you here alone?' asked Rose, praying that the hope she so strongly felt would not show.

'Yes, Judith is still in Iran . . . she lives there.' His voice trailed off. 'The kids are grown now, and they are in college.'

'Hmm . . . I see,' responded Rose, again praying that her relief would not show.

'So . . . is there a chance that we can meet?' asked Scott.

'Well, yes, today is pretty open,' said Rose looking at her calendar for the day, which was filled with Maryanne's neat penmanship. Just about every hour was taken with either a presentation or a staff–client meeting, or meetings with lawyers. 'I could see you for an early lunch or something if you like,' she said hesitantly, her heart beating fast.

'Sounds great. I'll see you at the coffeehouse downstairs, or would you prefer that I come up there?' he asked pleasantly.

'No, I'll be there in twenty minutes,' she responded decisively and stood up.

Hanging up, she picked up her purse, which lay on the sideboard next to her desk, and briskly walked out of her room. 'Maryanne, can you have Maniam come around with the car, and please tell Simon that he can handle all my appointments today.'

'B-but Ms Rose . . . You have a meeting with the lawyers in half an hour and then some urgent calls to return and . . .' trailed off Maryanne when she realized that the boss was not stopping to listen.

'Simon is quite capable of handling all that. He knows what to do.' Maryanne watched Rose walk away quickly. It was after the door had closed behind her that Maryanne closed her mouth, which she suddenly realized had been open.

When Clouds Gather

Chapter Six

'I'll handle it, Linda. Take it easy. It will work out,' Ethan said softly into the mouthpiece. His cubicle was right next to Ean's, and he couldn't risk his brother listening in to the conversation. When he hung up, his face was flushed with exasperation. Linda was furious at having been what she saw as 'humiliated in front of the whole office'. She had stayed up almost all night smouldering in the dark, waiting for morning when she could talk about it or do something about it. Of course, when morning came, it was most convenient and easiest to unleash the fury that had burnt within her all night on Ethan as soon as she got him on the phone. When Ethan finally responded saying, 'Come on Lin, you're exaggerating. The whole office wasn't there, and my mother did not intend to humiliate you,' she slammed down the receiver at her end.

Ethan sighed loudly and irritably and ran a hand roughly over his eyes. He hated confrontations like this and never handled them well. But this was exactly what he had feared when Linda had badgered him for a position in the company, and she had told him what a great fit she would be for the position of Senior Marketing Manager. 'Business and relationships don't exactly mix well, darling. Uh . . . I really don't think it would be a good idea. My mother is very demanding, and I . . . uh . . . I'm not sure your personalities would match well,' had been his slightly nervous but laughing protest. 'I have tons of contacts in the industry, and I'm pretty sure I can place you somewhere else.'

'What? Place me in an organization that is second-best? You know this job profile is exactly what I'm looking for, and Lee Constructions is the best in the industry,' she had replied earnestly. Deep within, Ethan had a nagging feeling that being a son of Rose Lee and therefore a strong connection to Lee Constructions was part of what Linda found attractive about him. Realistically, except for the fact that he was Rose Lee's son, he was too nondescript for a woman like Linda, who was, simply put, stunning with her tall, lithe figure, her flawless complexion, and her excellent sense of style. And, as much as he was thankful, there were also many pensive moments when he wondered why she had picked him and not Ean.

Growing up in the shadow of his more athletic and popular twin, Ethan had always worked harder to be noticed by anyone, leave alone the girls. He and Ean were not identical. They both looked pleasant, a little like their father, but Ean seemed to have a fairer share of their mother's good looks. Ean was also the more intelligent and the more articulate of the two, and so he often took the lead even in social situations. If Ethan had not been Rose Lee's son, he would have ended up as middle management in some large corporation—faceless and unnoticed. Unlike Ean, who had always been excited about joining the family business even while growing up, Ethan had wandered through his adolescence a little aimlessly, with reasonable but not exactly outstanding grades. As he grew older, he found calm and solace in painting and classical music as hobbies but nothing ever grabbed him as a passion.

He enjoyed being an heir to Lee Constructions because it gained him entry into circles that he would not have been able to access on his own. He knew people noticed him because they knew and admired his mother. Growing up, he had warmed to his father more than his mother because the man was far less demanding, but he was always in complete awe of his mother. He sought her approval and strove for it, often with Simon's help. Unlike Ean, Ethan was not convinced that Simon was all competition. He had pleasant memories of Simon as the protective older brother, and more than anything, he needed him. He wasn't always up to the demands of his job as Senior Director of Operations, and Simon was always willing to step in to cover for him or guide him. But these days, he had a sense that he was being pushed into some sort of a conspiracy, with Ean and Linda against Simon and his mother. Ean constantly talked about Simon like he was an enemy, and Linda needled him about his mother and didn't really trust Ean either. He didn't care about the things that Linda and Ean fretted about. Ethan really couldn't care less who took the reins from his mother. He was quite happy to be in his present position for the rest of his life and then retire to his apartment to paint while listening to classical music. But Linda was getting impatient. She wanted a commitment and she wanted Ethan to tell Rose about them. She wanted him to ask for the Malaysian operations for themselves. The thought of approaching his mother for something like that nauseated Ethan. He couldn't even imagine how she would react, especially now that she had been betrayed by his father. Ethan was also painfully aware that his mother did not like Linda. He wondered if she knew about his relationship with Linda. His gut told him that Rose suspected it, and his stomach churned a little more.

This conundrum that he was in with Linda and his mother, coupled with the silent feud between Ean and Simon that he was unwillingly being dragged into, felt like a black cloak that had settled on Ethan's head and weighed him down. He didn't know what to believe, despite a niggling feeling that Simon was not what Ean made him out to be. But he wasn't sure. Ethan had never been the type with a clear vision of his own, and now, being pulled in so many different directions, he often felt like his head was going to explode. So it was a deeply troubled Ethan that irritably snatched up the receiver of the buzzing phone. 'Ya! What is it?' he snapped, frowning.

'Mr Ethan, Mr Simon, and Mr Ean are waiting for you in Mrs Lee's private conference room,' said Maryanne.

'What? Was I supposed to meet them?' retorted Ethan, impatiently scanning his calendar.

'No, nothing was planned. The meeting was just arranged, and I think you were speaking on the phone when they tried to call you,' Maryanne said in a soothing voice.

Simon and Ean were already speaking in low tones when Ethan entered the thickly carpeted room where Rose held her private meetings with clients and the senior management. 'What? Are you both conspiring a takeover without me?' asked Ethan with a laugh that sounded false to everyone. Both Simon and Ean looked up. Simon chuckled while Ean frowned. But that was Ean. He rarely smiled. Simon looked at the two of them and wondered how twins could be so different in appearance and personality. Ethan was tall but slightly built, with a smile that was mostly ready but almost always somewhat nervous. The better looking of the two, Ean was about an inch shorter but muscular, because he was a sportsman—a very keen and competitive sportsman. He often wore an expression that could be construed as churlish. There wasn't a shred of softness in his eyes. The fact that he was very intense was obvious by the way he held himself, always erect and alert, with eyes that took in everything around him. When he met someone for the first time and shook their hand, he quickly gave them a once over, like he was mentally evaluating their usefulness. Whether it was sports or business, he played to win. They both wore their hair short, but Ean slicked it back as if he didn't even want his hair to get in the way of his focus, while Ethan's hair lay in soft waves, like Simon's. Simon's, more often than not, needed a cut, much to his mother's chagrin.

Unlike Simon, the twins had one thing in common with each other and that was their love for fine things. Their taste in clothing, watches, and accessories was always expensive. They were both very conscious of the way they looked, unlike Simon. 'Lose some weight, Simon, it's bad for your health, and besides, you look a lot older than thirty-five. And get yourself some nice clothes. You look like you slept in that shirt,' Rose would say when she met him in the evenings.

'Well, yes Ma, I did. You never let me out of here,' would be his laughing response. He could always feel his mother's eyes boring into him when he reached out for a third helping of roasted pork belly during their weekend dinners with Sylvia. 'Not everyone wants to have their collar bones stick out like yours. Stop staring at him like he is committing a crime,' Sylvia would chide Rose during family dinners.

'Come, sit down, Ethan. We were waiting for you to start the meeting. Ean and I were just discussing some ads that were placed in some publications last week. We are wondering if we need to continue with them because they are very expensive,' said Simon. He knew his step-brothers well and was good at smoothening their ruffled feathers, an art that was becoming increasingly tedious for him. 'The real reason we called a meeting, actually I called it, and I did call you first, is that Mother is out for the day, and she has asked me to take charge with your help … both of you,' said Simon, carefully stressing on the 'both of you' while looking at each twin slowly and deliberately, although everyone in the room knew that their mother would have said no such thing.

The three men knew that their mother only trusted Simon to be in charge in her absence, and therein lay the problem for all three of them in different ways. Simon was uncomfortable, Ean was distrustful, and Ethan was unsure of what to think but felt he should go along with his twin only for the sake of loyalty, because he definitely did not dislike Simon, who was his safe conduit to his mother. An irritated Ean would often scold him saying, 'You don't have to keep running to him. Ask me!' But Ean's competitiveness and his desire to be ahead secretly made Ethan very nervous. He couldn't help thinking that Linda was justified in fretting about Ean. Ethan was well aware that his twin was extremely aggressive. Given half a chance, he suspected that Ean would carve even him out of Lee Constructions.

'She seems to be out most of the time these days,' complained Ean. It irked him that Simon was sitting on his mother's chair, at her desk. He liked that desk, that chair, and the painting that adorned one wall. He liked the whole room, especially since it had the best view. He could see himself here, easily. 'I find it so hard to get her approvals on launches and marketing strategies,' he grumbled. Simon knew that Ean was making a point by going directly to their mother for approvals, although she had made it clear about two years ago that as long as Simon vetted it, she wouldn't need to see it. She had scolded Ean many a time for coming to her with what she felt was purely routine. 'You don't need to see me for this. Has Simon seen it? If he has, don't waste my time and yours,' she would say. To this, Ean would simply respond, 'I report to you, Ma. You know that. If all it needs is Simon's approval, then I can approve it myself.' Rose would just shake her head with a sigh that was ignored by Ean. She could have easily told him again that Simon was in charge when she was away and that matters concerning routine marketing campaigns were Simon's responsibility, but she felt it wasn't necessary, just as she felt that it wasn't necessary to inform the twins if she wasn't going to be in the office.

As far as she was concerned, she had made it clear once, and it was cast in stone in legal documents pertaining to the company. If the twins, especially Ean, refused to recognize it, in Rose's eyes, he was just making his path to leadership more difficult and thorny. 'There is so much more for him to learn and experience before he can take charge of this business, and if he would just leave the decisions to you, then he will probably grow into a leadership role himself more quickly just by observing. I look forward to the day when he doesn't have to get approval from you or me for his decisions. He does not realize that,' she argued when Simon chided her for harshness with the twins.

Rose was quite clear about the roles that she had in mind for her sons. Ethan was not for the leadership of the business. He was too nervous and too easily influenced by those around him. He was best where he was, in charge of operations. Even there, he often needed Simon to step in, especially when it came to negotiations with the staff or vendors. Ean was another matter altogether. He had amazing potential and Rose's shrewdness and eye for a good deal. But he had what she had never had, and still did not despite her phenomenal success, a raw ruthlessness and greed that was disconcerting and a little frightening. She was afraid that someday it would lead him and the company to disaster. 'How can I even think of letting Simon walk away? All I will have left will be Ethan, who knows nothing about the business, and Ean, who will think nothing of stamping on even Ethan and anyone else who gets in his way, just to get ahead,' was Rose's oft-repeated lament to herself on sleepless nights.

The thick tension that separated Simon from his step-brothers was palpable in Rose's room where the three men sat. 'Well, I think she had some urgent business that couldn't wait and that's what Maryanne tells me,' said Simon, sitting up straight in his mother's chair. He always did this when he felt that his brothers were angling for a discussion on their mother's behaviour and choices, and the conversation would then move into where the twins stood in her mind as opposed to Simon. Simon made every effort he could to avoid such conversations, and the only way he could do it was to assume his second-in-command stance, even with his brothers. Although he knew it annoyed them, especially Ean, when he spoke like a boss, there was no choice. If they questioned his decisions, he would simply smile and say, 'We could bring that up when we meet the boss next but work needs to get done now.'

Simon smiled at his brothers. 'Well, um . . . I think she is going to be out tomorrow as well. Let's look at her calendar, and we can split up her meetings between us. Then we can decide what else we can complete without taking us away from our own calendars.' Ethan nodded glancing at his twin while Ean studied his mother's calendar intently. He planned to pick the most important meetings, especially with the financiers and suppliers. They needed to know him as his mother's successor. But Simon was experienced enough to read his mind. He knew what his mother wanted, at least for now, and he knew that Ean, with his intensity and his pushiness that bordered on insolence, could spoil relationships that she had nurtured over the years. As usual, Ethan hung back a tad sulkily.

Ean's pick was, of course, the most important meeting with the CEO of the Yong Brothers, the biggest builders in Malaysia. Rose was in talks with them for a joint effort to build what would probably be the largest mall in Asia. While Simon couldn't imagine how his mother could brush off such an important meeting to go off on some random errand, he had to think of something that would distract Ean.

Simon cleared his throat and was about to speak when Ean spoke first.

'I think I should meet with Wilson Yong. I have met him before and he knows me. I think I can—'

Simon cut in smoothly saying, 'Yes, that would have been great. But I have to tell you that Wilson Yong will not be coming. He is sending one of his vice presidents instead to meet with Ma. Apparently, Wilson was called away to Melbourne on some urgent matter . . .' and as he spoke, he buzzed Maryanne and asked her, 'Maryanne, what was the message from the Yongs again, please?'

Maryanne sounded like she was checking, and then came back on the line, 'Mr Wilson Yong will not be coming. Instead, it will be Mr Karim Abdullah, Vice President of Sales and Marketing. Mr Yong is in Melbourne now. Ms Rose knows about it, and she wanted Mr Ean to meet with Mr Abdullah.' Ean's face darkened.

It was enough for him that his mother thought that the meeting was so unimportant that she was relegating it to him. 'I think you're better off seeing Karim Abdullah. I'm not sure that much can be achieved by this meeting, since the man himself is not going to be here.'

Ean frowned at the calendar before pushing it away from him. 'I really don't think there is anything here that can't wait till Ma returns,' he said, barely able to conceal his exasperation at the waste of an opportunity to project himself.

Ethan glanced at his twin, and then looked hesitantly at Simon. Perhaps this was the best time to talk about Linda and her position in the office and what she perceived as Rose's unreasonable demands on her. His brothers would be more empathetic, or so he thought. He cleared his throat as he prepared to talk. 'Linda is really unhappy about the way the presentation . . .'

Simon smoothly interrupted him. 'Actually, Ma spoke with me this morning, and she wants to talk to Linda when she comes back tomorrow. I think she looked over the presentation last night and came up with some ideas about how to make things work. It isn't Ma's intention to give Linda a hard time,' said Simon smiling conciliatorily.

'It looks like only you know everything about Ma, although she is our mother as well,' said Ean chuckling cynically.

'It just looks that way Ean, because I'm older. But . . .' began Simon, uncertainly. He didn't know what to say because there was some truth in what his brother had expressed.

Ean interrupted irritably, 'Ma seems to be getting more and more demanding as she grows older. It could be that the stress is getting too much for her—' He stopped short when he caught Simon's frown. He himself was a little mortified by his inadvertent revelation of what was playing on his mind, that it was time his mother stepped aside and let him and well, yes, his brothers take over the leadership.

'Ma is completely capable of handling herself extremely well here in the organization, or anywhere else. She built this and everything that this company is about, is due to her and no one else. This company is hers, and we work for her. Even Baba would have said the same thing, and you both know that,' said Simon, the steely edge in his voice slicing through the quietness in the room.

The twins looked away, unable to meet the chilling hardness in his gaze. 'If she is demanding, it is because she has achieved a great deal and knows what hard work and drive can do. I don't think any one of us in this room can come close to what she is. Believe me, we just don't have it in us,' said Simon with a coldness that was not entirely new to the twins. They had been at the receiving end of his anger once before. Simon was never angry. His congenial temperament was well known both inside and outside the office. There were even some snide remarks that were passed around that Simon's other role was damage control. He put right the damage created by his mother's demanding nature, Ean's brashness, and Ethan's ineffectiveness. However, on the extremely rare occasion when he did get angry, his quietness and razor-sharp choice of words were enough to cut deeper than any explosion of temper.

The twins glanced at each other. Ethan looked clearly nervous, and Ean seemed discomfited at being abruptly put in his place. Simon's anger today rudely brought back to their minds the last time they had been subjected to it some years ago. He had had to cover up for them with their mother when they had been caught cheating during their university exams. They had been threatened with expulsion, and the twins had pleaded with the university authorities to contact their brother instead of their parents to speak on their behalf. Simon had flown to Australia, where the twins were at college, telling his mother that he needed a quick vacation. It had taken all of his communication skills and his reassurances to convince the university authorities that the punishment would be harsher for the twins if they were retained. Expulsion would have meant nothing to them as they had jobs waiting for them in a family business. After Simon had successfully sorted out the mess, he had informed the twins curtly that it was up to him whether or not they had a place in the family business, and that if they acted in a manner that would be embarrassing to their mother and their family, he would ensure that they didn't get a foot into Lee Constructions.

The twins had stayed back a year and finally graduated by the skin of their teeth. Their father had laughed and applauded his sons for negotiating their way to success. But Rose had been furious about the wasted year and even refused to let them work in the company, telling them to prove themselves somewhere else and earn their place in her organization. It was then that her distrust of Ean had begun. She knew even then that it would have been Ean's, not Ethan's, idea to cheat. 'Ethan will always be too afraid to cross the line, but his twin knows no fear. That is the problem,' she had confided in Simon.

'Come on, Ma, that's a little unfair, don't you think? He's young and brash. Surely he will grow out of it,' Simon had argued. Rose had merely looked at him doubtfully and said, 'I hope.' While the twins had been grateful to him for covering for them and speaking up for them, they had also begun to see the power that Simon had within the company and the influence that he had on their mother. Minute seeds of realization that their mother listened to Simon and respected his opinion were sown in their minds then. The seeds sprouted when they saw, after beginning to work for Lee Constructions, that even their own father, Peter Lee, who was Simon's stepfather, liked and trusted Simon immensely and looked to him for counsel and sometimes even as a mediator with their mother.

* * *

A heavy and uneasy silence hung in the air after Simon had spoken that morning. He focused on arranging the folders in front of him, refusing to make eye contact with the twins or engage in any more conversation. The twins, uncomfortably aware that their brother had dismissed them with his stony silence, rose one after the other. 'Um . . . I guess we should get busy. I have a staff meeting with my sales team,' said Ean, and made for the door, while Ethan mumbled something about having to speak with vendors somewhere in Jurong. Simon merely nodded without looking at them, the masklike demeanour hiding the agitation that raged within him. Scenes like this, where the twins displayed their misgivings about him and their mother, were becoming too frequent, too disturbing, and too draining for him. All he wanted was to travel and follow his heart.

His thoughts were interrupted by the buzzing of the phone. When he reached forward across Rose's desk and answered it, Maryanne informed him that Ms Rose had a call waiting on her personal line. He sighed in response. He knew who it was. He had arranged it with Maryanne. 'Hello, Mr Yong, my mother informed me that you would be calling. She is out for the day, but I know the details. When and where can we meet?' This was the real meeting with Wilson Yong and Rose had instructed Simon privately to attend the meeting in her place. 'We cannot risk Ean insisting on meeting this man and ruining what I have worked on for a whole year. So you go in my place. You can make up something to Ean because you know that he would want to meet Wilson Yong. Just take care of it.' After agreeing on a venue for the meeting with Wilson Yong, Simon walked out of the room 'to take care of things'—as he was supposed to in place of his mother—slapping the folder of papers against his thigh resignedly. *More deceit and more reason for the twins to distrust me.* Simon hoped that he would not meet either of them as he left the office. He needed to have a serious conversation with his mother.

Chapter Seven

Rose stretched lazily and turned over to face the window. She closed her eyes and listened to the rhythmic drumming of water in the shower with a lazy smile playing on her lips. After all these years, nothing had changed between them. They still shared a closeness that she had never felt for Peter or even Stanley before him. With Scott, there was no holding back, no secrets, and so this time, like all the other times, nothing was lost in the time that they had not seen each other. All her fears, inhibitions, and guard had melted the minute she had set eyes on him from a distance. All she had wanted to do was to run up to him, fling her arms around him, and bury her face in his shoulder.

But she couldn't because of who she was and the fact that several heads turned and eyes lit up with recognition the minute she stepped into the hotel lobby, which was, much to her dismay, filled with people from a conference taking place at the hotel. If only she had known, she would have fixed the meeting elsewhere. She had had Maniam drop her off at the Shangri-la and then taken a taxi to the Hyatt. She was less mortified by the cloak and dagger game she was playing than by the possibility of being seen by her sons while meeting an old boyfriend. It would have been impossible for Maniam to guess anything, but she wasn't taking any chances. It was best that he was unaware of where she was really going, so he wouldn't have to lie to Simon or the twins. She was convinced that she couldn't face her sons if they knew.

Scott's face, too, lit up the minute he saw her, and he greeted her with the broad smile that she had always loved about him. Never forgetting who she was, she had returned the smile with the slightest of smiles and nods. She hugged him lightly, reaching up as always as he was a full head taller. Immediately sensing her restraint, he had responded just as lightly. And that was Scott, always empathetic, never forcing himself or his views on her. For a fleeting second, the stark difference between Scott and Peter stood out in her mind. Had it been Peter, he would have wanted not just the people in the lobby, but the whole world to know that he knew Rose Lee, the leading lady of a multi-million-dollar construction business. That was Peter, always looking to be noticed for who he knew.

'It's so good to see you, Rose,' said Scott, smiling down at her, his eyes reflecting the sheer happiness that he felt. 'I've thought about you a lot. I heard about Peter, and I'm really sorry about everything.' Rose felt hot colour rushing up to her face. A wild combination of embarrassment, anger, sadness and despair burnt within.

She smiled stiffly at Scott and nodded. 'I'm really happy to see you too, Scott. It's been so long. We have so much to catch up on.' Scott had smiled down at her, his eyes knowing. The charade was not lost on him.

'So what would you like to do now? Have some lunch or a drink first?' asked Scott holding her hand lightly and leading her to the restaurant, which was relatively quiet since it was not yet lunchtime.

The small talk that Rose insisted on began to be exhausting for both. She resisted talking about Peter and his death, her marriage, or anything else that was painful to her. The conversation was merely a series of questions and answers about what each one had been doing. Sensing her reluctance to venture beyond trivialities, Scott dutifully played the game and asked the right questions and answered her questions about himself. He was now living in Indonesia and was still married, but he and his wife lived separate lives. She lived and worked in Iran and had no plans to join him in Indonesia. In fact, of late she had been talking about returning to the US to be closer to their children, who were both at different stages of their doctoral programmes in Berkeley. 'They're just lovely, aren't they?' he said proudly, showing Rose a picture of two pretty young women together, laughing at the camera.

Rose looked at the picture, smiling gently and nodded. 'Yes, they are lovely. I hope to meet them sometime.' She felt a slight pang of hurt somewhere within. He was a family man after all. He just hadn't thought that she was the one with whom he wanted that family.

Reading her mind, he said gently, 'I wasn't ready for a long time. But when I was ready, you had made your choice Rose, and I had to look somewhere else.'

Rose glanced at him quickly, a little self-conscious that she had made her thoughts so obvious, and then laughed nervously, looking down at her plate. 'We have both travelled a long way since then . . . clearly,' she said, softly and hesitantly.

Scott looked at her with a slight smile, and said, 'Yes, we have. But we haven't moved so far apart from each other that we have to pretend. I can see that you're hurting, and I'm here now,' said Scott gently. Rose kept her eyes steadfastly on her plate because she felt tears pooling in them. 'I lied. I don't have to be here today. My meeting was over yesterday. I chose to stay on because I wanted to see you. I have come at least forty times to Singapore since we last spoke, and it took all my restraint to stop myself from calling you. If I'd called you then, I would have ruined things for you,' he continued. 'For both of us, I suppose. Judith was very much in my life then,' he added with a wry laugh. 'This time I heard about your husband . . . and well . . . his other family . . .' he added sounding faintly uncomfortable.

Rose looked at him with pained eyes, and he stopped for a moment. 'You don't have to feel shame or embarrassment with me. It's me, Rose. Scott. You never have to feel like you lost with me.' Rose felt the tears prickling in her eyes, and she looked down at her untouched plate. If any of her staff—or even Simon, who had seen her at her most vulnerable sobbing outside the ICU when Stanley died—had seen her now, they would have been astonished by the person who sat before Scott. This was the same person—the demanding boss who made the staff squirm when she as much as looked at them from over the rim of her reading glasses. But now she sat with her face reddened and lips that quivered as she tried to suppress the emotions that welled up within. 'Perhaps we should have coffee in my room. That would be best. You go ahead, and that way it won't look obvious,' said Scott slipping Rose his access card while signalling the waiter.

* * *

Rose heard the shower turn off and a door opening behind her. 'How about something to eat, Rose?' asked Scott rubbing his hair with a towel. Rose turned over to face him. His face had certainly aged. The once handsome, boyish face was now deeply lined and a little gaunt. He had also lost quite a bit of his dark hair. But he still looked arresting, mainly because of his height and athletic build.

'We just ate,' she laughed, her eyes dancing.

'What? I still run ten miles a day,' he said flopping down beside her on the bed and wrapping his arms around her.

'Well, I only eat one real meal a day. I graze after that,' she said, playfully twirling a lock of his hair with her fingers.

'Hmm . . . you certainly look fit. Although I must say you have become too thin,' he replied, stroking her cheek. Pulling her close, he kissed her eyelids gently as he caressed her arms. She moaned softly and drew him into her arms. He kissed her nose and her cheeks, and when he finally arrived at her mouth, his large hand rested on her breast, gently, like a feather, and she arched her back to meet his mouth.

'Oh! Rose, my lovely little Rose. I've missed you so much,' he groaned, his voice thick and deep. His confession triggered a rush of emotions in her, and he softly exclaimed when he tasted salt. His kisses became gentler as he began to kiss away her tears.

Her mind was a muddle of suppressed emotions and memories. Sex with Peter had always been just sex. With Scott, it had been, and still was, a union of their two selves. Scott was a gentle and considerate lover, who gave what she wanted and took what she gave willingly. Stanley had been able to unleash an untamed passion that surprised her. He was a playful lover and he teased, cajoled, withdrew, and gave till her whole being screamed for him. He was the only one who could get her to walk up to him wearing nothing but a pair of stilettoes and act the vamp without a hint of bashfulness. By the time Peter came into her life, she knew what she wanted, but very quickly and early in her relationship realized that sex with Peter was just that, sex.

Peter would reach out to her once or twice a week and quite often when he was inebriated. His idea of foreplay did nothing for her, and it was over when it was over for him. He would roll off of her like he had achieved something while she would turn away to hide her disappointment. It was disheartening in the first few months, and she was not sure if it was something that she could live with. But in due course, she trained her mind to look at the other advantages of the marriage and soon became accustomed to it. The twins came along, and in time, their sex nights dwindled to once a month or even once in two months. When she hadn't known any better, Rose had breathed a sigh of relief. She was focused on juggling the business and raising her sons, and sex with Peter was more of an irritation. When the real reason was uncovered after Peter's death, she was humiliated because 'that woman' had been more than enough woman for Peter.

As she lay in Scott's arms now, Rose felt a stillness and satisfaction she hadn't felt in many years. She realized that the last thing she wanted was to go back to being the Rose Lee who headed Lee Constructions. The knot that was always tight in her stomach, nudging her along the endless road of perfection had suddenly dissolved. Closing her eyes, she tried to think of herself without the numerous responsibilities that tied her to being the Rose Lee that the world knew—razor sharp in her business dealings, unsmiling more often than not, aloof with her staff and these days even with her sons, impatient with her mother for being the voice of reason, and most of all still feeling humiliated by a dead husband who had cheated on her.

* * *

Rose woke up with a start. Both Scott and she had fallen asleep, and Scott still had his arms around her. She could hear his regular breathing and feel his gentle, warm breath on the nape of her neck. The clock that glowed in the dark showed 8:30 p.m. Rose sighed and carefully extricated herself from Scott's embrace. Her sons, especially Simon, and Sylvia would have tried to call her and Maniam at least twenty times by now. She had left strict instructions with Maniam to switch off his office cell phone. Only she and Maryanne had Maniam's private number, and he was not allowed to give it to anyone from the office. If his office cell phone was switched off, no one could connect with him to try and find her, so he wouldn't have to struggle to find excuses for her absences. She had switched off her phones, both private and business.

Swinging her feet lightly off the bed, Rose stood up and reached for the robe that lay on the chair next to the bed. Wrapping herself in it, she walked up to her purse and pulled out her cell phone meant for personal calls only. She gasped softly when she saw the close to forty calls from Simon, Maryanne, Maniam, the twins, and her friends since four-thirty in the afternoon. There were five messages from Maryanne alone which read: *Please call immediately. Very urgent.* There was also a voice message from Maniam: *Rose Mam, where are you? I talked to the receptionist at the Shangri-la. They never saw you.* Rose's forehead was etched with a deep frown, and her icy hands fumbled with the phone as she tried to listen to and look at the numerous messages.

'For heaven's sake! Where the hell are you?' asked Penny. 'What's wrong with you? Why can't you call back?' demanded Nalini in her message. Rose couldn't imagine what all the urgency was about that even Penelope and Nalini were demanding that she call back. Rose's breath became shorter as she switched on her business phone. Her sons would have called her there if there was an emergency at the office. As soon as she switched on the phone, it repeatedly beeped with messages, again from Maryanne, Simon, Maniam, and the twins. *Where are you?* asked Simon *Please call,* said another message. *Please call me now,* he repeated. *Mom, please call one of us back now,* said Ethan in his message. Something had happened! Despite her racing heart and breath that had become faintly ragged, her characteristic ability to take charge, stay calm in the most unsettling situations, and choose the most effective means to achieve the fastest results prevailed. Rose called Penelope. She didn't want to call her sons because of the questions that they would have. It was easier to manage friends.

As soon as Penelope came on the line she snapped, 'Rose! Where on earth are you? We've all been trying to call you all evening . . .' Rose's half-smile, which had played around her mouth at the start of the call, froze as she listened to Penelope. Scott had silently awoken and was now behind her. 'What's happened, Rose?' he asked, his voice filled with quiet concern.

Rose looked up from listening to Penelope. 'I'm coming now,' she said to her friend before she hung up. She looked at Scott, frowning a little and biting her lower lip as tears gathered in her almond-shaped, brown eyes that almost always drew a second look from anyone that they saw.

Chapter Eight

Sylvia's routine was so predictable that everyone who knew her well knew exactly where she was or what she was doing depending on the day of the week. Monday mornings were for Mahjong with her friends from her sewing days. In the afternoons, Keng San, the chauffeur that Rose had engaged specifically for her mother's afternoon drives, took Sylvia and Ming to the Kuan Yin Temple on Waterloo Street. After the temple visit, the two would take a slow walk around Waterloo Street, just to take in the sights a little before heading home. Sylvia would then spend the evening watching Korean soaps.

On Tuesdays, she would spend the morning at home doing this and that, but afternoons were spent having coffee with her old neighbours and customers in the Commonwealth Food Court. She looked forward to her weekly journey back to the days when her husband had a noodle stall there. On Wednesdays, she would spend the day at home, resting or playing Mahjong with herself on her laptop. Sometimes, Rose would have lunch or dinner with her. But it was Sylvia's special day because it was Simon's day to come to dinner. It was the one day of the week when she hovered around in the kitchen keeping a close eye on dinner preparations by Ming for her ' . . . dear sweet Simon'. Thursday was Sylvia's day to go over to another friend's home to play Mahjong again, and Fridays and the weekend were when Rose or Simon or, on very rare occasions, one of the twins, mostly Ethan, would take her out for a meal. Though, as Sylvia often sadly mused, 'The twins rarely come these days.'

Today was Wednesday, her special day, but she was dead. It was almost like destiny had decided that Wednesday would be the best day for Sylvia to die because that was the day she would be happily comfortable at home, eagerly waiting for her Simon to have dinner with her. And, indeed, she had looked like she was sleeping peacefully when Ming, who had returned from Melaka in the afternoon, had tried to wake her. 'After I came back, I looked into her room,' cried Ming, her usually expressionless face now drawn and white with the anguish that she felt. Simon reached out to pat her arm in empathy. 'She looked like she was fast asleep. So I left her. But when I went to wake her one hour later, at three-thirty, she was gone,' Ming had related this to him in short staccato sentences before breaking down in sobs. The uncharacteristic display of emotion would have been surprising if not for the circumstances. As soon as Ming had found Sylvia, stone-cold and unresponsive, she had frantically called Simon first, and he had been hard put to understand her disjointed sentences amid her ragged sobs. Ming never called Rose. If she wanted to communicate anything at all to Rose, it was always through Simon, whom she liked and who liked her in return.

By the time Rose walked into her mother's house that night, a few of her staff, especially the senior management and some friends of Sylvia, were already there. Some who had come to pay their respects were leaving when she walked in. They nodded respectfully as they passed her, but Rose felt like they looked at her rather quizzically. In fact, she felt the weight of hushed whispers in the quiet room and the relentless stabs in the twins' eyes filled with a thousand questions, as she slowly walked up to her dead mother. Choosing to ignore the stares, she fixed her eyes on the body of the woman that lay in the middle of the room. Sylvia lay peacefully with her hair perfectly arranged and her lips coloured in the beautiful rose pink that she loved. The fragrance from the

flowers and wreaths that surrounded Sylvia hung heavily in the
air. Rose laid a hand on her mother's cold forehead. Although the
anguish inside her was unbearable, the tears didn't flow.

The pain, coupled with the intense guilt that filled her, felt like
lead in her heart and froze her emotions, only serving to confirm
what must have been on the minds of all those who stood staring.
Rose is cold and unfeeling. The guilt that she felt gnawed at her
because she had chosen to spend the afternoon in the arms of an
old lover instead of being available to rush to her mother's side
sooner. Ethan and Ean looked on sullenly, and Linda, who stood
by Ethan, had the hint of a smirk that spoke of what she was
thinking. Rose was now alone, save for Simon, whose hand she felt
rest firmly on her shoulder despite the questions he might have
had in his mind.

'Ma,' he whispered. 'Do you need to sit down?' he asked. Rose
didn't respond. What she didn't realize was that to those who
were observing her, she looked like she was swaying, on the verge
of falling. Rose simply closed her eyes and shook her head, her
hand still on her mother's forehead. She licked her dry lips and
opened her mouth as if to speak but could merely sigh slowly. She
swallowed and tried again. Her voice was so soft that it was barely
a whisper, and Simon had to lean forward close to her mouth and
still strain to hear her.

'Are the formalities over? Did you have to take her to the
hospital?'

'No, Ma. Dr Chang next door just came over and signed the
death certificate. The embalmers finished a couple of hours ago,'
responded Simon, uncomfortable about these details because they
underlined the reality that his beloved Popo was dead. He had
been so busy taking care of the details in his mother's absence that
they had seemed merely items to be checked off, as always when
she was not there.

Now that Rose was here, the truth coldly descended on him,
and it took all of his grit to suppress his desire to just cling to Sylvia

and cry. That voice that was only caring, fiercely protective, and unwaveringly supportive was now silent. His grip on his mother's shoulder tightened as they both stood staring at the dead woman. Rose's hand sought Simon's hand that held her shoulder and rested on it. She squeezed her son's hand. They were once again mother and son sitting alone outside that hospital room when Stanley had died. Only this time, Sylvia was not going to burst in and hold them both.

* * *

In the days after the funeral, Rose spent most of her time in her mother's home, listlessly going through Sylvia's things, working constantly but achieving very little. She kept taking things out of the closets, drawers and cupboards, looking at them blankly and putting them back because she didn't quite know what she wanted to do with them. Sylvia had loved clothes and baubles. In the early days, when money had been short, she had sewn her own clothes and worn costume jewellery. When money ceased to be an issue because of Rose's success and her generosity, Sylvia had her clothes custom-made. When she was younger, she wore cheongsams, and as she grew older she wore blouses and loose trousers, fashioned like the samfoo in silk or soft cotton. Her closet held about thirty or forty sets of these in different shades and designs, all neatly hung on hangers by Ming and scented with rose and lemon essential oils. A few unopened packages of new sets of clothing lay at the bottom of the closet. Rose couldn't stop a wan half-smile when she thought of her mother and her love of clothing. 'She had more clothes than I do, and she left the house only for a few hours every week.'

The scent of rose and lemon wafted out of all the drawers of the beautiful Chinese lacquer jewellery cabinet that Rose opened. Every drawer contained velvet boxes and silken bags of Sylvia's jewellery. Earrings, necklaces, bangles, and bracelets of jade, gold, and diamonds twinkled and glittered as Rose opened the boxes and pouches one by one. Sylvia loved to show off her jewellery to her friends as gifts from her daughter. 'My Rosie bought this for me. She spoils me too much,' she would say smiling proudly. More often than not, Sylvia would buy these presents for herself and have the jeweller send the bill to Rose.

Rose picked up a bangle and held it up in the sun. Sparkling and winking, almost preening in the light, it seemed to be taunting her. This was probably the most expensive piece that Sylvia had owned. Rose had baulked at the bill. When she had asked Sylvia about it on the phone, her mother had laughed, 'Not sure how much longer I have Rosie, you better be nice to me.'

'At this rate, Ma, I may be the one to go first. So you better be nice to me,' Rose had grumbled.

Sylvia had simply laughed some more in response and said, '*Haiya* Rosie! Talking nonsense as usual!'

Rose tried on the bangle and held it against the light again. Just as she didn't quite like many of Sylvia's pieces of jewellery, she didn't like this one either. Almost all of them were designed with dragons, frogs, goldfish and butterflies, which Sylvia considered lucky. And she loved butterflies. But they didn't appeal to Rose, who preferred clean lines; images of animals or people on her clothing or her jewellery were just not her style. But she decided to keep this piece and wear it always. It was Sylvia's favourite dragon bangle, with a jade bead in the dragon's mouth. It was not something that Rose would typically wear, but when she felt the bangle against her skin, she felt Sylvia's presence.

Rose went through a few more boxes mechanically, all containing a bangle, a necklace, a pair of earrings, or a ring. Without a clue as to what she would do with them, she gathered them all in a large bag. She couldn't bring herself to sell the pieces. *I can't imagine strangers evaluating them and judging their worth or their beauty. She bought them because she loved them and enjoyed wearing them. I'll just place them in a safe deposit box. Maybe someday the boys' wives can have them.* Just as she was getting back on her feet, she heard Simon speaking with Ming in the courtyard. He had been visiting every day at lunchtime hoping that his mother would be ready to return to the office.

It had been three weeks since Sylvia's funeral, and Rose showed no such inclination. She rarely even called the office to check on matters. Other than her sons, especially Simon who kept her abreast of what was happening in the office, she spoke with Scott every day. He had returned to Jakarta after briefly attending Sylvia's funeral. The day Sylvia died strangely served as the day Rose would experience the end of one relationship and the renewal of another. She and Scott had finally moved towards permanence.

Meanwhile, Simon was managing the office, the staff and his brothers, and the extreme fatigue showed on his face. His partner, Luis, wanted to come to Singapore to be with him, and Simon would have liked that, but given the situation and the fact that he had never spoken about his private life to anyone, it seemed impossible. The frustration and stress of that showed as well. Simon was ready to tell Rose everything that was on his mind and his desire to quit the business, but he couldn't because she wasn't even speaking whole sentences. She was simply wandering around his grandmother's home, distracted. She hardly ate or slept. When he spoke with her, she responded in monosyllables or with just a 'hmm . . .' or a nod. Mixed in with his grief for Sylvia was his anxiety for Rose, who he feared was never going to be her old self, and his irritation with having to deal with his brothers, who were becoming more and more distrustful.

Simon couldn't help it, but he was beginning to feel a little bit of resentment and impatience. He had never felt it before and was uncomfortable feeling it now. He considered himself ungrateful and unappreciative of everything that his mother had done for him. But the feeling overwhelmed him, especially since his mother seemed to be on a journey that was taking her further and further away from the business while leaving him to unwillingly hold the reins and keep his brothers in check. He had held her hand from the day Stanley, his father had died, and that was when he was barely ten. These days, the trust that she had in him felt more like a burden. He was going to talk to her frankly. She had to make a decision one way or another. If she planned to return and take charge, she had to provide him with a date, and if she didn't plan to return, then she would have to trust the twins and give them the business. He wanted out.

'Have you eaten, son?' asked Rose, glancing at Simon and sensing a seriousness that she didn't want to deal with yet. 'I haven't eaten yet. Let's have lunch together. I think Ming has something ready.' She walked towards the stone table in the sunny courtyard. Ling Ling the parrot expressed loud delight at the sight of Simon. 'Simon Boy! Simon Boy!' squawked the bird, parroting Sylvia, who called him that, much to his annoyance, till the day she died.

'I'm not hungry, Ma,' grumbled Simon.

Rose glanced at her son and sensed his dourness but refused to succumb to it. Instead, she simply said, 'Well, then why don't you sit with me while I eat? I'm hungry.' Ming silently slid in and out of the dining area, laying bowls and plates on the table while stealing glances at the mother and son.

Rose sat down and dished out the soup for herself, ignoring Simon, who continued to stand at a little distance before slowly walking towards the table and sitting down. Rose placed the bowl of soup in front of him.

'Come on, you will like this. You have always liked her dried vegetable and pork rib soup, and I know you are hungry ...'

'I'm a grown man, Ma. If I'm hungry, I know how to take care of myself,' interjected Simon, frowning. If Rose was surprised by Simon's tone, she didn't show it. She merely glanced at her son and dished out another bowl for herself. She had an idea of what was on her son's mind as she had seen it coming for a while, but she now feared that he was going to force her hand.

Rose had known all along, even before Simon had told her, that the business was not his cup of tea. His love for art, his love for travel, and his boredom with numbers had made it all obvious. She had known that he would never want to take charge of the business even if she had handed it to him on a silver platter and disinherited her two other sons. Her two other sons irritated her because they couldn't see the obvious, that they would inherit the business whether they liked it or not since Simon had no interest in stepping into her shoes. What she had hoped was that they would learn as much as they could from him so that they would be ready. Through his long association with her, Simon had acquired the skills and acumen that he did not naturally have. He held the reins well because he did what he knew she would do. 'They are too stupid to figure things out the way he did and too proud to learn from him. How can I entrust them with such a huge responsibility?' she frequently asked herself when she was alone and pensive.

Rose ate slowly while Simon sat in stony silence. His mind was fraught with what had happened at the office that morning. His brothers had been openly antagonistic, embarrassing him in front of the staff by refusing to attend the monthly all-hands meeting that he had chaired that morning in Rose's place. Ethan had feigned ignorance of the meeting, while Ean had openly refused to come. Their complaint was that Simon was assuming powers that had never been given to him. 'Where's Ma? Is she ever coming back? If she is not, then isn't it time for her to name her successor before we continue? Or, has she already secretly appointed you? Whatever it is, we need to know.' They had questioned unrelentingly when he had spoken with them. Since it was an all-hands meeting, where some major projects, appointments and cutbacks had been announced, his brothers' absence had been glaring. They had even left it to their staff to inform him that they were not attending.

And, when he had spoken to them after the meeting, Ean, in particular, had been belligerent, while Ethan had sullenly stood by and listened. Ean had openly expressed his hope that their mother would see it fit to finally retire so that everything could be streamlined, and their rights and responsibilities clearly demarcated. Simon had angrily retorted, 'Aren't you ashamed to even voice something like that? Look, I have no desire to inherit any of this. I'm Ma's employee. I know that's what you are constantly afraid of, and let me assure you that the two of you will get every last brick of this bloody damn business!' Simon had exploded loudly, slamming his hands on his desk.

This explosion of anger was so out of character for Simon that Ean had taken a step back, and Ethan, who had been silent and uncomfortable, had stared wide-eyed, stunned. The staff outside had cast furtive and worried glances at the brothers through the glass walls of Simon's cabin because they had never heard him raise his voice so harshly. Typically, they only heard him laughing loudly. Simon had left his room in a huff, slamming the door behind him and leaving his brothers alone inside. He had driven directly to his grandmother's home where his mother was, determined to force a resolution.

The discord was so obvious now that the staff could guess what was happening. Even the company's clients, business associates, and partners were beginning to question Simon about where they were heading and what was going to happen after his mother. And Simon was tired of fielding these questions while Rose absently floated around with her depression—first about Peter and now about Sylvia's death. There had been many times when he had questioned his mother, stood up to her, argued with her about her decisions, and disagreed with her, but there had never been any doubt in his mind that his mother could always depend on him as a son and as someone who cared about her immensely. For once though, he wanted something for himself. He wanted his freedom.

'What happened at the office? Why the bad mood?' asked Rose, looking at the soup in her spoon, doing her best to keep her manner light. Her questions hung in the air without a response as Simon sighed impatiently and stared in front of him. Then, when he spoke, there was a decisiveness and finality in his voice that she had never heard before. 'I don't want to continue with this. I have tried telling you many times and in many different ways but you have always ignored me. I have no interest in working for this business. I think the time has come for you to pay attention to what I want . . . for a change,' he said looking directly at his mother, who avoided his gaze, preferring to focus on the soup in front of her. He was using every ounce of his restraint to contain his profound exasperation, while she was doing her best to hide her agitation. She had never imagined that it would come to this, where her sons just could not get along, and the twins were almost completely estranged from her. They had not even come to see her after Sylvia's funeral.

'Ma, you need to come back to work. And, I would like to stop coming into the office when you do that.' Simon enunciated his words deliberately. When Rose finally looked up, the fatigue in her red-rimmed eyes was not lost on him, and his heart went out to her but for once he held back. If he weakened now, he would be lost forever. In some ways, it was already too late. He knew that his relationship with his brothers was ruined forever. They didn't trust him, and they didn't trust their mother. 'It's really up to you how you wish to divide up the company between the twins, but I think it's time you did it. I want no part of it. You already know that,' he persisted stubbornly. 'It would be best for everyone, Ma,' he continued, his voice softening a little. 'I'm your son, and I will be there for you, always. I just don't want the business.'

Rose smiled a little at Simon's final sentence. She reached out and held his forearm that was resting on the table.

Sighing, she said, 'I know. And I'm sorry you've had to put up with all this for so long. I thought, or rather hoped, that you would change your mind eventually, but it looks like you are pretty sure about what you don't want,' she chuckled with resignation. 'I'm not sure the boys are the best choice to lead the business, but I'm left with no other option. I will stick around a little longer just to make sure that they don't sink the whole ship.'

'Come on, Ma. You know that they will not do that. They have worked with us long enough,' said Simon, his tone immediately a lot lighter and conciliatory because of the new hope that he now felt.

Rose simply smiled in response. She knew all her sons well. 'I will return to work on Monday ... it's only Wednesday. Do you think you can stay till Monday next week?' she asked, glancing at her son impishly despite her fatigue.

Simon laughed softly and began to eat his soup. 'I would like to go away at the end of next week. I haven't taken a vacation for a whole year,' he said in between mouthfuls. After a brief pause, when only the clinking of cutlery and the sounds of eating could be heard, she said, focusing on her soup, 'I think it's time you introduced Luis to me.' Simon's spoonful of soup remained in mid-air between his mouth and the bowl. He looked up, perplexed, at his mother.

'How did you ... ?' he began.

'You're my son. You manage my entire business. I'm sure you would agree that I need to be careful about who gets close to you?' she replied, smiling but still without looking at him.

Chapter Nine

Rose stayed on in Sylvia's home, with a plan to move back to her apartment in a day or two. She was still in two minds about what should be done with Sylvia's place since it was a little too large for her. But she loved the house because it had been her mother's, and so she couldn't yet bring herself to sell it or rent it out to strangers.

'What are your plans, Ming?' she asked the silent little woman in the evening after her conversation with Simon. 'I will close up this house for a while but that doesn't mean you have to move back to Melaka. I have more than enough room for another person in my house,' she said to Ming, while uncertain about whether or not she wanted the woman in her house. She was never comfortable with Ming and didn't see why she had to prolong contact with her now that Sylvia was gone. 'You can do what you have always been doing here. Lisa, my Indonesian helper, can clean, and you can cook,' she said, assuming that Ming would accept the slot that she had in mind for her. Rose slotted people into different categories in her mind, depending on the amount of time and energy she wanted to spend on them. In Rose's mind, if Ming accepted her offer, Lisa would deal with Ming.

Given that it had been a very long time since Rose had had to face rejection or even opposition, she was naturally taken aback when Ming firmly and decisively said, 'No, my work is finished. I came to live with Sylvia to keep her company and help her in any way I could. And she helped me when I needed it. Now that she is gone, I go too. I will return to Melaka.' Rose was stumped for a few minutes, largely because this was the first time Ming had spoken so many sentences to her. There was a thick silence in the room as a bemused Rose thought about what this diminutive woman, whom she barely knew, had just said. In all the years that Ming had lived with Sylvia, they had always spoken to each other through Sylvia. In the last couple of weeks, they had exchanged about a hundred words altogether, usually involving meals or cleaning. The older woman had literally slipped in and out of rooms so silently that it was only when the food appeared on the table, or when freshly laundered clothes, neatly ironed and folded, appeared in the closet, or when the bed was miraculously made in the morning while Rose was in the bathroom brushing her teeth and showering, that Rose was aware of another person's presence in the house. So Ming's quiet assertiveness, which established that she was not looking to discuss her plans, was a surprise. This woman was not about to let herself be slotted in anywhere.

Rose cleared her throat and swallowed before she spoke again. 'Why the sudden decision to leave? You can continue to live here in Singapore, in my house. My mother would have wanted that,' said Rose looking directly at Ming.

Ming met Rose's gaze before chuckling resignedly. 'I know what she would have wanted. At least, I know what she would have wanted for me. And I think she would have preferred that I return to Melaka.' Although a little perplexed by what Ming had said, Rose didn't respond to this. The woman wanted to leave; then so be it. She would have Maryanne settle her dues. Maryanne also dealt with a lot of Rose's personal matters, such as managing Rose's personal staff, like Lisa her helper, and Maniam and Keng San, the chauffeurs, among other things. She would do this too.

'Well, if you have to leave, then that's fine. Please let me know what I have to pay you. I will have my secretary pay you,' said Rose, and made to leave the dining area while dismissing the older woman in her mind as a matter settled. But Ming wasn't done, and Rose was unprepared for the conversation that ensued.

'Please sit down. I would like to speak with you,' said Ming, her voice steady and calm, not demanding, but definitely firm. Ming was unafraid and displayed none of the nervousness or hesitation that other members of Rose's staff showed when they spoke with her. She merely stood where she was, ignoring Rose's cool gaze that hid a rising annoyance. After a couple of minutes, Rose began to repeat her question about how much she needed to pay as a settlement, 'As I said, let me know—'

'I don't need any money from you. I have enough,' interjected Ming, and Rose was silenced by the firmness in the tone. 'But I need to speak with you before I leave. I have some things to say to you.' The old black clock on the wall ticked loudly as if it was counting the minutes of pregnant silence in the room. Sylvia had bought the clock in an antique store in Chinatown soon after she had moved into the house. It had belonged to a Chinese coffee shop in the area in the pre-war days. Then suddenly its metallic chime pierced through the silence, startling the two women— interestingly, Rose more than the older woman.

'I have been meaning to talk to you since the day your mother passed away, but I was waiting for the right time,' continued Ming, like she was taking her cue from the old clock. If Rose was surprised there was nothing in her expression that suggested it. She glanced at the older woman, simply waiting to be spoken to, her expression revealing none of the impatience and irritation that was rising inside her. Simon had told her many times to be a little more people-friendly. 'Your lack of expression can be quite unnerving, especially for the junior staff,' he would grumble. 'Well . . . that's why I have you. You're the nice one,' she would chortle. But there was no hesitation or fear in Ming, and that was obvious to Rose. The evenness in the woman's manner and tone matched her own. *Were there no right moments all this while when we were the only two in the house*, Rose thought to herself. As if reading her thoughts, Ming continued, 'I didn't speak with you all these days because I wanted to give you time to get over Hui Fen . . . Sylvia's death. So, I needed to wait for the right opportunity. I will leave in the morning.'

For the first time in many years, Rose Lee struggled to find the right response. This was her mother's helper, who had referred to Sylvia by a name that no one ever used, not even Sylvia. Rose had a vague memory of some relationship that Ming shared with her mother, but over the years so little had been talked about that, that it was forgotten. Rose couldn't for the life of her remember what the connection was. 'I know what you must be thinking,' said Ming softly. Her white face looked whiter. The harsh afternoon sun that streamed in from above made the deep lines on her dry cheeks look more pronounced. 'What on earth do I have to say to you? Well, I have plenty to say to you. Nothing is going to change but there are some truths that you need to know. I need to be at peace,' said the woman resolutely.

'Sylvia, your mother, was my cousin, and her Chinese name is Hui Fen. Our fathers were brothers. My name is Hui Ming,' said Ming slowly. Rose's mouth opened slightly, as if she was about to speak, but she said nothing, continuing to stare in disbelief. 'We grew up together in Melaka, or Malacca as it was known then,' said Ming matter-of-factly. 'But we were originally from Perak. We belonged to a wealthy tin miner's family. Like many others during the war, we lost everything and had to leave our family home in Perak. We lost more than wealth. Our fathers were killed. The two young sons were the only men left in our family. During the journey to Malacca, we lost our grandmother, who could not bear the grief and the long journey—'

'Wait a minute,' Rose interrupted. 'My mother was born in Singapore,' she said hesitantly, while staring at Ming with a frown like she was now unsure. As far as she knew, Sylvia had been born and raised in Singapore by a dockyard worker and his vegetable vendor wife. Sylvia had told Rose that her parents had died just before Rose had been born.

'Hui Fen preferred to keep her past buried. And I don't blame her. So much of our past was so full of sorrow that it is best forgotten,' replied Hui Ming, looking down at the floor.

'So why are you telling me now?' demanded Rose, suddenly feeling a little warm and bothered by the afternoon heat.

'I need to. I don't wish to go to my grave without telling you. I owe it to myself. I owe it to you,' replied Ming determinedly. Very clearly, the older woman was not afraid. She responded to Rose's questions while looking away, like she was looking at something beyond the present. Without waiting for a response, she continued, 'Hui Fen lost her mother and older sister in a fire that broke out in our home in Malacca. My mother, Wang Shu, raised Hui Fen and her brother as her own with me and my brother. My mother, who first made a living doing odd jobs, became a seamstress. Hui Fen and I learnt how to sew from her. Hui Fen was better than I was as a seamstress. She was better at everything, prettier . . . just better . . . .' The ache that had burrowed deep into the woman's heart was not lost on Rose.

'My mother, who had learnt how to sew and embroider from her governesses in Suzhou where she was born and raised, was skilled in Su embroidery. She taught both of us, Hui Fen and me, but Hui Fen became very skilful at it . . . ' Ming trailed off pensively, a faraway look in her eyes, like she was watching her gentle mother taking special pains to teach her prettier cousin. Ming was now leaning against the doorway. The expressionless face that she typically presented to Rose and the rest of the world now softened with sad nostalgia. The past was too far away for tears but apparently not distant enough to remove a lingering feeling of loss and pain. 'After the war, when we thought our life would get better with the British coming back, both the boys, my brother and Hui Fen's brother, chose to join the communists, like their fathers. Hui Fen's brother died in jail. We were told that it was cholera. The one remaining male member of our family was my brother, whom you knew as Uncle Benny. His name was actually Hui Beng.' Rose had a vague memory of Uncle Benny.

He walked with a limp and smoked numerous cigarettes, and that was really all she remembered of him. When she was about eight years old, Sylvia had left her in the care of her father for a few days and gone away somewhere. She had returned tired and sombre. Her father had explained that Uncle Benny, who had visited them once in a while, had died in an accident while riding his motorcycle in Malaysia, where he lived.

'Hui Beng wanted to move to Singapore, and that's how we came here,' continued Ming softly. 'Unfortunately, my mother had seen and lived through so much in life that she had just about had enough of it by the time we moved. She died a few weeks after the move. In a way, it was good that she died when she did because she would have died anyway if she had known about the jobs that we had to take in Singapore.' Rose's eyes widened. Ming merely continued. 'She would have never allowed us, Hui Fen and me, to work as taxi girls. She had spent so much of her life protecting us, and the family "honour" as she called it.' Ming laughed softly and without humour when she continued, 'My poor mother never ceased to see herself and us as members of a wealthy and respectable family till the day she died. We didn't know anyone here. But Hui Beng managed to find work in New World, the amusement park.' Rose looked up sharply. She remembered Sylvia talking about the New World. 'His towkay, who owned the bar, liked him a lot and left the running of the bar to him . . .'

'But what about my mother and you? Where were you?' asked Rose, interrupting Ming, who glanced at her before continuing.

'My brother ran the bar well, and soon, he was making money for the towkay, who was a generous man. He paid my brother well. Hui Fen and I worked as taxi girls in New World and then helped him at the bar when we could. Taxi girls danced for a living. Men would buy tokens to dance with us. We were okay, all three of us. Hui Fen and I tried not to think about what my mother would have said because we were eating more than we had in years.'

The term 'taxi girls' sounded familiar to Rose. She had heard it before but she just couldn't remember where. Frowning, she was about to ask Ming, but, oblivious to Rose, the older woman continued, like she was narrating the story of a movie she was watching. There was silence again for a while. Rose suddenly felt like she had had enough. Perhaps it was the constant hum of the traffic outside, the quietness inside the home, or Ming's low emotionless monotone that gave Rose a portentous feeling. She was a little fearful of listening to any more of this tale. While everything that Ming narrated now sounded like it was someone else's story, she began to have an uneasy and gnawing fear that it was hers.

The older woman continued. 'We lived in Potong Pasir. We had dreams, your mother and I. We didn't care to be taxi girls forever, obviously. We wanted to start our sewing business again. But we needed to make a little money first, to start our lives here. As I said, we didn't know anyone here.' At this point, Rose felt a little bit of impatience rising within her. Perhaps it was having to simply sit and listen while the older woman rambled on. And then her innate inclination to question and doubt also made her suspicious of the story. How was she to believe this woman and why did she wait so long to tell her? What did she stand to gain from this revelation? So, Sylvia was not from Singapore. She was from Malaysia and had a bit of a chequered past. What did it matter? Many lives were unsettled and turbulent in the early days after the war. As if reading her thoughts, Ming spoke directly to Rose. 'You are wondering why I'm telling you all of this now. And how your mother's past matters now. Well, the truth is that you are not Hui Fen's daughter at all,' declared Ming, in a tone completely devoid of emotion.

She wasn't challenging and neither was she pleading to be believed. She was merely telling, and the look in her eyes was open and candid, like she didn't care if anyone believed her since she was stating an unchangeable truth. Rose flung an irritated and bemused glance at the older woman. Either Sylvia's death was affecting the woman more than was apparent or she was unloading some hidden vendetta that she had held all these years. Rose stood up abruptly, like she was preparing to leave. Looking directly and coolly at the older woman, she said quietly and without a trace of emotion, 'I don't know what you're talking about but whatever it is, I have no interest in it. As far as I know, my mother is Sylvia, and my father, Joseph Chen. You were my mother's helper, and she mentioned that you were a distant relative. You claim that your fathers were brothers. Well, I've never met any of her family, and now that she is gone there is no way of knowing if what you're telling me is true. Obviously, she didn't want me to know her family, which is why I never met anyone. She must have had her reasons. You mentioned that you're returning to Melaka. Well, when are you leaving, and how much should I be paying—'

'The truth is that you're *my* child, my daughter.'

The clock chimed again, shattering the silence with a vengeance. It had been a whole hour since Ming had started talking. A lifetime had been shrunk into that hour and presented to Rose, who merely stared back aghast. *This woman is completely insane! I need to get her out of this house.* Rose reached for her cell phone that lay on the dining table.

'Are you afraid that I'm crazy?' chuckled Ming. 'I have nothing to gain or lose by telling you the truth. Do you remember finding a photograph in an old trunk when you were a teenager? Do you remember the photograph at all? The laughing girls and the white army officer among the girls?' Rose stopped reaching for her phone and frowned at Ming. She was silent but her silence was an opportunity for Ming to continue talking. 'I know because Hui Fen told me. She told me that she had had a difficult time explaining the photograph. Well, that army officer was your father.'

The story that Ming revealed was too much for even Rose Lee to take in her characteristic cynical manner. Rose's eyes widened as she slowly sat back down on the chair. She remembered the incident with the photograph but had only a vague memory of the people in it. She remembered Sylvia sharply telling her to put the photograph back where she had found it, and that's as much as she remembered of something that had happened almost forty-five years ago. But there was something about Ming's earnest tone, her lack of desperation, her absence of fear, and the fact that she was calm and matter-of-fact instead of pleading that made Rose want to continue hearing the story. To Rose, it felt like the older woman was merely laying the facts down for her to see, as a parent would. It was suddenly difficult to disbelieve the woman.

'Hui Fen was a beautiful young woman. She was everyone's favourite because she was not only good at everything she did, she was also a good person. And since I was not as pretty or good at many things, I grew up in her shadow, always second best. But she loved me very much and was always protective. When she met your father in the bar, she was about twenty and I was about sixteen. She was crazy about him. He frequently came to the bar just to see her. While everyone except Hui Fen knew that he was just fooling around with a pretty Chinese girl, she hoped that he would marry her and take her back with him to England,' said Ming softly. 'She looked so happy and more beautiful because of that. He was a very handsome man. Gradually, I didn't want to be second best any more, especially when I realized that he had eyes for my freshness too,' she said with faintly discernible remorse. 'Sometimes when she was busy serving other customers, he would look at me, and I would smile back. Soon we found ways of being together in that dimly lit bar right under her nose. Or, perhaps, she was too much in love with him to notice anything amiss. Or maybe she never imagined I would betray her,' she added cynically.

After a brief pause that hung heavy in the silence that was only punctuated by the ticking of the old clock, she continued, 'My brother, Hui Beng, had his own problems in trying to keep his communist activities quiet. He never let that go, and he was more interested in that than in us; he just saw us as a burden. We had loved him more than he loved us right from the beginning. But everything came out in the open at least to Hui Fen when

I found myself pregnant. I had no idea I was pregnant until my stomach started to show. I simply thought I was getting fatter,' scoffed Ming. Rose felt the cold chill that gnawed at her stomach spread through her whole body; it weakened her limbs. She had an idea of where the story was going.

'Hui Fen soon guessed what had happened. As expected, the British officer stopped coming to the bar. He knew before Hui Fen. I remember him laughing nervously and telling me that I had grown fat. He stopped coming soon after that. We never heard from him again, and we didn't know where to find him. In those days, you trusted for no real reason.' She stopped talking for a few minutes and stood leaning against the wall with her eyes closed, her thoughts years away in a village in old Singapore, crying as her cousin Hui Fen questioned her first angrily then desperately.

Her own hopes and dreams crushed, Sylvia tried to find out from young Hui Ming how far gone she was in her pregnancy. Hui Beng did not know as yet. The girls had been raised to be afraid and deferential to the men in the family. Although they didn't see him much outside the bar, and even then he was often huddled in conversations with strange men, too preoccupied to notice them, they were still terrified because he had warned them about the white officer and all the other white men who came to the bar. 'They're just looking for a pastime. Stay away. Don't want to see you in any mess. We come from a good family.' This was what Wang Shu, Hui Ming's mother, used all the time. What she could not remember about the lifestyle of the 'good family', which was once hers, she made up, hoping that the story—even if embellished or imagined in parts—was enough for the girls and Hui Beng to do the right thing.

'We were afraid, Hui Fen and I, that Beng would find out. I was too scared and didn't know what was happening. Hui Fen tried to ask around discretely if I could get an abortion. My pregnancy was already quite far gone. There was a woman in the village who got rid of unwanted pregnancies. We tried that. I didn't think I would come out alive. But I lived, and so did the baby.' Ming smiled wryly before she said, 'You were a fighter even then. You wanted to live, and you did.' Rose merely gazed at her, a slight feeling of nausea churning in her stomach. She was the result of illicit caresses and romps on grimy sofas in a dimly lit bar. She was reminded of B-grade movies about Asian women ravaged and abandoned by white army officers. Hilarious, but that was really her own story.

'Hui Fen decided that the best thing we could do was to send me back to Malacca. We were still in regular touch with a majie who had been my mother's friend in Malacca. She had been like a sister to my mother during our most difficult years while we lived there, and once again, she helped us like a deity that appears out of nowhere. By that time, she had retired and shared a large house with her retired majie sisters. I had you there, and I named you Rose. I wanted to give you an English name because I felt it was appropriate since your father was British, and I got the name from the name of the bar, "The Mandarin Rose",' she said without emotion, calmly meeting Rose's gaze.

Rose had a ridiculous urge to laugh aloud now. So she was a bastard child, named after a bar, and her light brown eyes were finally explained. She could now go to her grave in peace. Ignoring the hint of a cynical smile that played on Rose's mouth as she thought about her true story, Ming continued. 'After you were born, I stayed on with the majie sisters for a while. They were very kind to me and took good care of me and you, and Hui Fen sent us whatever money she could. Hui Beng still did not know what had happened to me. Hui Fen had told him that I had gone back to Malacca because I did not like working in the bar any more, and that story was good enough for Hui Beng since it was one less burden for him. As long as Hui Fen said I was safe, he was contented and didn't try very hard to get me back to Singapore. About a year after you were born, I wanted to leave the sisters. I wanted to start a small sewing business in Malacca. But I didn't want you with me. I had not bargained for a child when I met your father. And I was very young, just seventeen. It was just too much of a responsibility for me.'

Had she been forty years younger, she would have been shattered with this knowledge. But at the age of sixty, with three grown sons and a construction empire that she had built on her own, she was just struck by how one's beginnings had so little to do with where one ended. She felt no bitterness or anger, just amazement at how successfully Sylvia had taken the truth with her to her grave. If Ming had never told her, she would have never known that she was the discarded child of some strange soldier and a seventeen-year-old girl. Her respect for Sylvia only doubled.

As if reading her thoughts once again, Ming said, 'Hui Fen was not as much a sister as a mother to me. It was no mistake that everyone who met her and knew her loved her dearly, because kindness flowed from her like warmth and light from the sun. She should have hated me for what I did to her, taking away her lover and having a child with him. But she was more concerned about me and the baby.' Rose smiled slightly at this. It was typically Sylvia. She would have known immediately that the man was not worth a single tear as soon as she found out that her Ming was pregnant. That was Sylvia, a strange combination of kindness and pragmatism. While she would go out of her way to help you in a bind, she wouldn't think twice about telling you if she thought you were an idiot.

'When I wanted to leave the sisters, I wrote to Hui Fen telling her that I was going to put you up for adoption and that I couldn't care for you. By that time, she had met the man she would marry, the man you knew as your father.' Rose thought of the only father she had ever known, and silently blessed the man who had abandoned a pregnant Ming. Rose didn't need to hear any more. But she indulged Ming, who needed to unburden herself of a lifetime of guilt. 'Hui Fen came with him to Malacca as soon as she received the letter. She tried her best to talk me into keeping you but I was by then bored with playing parent.' She closed her eyes as if the memory shamed her. Or perhaps it was the path that she chose to take instead of parenthood that shamed her.

Ming went on to reveal to Rose that she had planned to sell her to a childless couple. 'Luckily for you, Hui Fen and her husband decided to take you back with them. She loved you from the minute she set eyes on you, and there was no question of giving you away to anyone else,' said Ming quietly. 'She paid me the price that I had asked the couple for you,' she said in a whisper filled with mortification. As a young woman, Ming had felt a sense of entitlement for the money that she had been paid for the child. After all, she had done Hui Fen, who could not have children, a favour. But as the years had passed, and Hui Fen had stepped in more than once to lift her out of disaster, the significance of her perceived act of kindness had dissipated to nothingness. By the time she had arrived in Singapore as Sylvia's helper, it was obvious that it was Sylvia who had provided a life full of favours for Hui Ming.

It was about four o'clock in the afternoon, and the old clock chimed again. By this time, Rose had grown restless and weary of listening to Ming. Her origins didn't matter to her now since she knew her destiny. There was no fear or bitterness, just wonder about what could have happened and thankfulness for what hadn't. But she felt no surge of affection for this new-found parent. As far as she was concerned, the parents that she cared for were gone. They had loved her dearly while they had lived and she, them. They were the only parents she wanted to know. The woman who stood before her and claimed to be her true mother had wanted to sell her to strangers. Even after she came to live with Sylvia, she had not shown any real desire to get close to Rose. Perhaps Sylvia had asked her to stay aloof. Perhaps she herself had wanted to keep her distance. But the reason didn't matter to Rose. It might have, forty years ago.

Rose stood up resolutely. She moved to get out of the dining area. 'I know none of this will make any difference to you. I'm just five years younger than Hui Fen. I don't have that much longer. When I leave here, I want to leave the burden that's been in my heart all these years,' said Ming. Even now, the woman spoke of a burden. The irony was not lost on Rose, who smiled lightly and turned to gaze kindly at the older woman, who was a head shorter, with her grey hair drawn back in a tight bun. The white top and black trousers she always wore were immaculate as usual, a practice she had learnt from the majie sisters.

Rose felt pity for Ming, whose very demeanour and stance spoke of a lifetime of wrong turns and missteps. Sylvia, on the other hand, had lived a good life. Rose didn't care to wonder why Sylvia had chosen to keep the truth from her, but since it was her decision it must have been for the best. Rose merely nodded at Ming before walking past her towards the staircase. As she walked past Ming, she patted her gently on the shoulder and said, 'I would like you to continue staying with me for as long as you live. But if you have something more pressing to attend to in Melaka, I won't stop you.'

Chapter Ten

When Ming awoke the next morning, Rose was awake and sitting on Sylvia's rocking chair, which stood exactly where it had when she had been alive, with one of Sylvia's shawls draped around her shoulders, nursing a cup of Teh-C. Sylvia had loved to watch the traffic that plied along Tank Road from the little balcony just outside her bedroom. Rose sat like her mother, on a gently rocking chair, watching the early morning traffic, her thoughts miles away despite the morning chaos—the sound of the bell chiming from the temple across the street mingled with the constant buzz of the traffic filled the room. Unlike Sylvia, who had loved the noise and the bustle because it made her feel alive and a part of a community, Rose had always hated this part of the house. She couldn't stand the constant hum of traffic. 'It disturbs my yoga and meditation,' Rose would complain. 'Focus on the sound of the traffic and meditate,' Sylvia would chortle. 'After all, meditation is for mind control, right? Well, make your mind focus on the sound of the traffic, and it will be therapeutic.' Rose would shake her head and mumble, 'Nonsense.' But today, the hum of the traffic actually lulled her. It seemed to calm the multitude of images that flashed through her mind—images of the parents that she knew, of a faceless Caucasian man who was her real father, of Ming, of her own sons, of Stanley, and of Peter. Deception seemed to be the only truth in her life. Everything that she had seen as the truth seemed to have a deeper kernel of reality that taunted her.

Ming stood behind, watching the daughter she had once sold. After she had sold the child to Hui Fen, she had started a sewing business in Malacca. Hui Fen's disappointment in her had been deep and long-lasting.

'You're selfish and wilful,' she had scolded Ming. 'You took away my man, had his child, and now you're trying to sell the child without asking me. If I'd not come in time, you would have sold her.'

Ming had sulked and complained about the responsibility that she had never asked for. 'I'm too young to be a mother. Besides, I can't afford to take care of a child.'

'But you were not too young to sleep with my boyfriend! Not too young to cheat me!' Sylvia retorted with uncharacteristic anger.

'He never really wanted you. Isn't that obvious? If he had, he wouldn't have slept with me,' spat Ming with the venom that had been eating away at her as the less pretty, less talented, and less liked daughter of the family. Even her own mother had loved Hui Fen more.

The price that Ming had paid for that venom had been high. Sylvia had bought the child from Ming and returned to Singapore, turning her back on Ming. 'I don't want to see you again. You have hurt me too much. You obviously know what you wish to do with your life. Don't come in search of me again,' Sylvia had said with finality, her voice harder than Ming had ever heard. Sylvia had picked up the child and walked away from Ming's life without once turning to look at her.

What she had not known then was that Ming had had a very murky idea of what she wanted to do with her life because she had always relied on her mother, and then on Sylvia, to decide for her. She had never had a separate plan for herself and had not bargained for the outcome of her plan to sell her child. She had assumed that Sylvia—who had always been the kind, protective big sister and who always seemed to know what to do—would forgive her and take her back with her to Singapore. After all, she had forgiven the treachery and the subsequent pregnancy. Ming was very comfortable with the idea of continuing her life in her cousin's shadow, with her child being raised by Sylvia. She couldn't honestly say at that time that she felt any deep maternal affection for the child, who seemed more like an encumbrance. When Sylvia arrived and took away the child, it all seemed so perfectly convenient that the turn of events caught her by surprise. In fact, she was overwhelmed by anxiety when she saw Sylvia turn her back on her and walk away. She had wanted to run behind her as Sylvia was all she had—the only one who had cared about what happened to her. Ming's disbelief at Sylvia walking away and her pride held her back from rushing after her big sister and drew her into a disastrous tailspin.

After the showdown with Sylvia, Ming started the sewing business and found some success initially. But she was not as skilled or as disciplined as Sylvia to be perfect and to deliver on time. Her customers had tried her but not all had returned. The few that did weren't particularly impressed with Ming's less-than-perfect work and did little to spread the word of her business. In the midst of this, she struck up a relationship with a laundry business owner— an older married man with children and an opium addict. He kept Ming as a mistress for a while without his family's knowledge and then, after a while, openly, without caring if anyone knew. Life then took a miserable turn for Ming, with the man's wife and family constantly harassing her. When the man finally died because of his addiction, Ming was once again left out in the cold because his family saw to it that she got nothing in inheritance. By this time, her own tailoring business had dwindled due to her lack of focus. She tried reaching out unsuccessfully to Hui Fen. Youth, which had lent her a certain charm and allure, was by now fading, and she didn't have the admirers that she once did. Desperate to make a living, she slowly turned to the men who were willing to pay a few dollars for her sexual services. She managed that way for a few years until a chance meeting with Beng, her brother.

At the time Ming had run into Beng, he had already closed his bar in Singapore and was in hiding in Malacca because of his communist affiliations. His imprisonment during the time he had lived in Malacca with his mother and the two girls had done nothing to change his ideology. He was still strongly affiliated with the Communist Party of Malaya, and the bar, The Mandarin Rose, had been a mere cover, which had been blown. Several of his friends and acquaintances had been arrested when the government decided to crush communist activities in the state. By this time Malaya had become Malaysia and Singapore. Beng had slipped out of Singapore in the middle of the night without even informing Sylvia when an acquaintance that he had in the police force had tipped him off about a raid that had been planned for his bar for the next day. He had left behind everything that he owned and crossed the border into Malaysia with just fifty dollars in his pocket, escaping by the skin of his teeth.

Sylvia, who was by this time no longer connected to the bar and very sporadically in touch with Beng, had not even known about his disappearance. When she began to wonder about his whereabouts, she decided to pay him a visit at the bar. On reaching, she found it all boarded up and locked, with a huge iron lock sealed by the police. Her enquiries with neighbours had only drawn blank looks and frowns. Since she had always suspected that he was still active in the Communist Party, she guessed that he had probably slipped out of the country to avoid getting caught and let the matter lie. She felt he would turn up at some point. But it would be another two years before she made contact with him, and that would be when she would reconnect with Ming as well.

Ming discovered Beng through one of her regular clients. By then, her lifestyle and age had erased the reasonable good looks that she had had as a young woman, and she was now a portly prostitute with a few regular clients who were too old and too accustomed to her to engage the services of younger women in the business. These clients kept Ming reasonably comfortable in a shop house on Jonker Street. It was here that Ming met Beng. One of her clients brought Beng to her house and asked her if he could stay for a few days. Ming was aghast at the sight of her brother, who was a shadow of the large, loud, and ruddy man she had known. The man that stood before her looked old and thin, hunted and furtive. He had not eaten in days and grabbed the bowl of rice and meat that she offered him. His eyes darted furtively, and he sat on the edge of his seat. She learnt that he not only feared the law but also the feared men who were looking for him because he either owed them money or they were afraid that he would betray them.

Beng's stay with her, which was meant to be for a few days, extended indefinitely, and as the days went by no one came looking for him. Perhaps many in Singapore thought that he had died while fleeing, or perhaps he just wasn't important enough at the party. Whatever it was, Beng's courage grew as the days grew into months. Some of the loudness came back, and he started going about freely in the town of Malacca but continued to live with Ming. Ming was half happy about this as she felt like she had someone to call her own now, but her business was affected. Her clientele dwindled because people felt uncomfortable coming to the house where she lived with Beng.

While Beng frowned upon what she was doing, he did not complain as he had no means of an income. With Ming's income drying up, the two had no alternatives but to try and open a nightclub again. This was when Beng asked Ming to approach Sylvia for money. 'Are you crazy?' snapped Ming. 'She has not kept in touch with me since the time she walked away with my baby. Do you think she would want to help us now?'

'We don't have a choice. I can't contact her. It will alert the authorities. You have to contact her, and get her to send the money to us,' Beng had said decisively. Defenceless and poor, Ming could not stand up to her brother, so she wrote her cousin a letter dictated by Beng. There was no mention of Beng in the letter for fear of it falling into the hands of the authorities.

The letter was met with a silence that lasted for about six months. Then, one morning, the postman presented Ming with a money order for about five thousand dollars. He also had a short

terse letter in which Sylvia had made it clear that the money was
the repayment of the debt that she owed Aunty Wang Shu. 'She
would have wanted a better life for you. I don't know what you
are doing now, but knowing what I do of you, I can only guess.
And I'm humiliated. Had Aunty been alive, she would have burnt
with shame. So this money is for you to make a decent woman of
yourself. Don't write to me any more. I have nothing more to give
you. This money was hard-earned. Use it respectfully.' Somewhere
in a small corner of Ming's heart, the smallest glimmer of hope
had lingered for a mention of the baby. But there was none, and
the hope evaporated almost as quickly as it came. She didn't think
about the child after that.

With more money borrowed from clients and moneylenders,
The Mandarin Rose opened again—in Jonker Street, Malacca—
and times became a little easier for the siblings. The business
flourished downstairs, while they lived upstairs. Soon, the upstairs
too began to have its own business when Ming's old clients
wandered back to her. The bar helped to grow the business upstairs
too, so much that she even had to hire girls. The siblings became
reasonably prosperous and comfortable in their lives. Beng finally
gave up his communist affiliations, coming to terms with the fact
that financial well-being was alluring and that he could be far
happier without having to look over his shoulder all the time. Soon
Ming had a patron, an old and wealthy man, who took her under
his wing. She then stopped seeing clients, leaving them to the girls
that worked for her.

Life would have continued in that uneventful manner if not
for the fact that The Mandarin Rose was set on fire one day by a
disgruntled employee, who felt that the owners were taking more
than the lion's share of her earnings. All of the siblings' progress in
life from the time they had opened The Mandarin Rose in Malacca
went up in smoke on that day. It happened in the wee hours of the
morning when everyone was asleep. Saving themselves was just
about all they could do. Two girls were killed in the fire, and a

client was badly injured. Luckily it had been a quiet day, and so the client that was injured was the only one. While insurance covered some of the damage, a large part of the losses had to be borne by the owners, since a generous portion of the business was illegal. In addition to that, the dead girls' relatives and the injured client demanded compensation and threatened severe repercussions if the siblings didn't make good on their assurances.

Luckily for Ming, her patron, a devoted old man and the owner of a successful scrap iron business, provided for her in a somewhat comfortable manner until his death. He left her a small house and a little money with which to get by. Beng did this and that to earn a living, until he met with a motorcycle accident that killed him. This was the time when Sylvia came back into Ming's life. By this time, many years had gone by and frayed feelings had been somewhat assuaged, especially since Rose had grown to be the precious child that Sylvia could never have.

Although her letters were still cool, Sylvia began communicating with Ming after their meeting at Beng's funeral. Then, when Sylvia's husband died, she called Ming and invited her to come back to Singapore for good. Ming's heart raced because this was the relief she needed. Her money was running out, and soon all she would be left with was the house. She was managing by subletting the rooms in the house and doing some sewing. But she was getting old and tired. So when Sylvia reached out to her, Ming saw it as the hand of providence, and grabbed it. But Sylvia's invitation came with strict conditions.

Sylvia warned Ming that her stay in Singapore was dependent on her keeping a distance from Rose and never revealing who she really was. 'Rose is my daughter. I raised her. She has a beautiful life, and I want it to remain that way. Don't spoil things for her. If I ever sense that you're trying to get close to her, I will turn you out, and you will be back where you are now. I know you, and I know that your well-being matters most to you. So be mindful of that,' she said, her voice on the phone quiet and firm. Sylvia had been right about the fact that Ming's main concern was her own well-being. Ming readily accepted the conditions Sylvia had laid down and arrived in Singapore as quickly as she could wrap up her affairs in Malacca and put her house up for rent. 'No going out on your own. No meeting old friends here in Singapore. And, most of all, keep your distance from Rose and don't talk too much to her. You may reveal something if you get too chatty. I cannot have that because she is my daughter, and I still don't trust you. If you want a roof over your head, you do as I say.' Sylvia had reminded her.

Now, thirty years later, Ming had even less in Melaka. Many of the people she had known there had died. And the last trip she had made was to sell the house that the old scrap dealer had left her. She had not expected to return there. So there really was no pressing need to go back. Ming stood watching the figure of her daughter, who now stood alone, missing the only mother she had ever known. She still didn't feel a surge of maternal love for the daughter she barely knew, but something in her stirred, urging her to stay. Perhaps it was a strange connection to this woman who was her daughter, or perhaps it was self-preservation once again. She continued to stand at the door watching Rose, who still sat in Sylvia's chair. The sun had completely risen, and so had the heat and the noise from the morning traffic. Rose stood up slowly and stretched, while Ming busied herself with making the bed and clearing away the teacup. Rose stood watching the older woman for a few minutes before she said, 'The offer still stands. You can stay with me as you did with my mother. But we will move back to my apartment today,' and left the room.

And the Storm Begins

Chapter Eleven

Rose had come to see Simon off at the airport despite his protestations about how she was being silly. 'This is not the first time I'm going away, Ma,' he said, pulling his luggage out of the trunk of the car. 'I don't understand why you had to come all the way to the airport.'

'You did say that you were going to be away for a couple of months. You haven't done that before. And . . . well, hopefully, when you come back, you will finally bring Luis with you. It's time he met me and your brothers.' Simon looked away and smiled to himself. He was at peace at last. He had told Luis that his mother knew and that she would be expecting them when they returned together to Singapore. He looked forward to the beginning of his own life.

Simon looked at his mother for a long while from where he stood checking in at the airport, and then smiled gently at her when she caught his eye. While his heart felt light, there was a lingering sadness in him. He knew he was abandoning her. And he was lying to her. He planned to be away for at least six months or maybe even more, but he had told her that he would be away for just two. As far as he was concerned, this was the final break with Lee Constructions. But he had revealed none of this to her because he knew Rose still hoped that the vacation in Europe would make him see things differently and that he would come back to the business. He was afraid that if he told her he was never going to go back to the office for anything other than to say hello to the staff, she would convince him to change his mind. And he might have, had she pleaded with him. He would tell her from Europe, in stages. The distance would help them both.

Simon wistfully noticed the grey in her hair and the fatigue on her face. For a fleeting moment, he remembered her as a young woman laughing heartily with him about a picture of her he had drawn in school, in first grade. The memory of her face flushed red, framed by her long silky black hair was clear in his mind. She had shown the picture, beaming with pride, to his father, who had made one of his occasional appearances in their home. Simon suddenly missed those simple days. He watched the older woman that his mother was now seat herself on one of the chairs in the waiting area and discreetly slip off one of her white Christian Louboutin stilettos to rub her heel. As always, Rose was immaculately dressed in her navy blue-and-white dress, with matching sapphire and diamond earrings and bracelet. Those who didn't know her would have never guessed the fatigue. 'I think she'll be okay,' Simon said to himself, chuckling, as he walked back towards her.

'Ma, take care of yourself when I'm away,' said Simon, sitting down next to his mother. 'Let the twins handle things for a change.' Simon reached for his mother's hand to hold in his own.

Rose cast a sidelong glance at her son and scoffed. 'Are you asking me to hand over and scurry off to a retirement home?' she asked, looking straight ahead of her.

'Ma, I know what you're thinking. They're just silly fellows. They will just . . . you know . . . just ignore these things. I know you will make the right decisions,' said Simon gently.

'Then why couldn't you ignore them, Simon? What are you running away from?' was Rose's quiet response.

It was Simon's turn to cast a sidelong glance before responding, 'Ma, you know I would like to do something for myself, for once. Are you going to grudge me that?' he asked, his honesty and frankness demanding her generosity. A pregnant silence hung between them before Rose gently squeezed her son's hand in response.

'You take care of yourself,' she said. 'Be careful wherever you are, and call me every day,' she said.

Simon glanced at his mother and smiled. Then, with a twinkle in his eye, he laughed, 'Even if you did retire to a senior citizens' home, you're not going to scurry there. Knowing you, you will buy it and walk in there in style as the owner and send everyone else scurrying!' Rose cast a sidelong glance at her son and laughed quietly.

'Ma, there's one more thing I have been meaning to talk to you about. Please hear me out. For a while, I thought I wouldn't say anything but then I decided that you should know,' Simon began hesitantly after a brief pause. Rose looked at her son, her calm brown eyes searching the face that she knew so well. There was nothing there that provided even the slightest hint of what he wanted to say. But because he was clearly uncomfortable, she had an inkling that it wouldn't be something about his position in the business or the twins since they had talked about those matters ad nauseum. This had to be something else and she had a faint suspicion that it had something to do with Peter.

Smiling faintly, Rose sighed and asked softly, 'What is it? Tell me. Something about your baba?' It was a busy evening at the airport, and there were people sitting on the seats on either side of them. There was a Chinese family of five standing in front of them, snapping pictures of themselves in the airport. Simon looked around him and asked his mother if she wanted coffee. Simon's hesitation confirmed what she had guessed. She nodded and stood up frowning. 'You can be assured that I'm not going to be screaming like a fishwife. Grant your mother some credit. She knows how to behave in public despite her public humiliation.' Simon's shoulders sank with his heart, and he pursed up his lower lip and sighed glumly. She hadn't forgotten.

'Just say it, son. I'm a big girl. I can handle it,' said Rose with a quiet laugh, linking her arm in his as they made their way to the coffee shop.

'Ma . . .' he began slowly, clearing his throat. Rose's gaze was fixed on her son, adding to his discomfort. 'The other lady . . . wrote a letter, which was really addressed to you but you were at Popo's place. I picked it up from your apartment when I went to pick up the mail for you. I knew who had written it, and so I took the liberty to open it,' said Simon quickly, a red flush spreading slowly over his face. 'I didn't want to upset you more since Popo had just passed. You had too much to deal with already,' Simon glanced nervously at his mother. Rose nodded. She didn't care that Simon had read the letter. But now her curiosity was piqued by her son's hesitation.

'Never mind that. What did she have to say to me?' asked Rose with a hint of impatience. 'Did she want more money? Or a share of Lee Constructions?'

'No, Ma,' replied Simon. 'She's not like that at all, Ma,' he said emphatically, his clear sense of right and wrong igniting his courage to speak up for the woman who had slipped into his mother's life as her husband's mistress. 'I have been interacting with her since the time Baba died. No, she's not like that at all. We misunderstood her.'

Rose stared at her son—her gaze unflinching and the warmth that she felt for her son cooling a little. She was beginning to feel annoyance at what vaguely appeared as treachery. But Simon was undeterred. 'She didn't want any of the money I offered her. She kept insisting that Baba had done enough for her. She just wanted her daughter, Evelyn, to be recognized as Baba's daughter, that's all. It was I who insisted that she take the money because at that time I thought I was paying her off. But she shamed me by insisting that I could deposit the money in her daughter's name. She wanted nothing to do with it.'

'If it is in her daughter's name, she has access to it. That works in her favour anyway,' sneered Rose.

'No, Ma. It's not like that at all. She is dying,' blurted Simon. 'She has fourth-stage cancer of the stomach.'

Rose stared at Simon silently; the colour draining from her face. Her mind, which had been hitherto fraught with hatred and betrayal, now felt a rush of shame. She closed her eyes, trying to make sense of the words that had just come out of his mouth. With her eyes still closed, she coughed a little and rubbed the corner of her left eye with her finger. Her heel throbbed now. 'Ma, I know you were hurt badly. But I think it is time for you to let it go,' said Simon, gently holding Rose's hand. 'Her life with Baba, like yours, didn't have a happy ending. I don't know if you can forgive her. But perhaps you can stop hurting.' He held a letter in his hand, which he pressed into hers. 'I think you need to read this. It might help you to stop loathing the very thought of her. Please do this for yourself. You will feel a lot better about everything.' Then, he reached forward, kissed his mother on her forehead, and held her face in his hands. Rose now felt like the child looking at her parent. 'I will call every day, Ma. You take care of yourself.' And he walked away. Rose watched the portly figure from behind, the pants and shirt creased badly. *As always*, she said to herself, shaking her head. She leant back in her chair as she continued to watch her son walk away from her. She waited till she couldn't see him any more, then picked up her purse from the seat next to her and walked towards the exit, a tall, solitary figure, amidst the peak hour airport crowd.

* * *

The days, weeks and months that followed were filled with meetings and business that demanded Rose's attention. Much to her surprise, as if to prove a point, Ean strove to work well with her, and Ethan did his best too. They seemed much more cooperative and far less sullen than when Simon had been around. For Rose, this time was bittersweet. She welcomed the time with her younger sons and revelled in the warmth that she shared with them after so many years. But it pained her to accept that this relationship had to do with Simon's departure, even if temporarily, from the business. And, two months after his departure, when she was happily looking forward to his return, he broke the news to her that he intended to extend his vacation by another month. She had agreed, but those three months then became four and five—each time with an excuse of one more photography project. He had pretty much covered every nook and corner of Europe.

Six months had passed when she asked him bluntly and angrily if he was planning to stay away for good. After an uncomfortable silence, Simon had said that he did not want to come back to the business and that he preferred to live in Europe. At first, Rose tried appealing to her son's sense of responsibility; then, when she found that he was satisfied that he had fulfilled it, she tried pleading with him but when that didn't work either, she had a heated argument with him and slammed down the phone. They stopped communicating for a whole month, her pride refusing to succumb to the need to speak with her son and check on his well-being. When he finally called, she agreed to release him completely from his responsibilities in the business but said she needed him to come back for at least a month so that they could tie up some unfinished matters. Simon agreed to return at the end of October. She warned him that if he didn't keep his word, she would go to Europe to get him. Simon laughed sheepishly and said, 'Don't worry, Ma. I will be back this time.'

It was now the middle of October, and Rose was looking forward to seeing her eldest again. By this time, however, she had also started getting accustomed to the twins' style of working. She had greater faith in them and felt less anxious about Simon's absence in the management. 'Maybe I was wrong. Maybe they can manage this place without Simon. Ean certainly can, but I need to watch him. It's Ethan I'm worried about. I need to ensure that Ean doesn't nudge him out,' she said to herself as she sat looking out through the glass windows of her office. It was about four-thirty in the afternoon, and it had been raining all day. The grey sky had cast its colour over the sea, making the view slightly dreary. But a weak sun, refusing to be beaten, shone through grey, providing hope for better weather. 'I wish this fellow would change his mind. Maybe I can talk him into it,' she mused, thinking of Simon. 'Maybe if these two felt more secure, they could all work together.'

The future looked better than it had in the last three or four years. She felt like she could bring her family back together, finally. And excitement about the future grew within her. She visualized a time when she would sit down for dinner once again with her sons. Maybe there would be wives and grandchildren too. A fleeting glimpse of Linda in this picture brought on a frown. 'But even that is tolerable, if it means we will be all together again,' she said to herself softly with a laugh. There would be banter, laughter and happiness. 'My sons . . .' she sighed to herself with contentment laced with a bit of pride. A hint of a smile played on her lips as her eyes sought the spire of the St Andrew's Cathedral that stood steadfast and bright no matter what the weather, defying the spanking new buildings that rose around it, much like a symbol of the values that are always held dear despite changing times. The smile on her lips widened a little when she thought of Simon, the stocky figure in his rumpled clothes. She counted the days before she would see him again. 'As Mama used to say, it will all work out,' she declared to herself firmly as she sat watching the rain that now began to streak the glass. What was even better was that Scott was back in her life now and for good. There would probably never be a marriage, but there was no longer a need for that. He was there for her and she for him and that was fulfilling enough.

The day gradually darkened and little dots of light appeared everywhere. The sun had receded unnoticed by Rose, who was so lost in the serenity of the life that she visualized for her family. In fact, she was so preoccupied with the rosy picture she saw for her family that she didn't hear the hurried knock on the door. Maryanne burst in without waiting for a response. 'Ms Rose,' she cried. Rose slowly swung around in her chair, a smile still lingering on her lips, to face a teary-eyed Maryanne. 'I'm afraid I have some very bad news for you,' cried Maryanne. Her usual composure was completely absent, and she looked flushed and harried. She was breathing heavily like she had run from her desk. The smile persisted, but a slight quizzical frown appeared on Rose's brow.

'Maryanne , what's going—'

'Mr Simon . . .' she said, her raised voice quivering with suppressed sobs.

Rose immediately stood up and walked quickly to her secretary. The smile vanished instantly, and the frown deepened, while her eyes widened with panic. 'What's happened to Simon, Maryanne?' she asked, her voice unusually shrill. Maryanne looked at her and drew a breath while shaking her head, tears streaming down her face.

'Mr Simon was in a car accident in the UK. Unfortunately . . .' and Maryanne began to cry softly. Breathing quickly, Rose stepped forward and held the crying woman by the shoulders.

'Maryanne, please! Tell me what happened. I need to know what's happened to my son,' cried Rose harshly, shaking Maryanne's shoulders gently. Struggling to compose herself, Maryanne related what the Lee Constructions country manager in the UK had told her on the phone. The manager had chosen to call Maryanne, not Rose. Simon had been driving in the countryside with Luis, and their car had been hit by a trailer that had lost control. Simon had died on the spot, while Luis was struggling to stay alive in a hospital in London. Simon had died on Saturday. The police had had some trouble tracing Simon's contacts because he did not have his passport with him. It was Monday today, almost nine months after he had turned around at the airport to wave and grin at his mother, the way he always had when he saw her, just before walking away to his gate.

The Storm Comes Crashing Down

Chapter Twelve

When Maryanne broke the news to her about Simon's death, Rose's first inclination, as Rose Lee, was to walk quickly back to her desk and grab her phone. Breathing heavily, she tried to make a call, but the phone dropped out of her shivering hands and clattered loudly on to her desk. Struggling desperately to make sense of the tangle of thoughts that screamed in her head, she stared helplessly at the phone and slumped heavily into her chair. She dragged a hand roughly through her perfectly coiffured hair and then rubbed her forehead and eyes like she was in pain. Maryanne, who had stood crying, quickly came around the desk to Rose, and held her by her shoulders, calling out, 'Ms Rose! Ms Rose!' and hurriedly called Ean on the phone.

Ean and Ethan entered Rose's room within minutes. As soon as they heard, given the gravity of the loss, Ean asked Maryanne to have the staff come in as well. As they streamed in, hushed whispers of speculation about what could have happened were heard. The staff very rarely assembled in the boss's room all together, unless it was news of great impact. Their whispers, however, were immediately silenced when the real reason for the emergency in the room came to be known. After a minute or so of shocked silence, sniffles could be heard, and several of the women started sobbing. Even Linda started to cry. While she had seen Simon as a threat to Ethan's inheritance and resented his influence over his mother, she had never imagined this. And he had been kind to her on numerous occasions, protecting her from his mother. Ean and Ethan had quickly walked up to their mother and knelt by her side, their faces red and flushed. For once, all they could think of was their brother—and that he had died. It appeared that it was indeed Simon's exit that had the power to draw the twins to their mother.

Both the twins asked Maryanne to make arrangements for them to travel to the UK to bring Simon home. But as Maryanne moved towards her desk outside the boss's room, Rose weakly raised her hand and whispered, frowning, 'I will bring my son home.' Despite the faintness of her voice and the weakness in her movements, her intention was clear. So, it was decided that Rose would travel to the UK with Ethan, while Ean would stay back to hold the fort and make the arrangements for the funeral. If Ean had been less than happy with Rose's choice of companion to London, it wasn't obvious. Later on, when his mind was calmer, his ambitious and practical side re-emerged. He welcomed the opportunity to run the show without Rose or Simon looking over his shoulder. It wasn't like he was happy that Simon had died, but he was not one to crumble in the face of the loss of a sibling. 'Life has to go on,' he said to himself, sighing resolutely. He decided that it now fell to him to fill Simon's shoes, in the business and in his mother's life.

Ethan though, simply put, was shattered. After his mother had decided that he would go with her to London to bring Simon's body back and tickets had been reserved for a flight the next morning, he had returned mechanically to the apartment that he shared with Ean. Ean had returned with their mother to her apartment and was staying with her for the night. Already exhausted physically and emotionally by the day's happenings, the ineffable sadness that was made more acute by intense guilt exploded and streamed down his red face as hot tears as soon as the door closed behind him. Simon's death was not what he had ever imagined. A weak, irresolute, and inept man buffeted by Ean's ambition and fear of the unknown, and Linda's eagerness for advancement for him and herself, Ethan had found himself dragged along, more often than not unwillingly, on a rough ride. 'I'm sorry, I'm sorry, I'm so sorry,' he gasped as he cried, covering his face with his trembling hands. He slid down to the floor and sat there crying. He lay in the same spot well into the night, thinking about his dead brother and his own childhood when he had turned to Simon ever so often for anything that he wanted from his mother.

When he finally went to bed, the headache that throbbed in his head made sleep impossible. He tossed and turned for a few hours before getting out of bed to get ready for a flight that was still several hours away. When Maniam finally called to inform him that the car was waiting downstairs, Ethan could barely drag himself out. The sleeplessness and the ache that still gnawed away at his head gave his face a pallor that Rose did not miss when he got into the car. She herself looked like she had not slept at all. Her face was completely colourless. Mother and son merely exchanged looks before turning to look ahead, as Maniam pulled out of the parking lot and on to the street. Rose didn't make an attempt to speak, and Ethan welcomed the silence.

Completely oblivious to the bleakness within the black Porsche that sped towards the airport, the morning was brilliantly sunny outside, with puffy white clouds floating merrily in the clear blue sky. Buses, cars, and people bustled about on the island as always, in contrast to the sombre stillness inside the vehicle. As the car neared the airport, Ethan reached for his mother's flaccid hand that lay on the seat and patted it gently without looking at her, and Rose turned to glance at him for the first time since they had left his apartment. When they finally got out of the car, checked in, and walked towards the waiting lounge, Ethan held his mother's elbow lightly, guiding her and leading the way while she simply followed, unseeing. The numerous faces that she passed and the voices that she heard blended to form a murmuring mass around her. She closed her eyes often and pressed her forehead with her hands in a manner that appeared as if she was trying to make sense of her surroundings. She barely spoke, and even when she did, she sounded so soft and weak that he had to strain to hear her.

Mother and son sat through the journey like they were bracing themselves to face the reality that awaited them at the end of the journey. Not a word escaped Rose's mouth, and not a morsel of food entered it throughout the journey to London. She simply sat with her eyes closed, enveloped by an impenetrable stillness; it was hard to tell if she was awake. Ethan did not attempt to speak to her. Perhaps he was fearful, or perhaps he was nursing his own grief. What struck him though was that his mother had not shed a single tear. Even when he had rushed to her office as soon as he had heard, Rose had been breathing heavily, and her face had displayed the anguish that she had felt, but not a single tear fell from those brown eyes.

And this was what he, even now as a twenty-seven-year-old, always found formidable about his mother—her unshakeable strength and resolve in the face of the gravest adversity. It dwarfed him and fuelled his anxiety in her presence. Exhibiting such strength was something Ethan couldn't imagine doing. He, of course, knew nothing of the young Rose who had sobbed uncontrollably in the cold hospital, with a bewildered ten-year-old Simon sitting beside her and trying desperately to comfort her. He had never seen the Rose who had trembled and cried while holding her young son close to her as loan sharks had banged on her door, or padlocked her in her apartment in the middle of the night. By the time he was born, she was transforming from a vulnerable, sweet young woman into a success story who strode through life with the self-assurance and confidence that achievement and an abundance of money had inspired. Rose had gradually taken to wearing a demeanour that displayed little of what she felt or thought, like a shield that protected her.

When they arrived in London, Lee Construction's country manager took them directly to the mortuary, where Simon's body was held. Just as they were about to enter the morgue, Rose held back. She gripped the frame of the heavy glass doors. Ethan waited by her side and said gently, 'Ma, you don't have to do this.

You can wait in the hotel room. I will finish all the formalities and call you when everything is done.' Rose leant forward and rested her head against the cool glass that soothed her throbbing head. She breathed heavily. The night she got the news, Rose had lain in bed all night waiting for daybreak and then throughout the journey, she had prayed fervently that there was some mistake and that it wasn't Simon. It was as if the prayer had remained frozen in her mind holding her back from crying. She was terrified that crying would make Simon's death a truth. 'It won't be him. This is just some horrible mistake. Nothing could happen to him,' she had repeated to herself at least a thousand times as she sat sphinx-like in her seat on the aircraft. The voices of the different people in her life who had assured her that if she wished for something badly enough, it would come true echoed in her ears. Although she had learnt over her sixty-plus years that wishing hard for something didn't always translate to reality, she prayed that just this once, it would.

A technician stepped out of the morgue to hand them some papers. Ethan signed the papers and handed them back to the man. Once again Ethan said to Rose, 'Ma, you could wait here and I can go inside. You can sit—' He didn't finish because Rose was shaking her head decisively with a frown etched on her ashen forehead. She removed her sunglasses and her eyes, which were red and tired, looked straight ahead, refusing to acknowledge her surroundings. The door of the morgue opened, and Ethan made to enter ahead of Rose, but she held him back. 'I will see him alone,' she whispered. 'Please,' she pleaded without looking at him. Ethan stepped back. He stood watching his mother slowly make her way into the cold chamber that the autopsy technician held open. This was not the mother he knew whose back was always straight and whose gait always quick and purposeful. This woman had aged in a night, and all her betrayals, losses and sorrows seemed to have descended with a vengeance on the shoulders that now drooped as she slowly walked towards the technician, her heels sounding heavy on the cold stone floor.

Her heart sank hopelessly when she recognized the familiar form—her Simon—and the starkness of what was real stared back at her. His death was the truth after all. There was no mistake. Everything that she had struggled for all her life, her work, her business, the empire that she had built from scratch, and everything that was meaningful to her crumbled in that one moment when she recognized the lifeless body of her Simon. Ethan, who was watching his mother from the door, saw her stop and rest her hand on the wall next to her. He knew then that what he, too, had been hoping would be a mistake, was real. What he did not see were the tears that streamed uncontrollably down his mother's face as she softly repeated Simon's name again and again and made her way to her son. Due to the severe head injuries that he had sustained, his head was swathed in bandages. Rose felt like her whole being was on the verge of exploding as she laid a timid hand on his forehead. The urge to cry out aloud was excruciatingly strong, but the numbness that she felt at the sight of her dead son was crushing. The cries stopped at her throat making her breath ragged and heavy.

Ethan, who was watching his mother, quickly walked up to her and held her as she collapsed into his arms, shaking. For the first time in his life, he saw cracks everywhere on the mask that had shielded the real Rose Lee. Shrouded in aloneness and vulnerability, Ethan saw Rose as a woman who had lost much more than what she had gained in life. As she sobbed uncontrollably, for the first time, Ethan saw his mother as anything but invulnerable, and he decided on that day that his mother would never be alone for as long as he was alive. He didn't know if he could step into Simon's place in her trust, but he was willing to be close at hand, faithful and loyal if she needed him.

The tears that streamed down her face released the sadness that had lain buried within her for years—the death of Stanley, the man on whom she had pinned her youth; the treachery of Peter, the man whom she had trusted blindly; the death of her mother; and now the most unbearable of all, the death of her Simon, who had been a son, a parent, and a friend whom she had trusted beyond anyone else. She had lost everything. Ethan held his mother with his chin resting gently on her head, his free hand stroking her head, his own tears flowing. He had been wrong about her all along and had wasted so many years being fearful of her, fearful of having failed her. 'Ma,' he said softly. 'Perhaps you should go back to the hotel and rest a little. I will finish up here. The chauffeur will take you back. You need to sleep a little, Ma.' Rose shook her head, a limp hand still on her dead son's head. Born out of a hopeless union, for thirty-five years, he had given her the strength and support that she had needed to live and flourish. Now, he had moved on without warning. But not before nudging towards someone else who could take his place.

A few weeks later, as Rose thought over the unfolding of events from the days before Simon's body was taken home to Singapore, she realized with surprise that it was Ethan who had stepped up and taken charge. The Ethan she had known before Simon's demise was indecisive and had a lacklustre approach to work, which fuelled her disappointment and frustration with him. The fact that he was always slightly nervous around her, especially if they were alone without his brothers only made things worse. She was well aware that he was always afraid of being asked about work and his inability to respond appropriately. Rose had often chuckled resignedly whenever Simon had covered up for Ethan. She knew that Ethan always looked to someone else for direction, and that part of his resentment towards her and Simon stemmed from his own incompetence. But the Ethan that stood before her now was in charge. He made the calls and the arrangements, and, when they were finally on the flight back to Singapore with Simon's body, she felt immense gratitude towards him because it was Ethan who supported her when her own strength abandoned her at the sight of Simon's remains.

Chapter Thirteen

Rose pleasantly surprised some, while dashing the hopes of others when she walked into the office on Monday morning, just a week after Simon's funeral, immaculate as always. She seemed to be much like her usual self before Peter's death—business-like, reserved, and focused on matters at hand. And she worked as she had before Peter's death, like a demon. Her work, in which she had earlier lost interest, was now her panacea and her sole purpose to live, and so she threw herself into it for twelve to fourteen hours again. Many of the staff, especially the younger ones, had expected Rose to stay away for good and had murmured about her retiring.

The general assumption was that after so many consecutive tragedies, and especially after Simon's death, it would be impossible for Rose to continue as the head of a huge business. So, when she returned for business as usual, Ean could barely conceal his disappointment and thus sealed her distrust of him. The warm and concerned self that he had shown her during Simon's funeral had merely been a front to conceal his real intentions. His almost sulking and reluctant greeting on the first day of her return said it all. His first comment was, 'I could have handled it all, Ma. There is no need for you to do this any . . . I mean so soon.' She merely smiled at him in return and asked him to give her a briefing on all that had happened in the office in her absence. The truth was that she didn't have a shred of choice. She had seen enough in the last two weeks. She knew what Ean was capable of, just as she knew how incapable Ethan was of protecting his position in the business.

It was much like the old days when she would stay in the suite behind her office. Maryanne worried about this because now there was no Simon to barge into her suite in the morning and demand that she go home to rest, or Sylvia to call her incessantly and nag her about her health. Rose was pretty much on her own, except perhaps for Ethan. But the problem was that though he had in many ways pushed himself to be like Simon, when it came to managing things the way she liked and being the rock that she could depend on, Ethan was still not quite as bold as Simon when it came to dealing with his mother. Maryanne would watch from the corner of her eye, faintly amused when he hovered in her suite outside Rose's room. 'She is available now, you can go in,' she would say gently without looking away from her laptop screen. And he would look at her almost gratefully for reassurance before knocking softly on Rose's door. Rose was getting used to the hesitant tap, and the silence before she had to call out, 'Come in!' It would take Ethan another six months before he could bring himself to do what Simon used to do, barely tap before going in without waiting for an invitation. But his earnestness and his genuineness to be supportive were not lost on Rose. *I just wish it hadn't taken the loss of one son to realize the strength of another*, she thought wistfully. Several years later, when Rose finally retired from the business of building, she would tell Ethan that when Simon had died, there had been just two reasons for her to force herself to continue to live. One had been her work and the other had been him.

While Ethan clearly lacked Simon's aptitude and Ean's drive, he gradually grew in his mother's esteem in many other ways with his hard work and his loyalty towards her. He didn't cut corners with what he did, and he did his best to do things the way he thought Rose would. He wasn't always right, but Rose was now a little more empathetic and patient, and with that, his confidence and self-assurance grew. Even the staff saw the difference, much to the growing consternation of Ean, who was used to a younger twin who was quieter, more reserved, and more dependent on him for leadership. 'Looks like you're walking in Simon's shoes these days,' he would quip with a smirk if he ran into Ethan while walking down the hallway in the office on his way to Rose's office. Ethan would smile uncomfortably, but he knew his brother well enough to know that their relationship had now changed forever and that there was a wall slowly but surely developing between them. Ean no longer called him around six in the evening to step out for a drink before dinner. They still shared an apartment in the heart of the city, but they barely saw each other at home, and they hardly spoke at work except at meetings. Ethan had had an inkling that it would come to this the day his mother had picked him to accompany her to London.

If there was anyone who watched the new closeness that Ethan shared with Rose with quiet glee, it was Linda, although it was not lost on her that this good fortune had a price. She hardly saw Ethan these days. But she quickly brushed that off as temporary. Linda was too sure of herself to think, even fleetingly, that Ethan could permanently move away from her. And besides, it suited her to take a step back too. She liked him well enough, but she intended to marry him because he was Ethan Lee of Lee Constructions. When she had first met him, that had been what she had found most attractive about him. She sometimes wondered if Ean would have been a more suitable match since they were often like-minded about the business. But there were times when she wondered if Ean even noticed her, and it was clear to her that Ean loved Ean the most; everyone else would have to take second or third place in his life. He and his well-being was the main focus of his life. He dated the best-looking girls and was seen in all the best places in town, mainly because it made him look good. Ethan was far more malleable and easier to convince about her worth.

* * *

Four months had passed since Simon's death. It was around five in the evening on a Friday before a long weekend. The National Day holiday was on Monday. The weekend traffic was heavier than usual. Rose leant back against the cool leather of her car, with her eyes closed. She liked to do that these days because the minute she closed her eyes, Simon appeared either as a smiling young child, or as the child that had held her hand as she sat in the hospital waiting for news about Stanley, or as the portly man who had waved goodbye to her as he had departed to his end. These moments, when she could visualize her dead son, were her moments with him again. Tears pooled in her eyes and burnt them as she kept them stubbornly closed, refusing to lose the picture of the happiness that was forever lost to her.

'Do you want to go back to the office?' asked Maniam, looking at her through the rear-view mirror. He knew that she was crying. His helplessness frustrated him. There was nothing he could do for the woman who had been, on more than one occasion, a benefactor to him and his family. Rose drew a breath before she whispered, 'No, I will go home today. And you can leave after that, Maniam.' She dragged her purse to her from the other side of the seat where she had laid it and rummaged inside for a tissue. Her fingers brushed against some paper that lay at the bottom. She looked at it with a frown before pulling it out of her purse. It was when she had pulled it out completely that memories came rushing back. Simon had handed it to her just before he had left.

The torn envelope that contained a folded piece of paper brought back every detail of her last conversation with him. Rose stared at the piece of paper that she held in her fingers. Her first inclination was to toss it into the little wastebasket that Maniam had placed on the floor of the car. But she held back and continued to stare at it with a frown. 'I think you need to read this. Please do this for yourself. You will feel a lot better about everything,' she could still hear Simon say. Rose stared at the letter before she unfolded it.

The letter, which wasn't very long, was written in neat Mandarin script.

Rose,

I realize that I'm the last person you wish to hear from. But I'm hopeful that if you are reading this, you will also come to a point when you will stop hating me.

I worked in the ceramic factory that you and Peter owned in Malaysia. When I started working there I was just seventeen years old and fresh out of school. Peter was very kind to me, a girl who did not know much about the world outside my little town. The big car, the money that he flashed around, and the expensive meals and presents that he bought me were irresistible. Unfortunately, I also had a mother who thought the relationship would benefit me and her. There was nothing and no one to stop me or to advise me against the relationship. Besides, I soon found myself pregnant. I'm not going to make any excuses for myself. I knew he was a married man, but I had never seen the life that he showed me, and I went into it with my eyes open.

As Rose read the letter, what she felt was a dry resignation in place of the old bitterness of the past, especially now when Peter himself had faded in her mind like an unpleasant memory. The letter continued,

I know that you dislike me, but I must say that I'm thankful for my relationship with Peter, as I have a beautiful daughter because of him. I'm writing to you now because of her. Simon has been very kind to us. He has taken care of us very well. Evelyn is now in America studying. Coming from a small village, with very little education, I never imagined that someday my child would be in America, studying there. But she is, and that is because of Peter and now because of Simon. I know you must think of me as selfish. I can't blame you for that.

The next part of the letter came as a surprise to Rose. While she knew that Simon had managed the payments made to 'that woman', she had not known that he was funding her daughter's education in the US. She didn't care because Lee Constructions was generous, especially about education: several students benefitted from its benevolence, and this was just one more. But she wondered why Simon had not mentioned it to her. She continued reading the letter.

Simon might have told you that I will not live very long. I have cancer, and it is eating me up very quickly. I'm not even sure that I will be alive when you read this. The truth is that my Evelyn has no one except me. I lost my father many years ago, and my mother died some years ago. Now that Peter, too, is gone, Evelyn has no one. I would like to ask that you take care of her.

Rose stopped at this point and reread the paragraph. The message was not what she had expected. It was such a bold request to ask the wife of the man with whom she had an affair.

I cannot think of anyone else for my Evelyn. I know Simon will make sure she is taken care of financially. He is a very good man. But she needs someone who will be there for her as a mother, and, Rose, I will be very grateful if you could be there for her. I know I'm asking for too much, but please think about it before you decide. I hope you will decide quickly.

The letter was signed 'Mable'. Finally, 'that woman' had a name.

Rose laid the letter on the seat and sat back, staring out of the window. It had darkened, and they had almost reached her apartment on the East Coast. She could see the lights in the apartments that whizzed past, and she wondered about the families that lived in those apartments. She had had a family like that once, a complete beautiful family with a husband, three beautiful sons, and her mother. Just three or four years ago, she had had more than all of those people in those apartments. She had wealth as well, an enormous amount of wealth. The wealth remained now but everything else was gone, vanished. Yes, she still had two sons. But she was just getting to know one, while she wasn't sure if the other one even liked her. She wondered how Ean would relate to her if she suddenly lost Lee Constructions and all the money she had. Rose had an inkling of what the answer would be.

Her thoughts went back to 'that woman'—Mable. A semblance of a resigned smile lingered on her lips in the darkness. Now that she knew about her own origins, she felt less angry, less contemptuous towards Mable. How was Mable different from Ming? And how was Evelyn different from her, Rose Lee? She too, Rose Lee, who felt entitled to have it all, was the daughter of a woman who had cheated with her cousin's boyfriend. 'We're all the same, just in different bodies, walking in and out of life, at different times, through revolving doors. Who am I to judge?' said Rose softly in the dark, amused by the irony of it all. All the anger that she had once felt was meaningless. In any case, the man who had caused all that hurt was now gone, and she didn't care a jot, especially after Simon's death. She could hear Sylvia's voice, half scolding, half cajoling, '*Haiya* Rosie! There is no black or white in life. Let it go. Peter's chapter is closed in your life.' Sylvia had said that just a few weeks before she had died when the subject of Peter's other family had been broached. When Rose thought about it now, it struck her that Sylvia would have been thinking about Ming and her. She had accepted them both into her life despite Ming's betrayal. She had given Rose the best life she could afford and showered her with all the love that a mother could give her child.

A constant soft ringing from her purse intruded into her thoughts. Maniam looked at his boss through the rear-view mirror before he said, 'Phone, Ms Lee.' It was Ethan.

'Ma, we have a problem,' he said. She heard the concern in his voice.

Maniam had driven into the parking lot of her apartment complex and had just parked when he heard Rose snap, 'When?' Rose had a frown deeply etched on her forehead. 'I will be there in a few minutes.' She looked sharply at Maniam as she hung up and said, 'Maniam, I'm sorry, I can't let you go just yet. Can you take me back to the office quickly? We need to pick up Ethan.' Maniam glanced at his boss through his rear-view mirror. The urgency and anxiety in her voice were reflected in her eyes, which darted impatiently as he weaved through traffic.

Chapter Fourteen

Ean Lee's face was splashed across every Singapore news medium the next morning as the man who had bribed a government official for building permit approvals of a hotel that had collapsed in Jakarta, killing twenty and injuring at least fifty people. Pictures of Ean as the scion of Lee Constructions, with the rubble in the background, were flashed all day on television. And in that rubble lay Rose's hard work, her pride, and the reputation of Lee Constructions. Interviews with legal experts and industry experts were telecast, and Rose Lee, as the chief executive and chairman of Lee Constructions, and Lee Constructions itself, was extensively discussed, her character and ethics scrutinized and questioned.

Rose watched all of this, sitting up straight on the edge of a couch in her living room, her eyes darting and her mind jumping frantically from one image to another. The previous night had been long. She had met Ethan, and they had rushed to their lawyers' offices for legal counsel. It was way past midnight when an exhausted Rose had finally lain her head on a pillow only to stare up at the ceiling and get up to pace back and forth in her room, wretchedly tormented. When she had finally fallen asleep in the early hours of the morning, it was more like she had passed out of sheer exhaustion. She woke up startled by a nightmare. Ethan was already in the apartment, talking with the lawyers who had come with him. By the look of him, it was obvious that his night hadn't been any better. The television was on, and Rose could hear what was going on while dressing.

TV journalists and reporters who knew nothing about her, the real Rose Lee, talked about her, analysed her company, and tore her reputation to shreds. A mixture of rage, hopelessness and acute sadness filled her as she watched her integrity, her company's credibility, and, more than anything, the validity of her life's work dragged through the mud because of one person, one person who was greedy, avaricious and 'Stupid!' she screamed in her head. She watched stone-faced as Ean was shown being led by law officers into the building of the Central Bureau of Investigations for questioning. Her hate for Ean as a person overwhelmed her, while a small voice at the back of her mind reminded her that the young man being led away was her son, and a fear about what would happen to him churned in her stomach.

Ean had been arrested at the immigration checkpoint just as he was attempting to drive across to Johore Bahru for the weekend with one of his on-and-off girlfriends. Ethan kept glancing at his mother while speaking to their lawyers. She was so distant in her demeanour that he couldn't fathom what was in her mind. She didn't participate in his discussions with the lawyers. 'We need to go and meet him, Ma,' Ethan said hesitantly, sitting down next to Rose, who shook her head slowly, her eyes still fixed on the news.

'No, I'm not coming,' she said decidedly.

'But Ma—'

'I'm not ready to see him. What do I say to him? That I will bail him out? That I will make this whole thing go away?' she said with chilling quiet fury. 'I have warned him, both of you, a million times about what could happen if you try to get easily what others have toiled to get. This is what I was afraid of. He was always too much in a hurry to get ahead. Now we have lost everything. Everything that took years to build. No, I'm not seeing him. I have nothing to say to him, for now anyway,' she declared with bitter decidedness.

Ethan was at a loss for words, wishing fervently for his dead brother's sense and rationality. He knew that if Simon had been alive, he would have done everything within his power to get Ean out of this mess, and he may have even succeeded. Simon went to any extent to protect his brothers while he lived. As if reading his thoughts, Rose said, 'Simon was too easy on both of you. Always covering up for everything. Thankfully, you saved yourself. I'm sorry. I cannot do what Simon would have done. I don't want to, and I won't. Ean will just have to take what's dished out to him for this. He made the bed. It's his to lie on now.' Ethan's heart sank. The penalties were heavy, especially since there were deaths involved. His twin was looking at several years in prison in Jakarta, and Lee Constructions was probably looking at huge monetary penalties. Their lawyers were not optimistic. Evidence weighed heavily against Lee Constructions and Ean in particular, as the official who had taken the bribe was arrested and had identified him. Relatives of the dead and injured were demanding that Ean be brought back to Jakarta to be tried, that Lee Constructions be held responsible, and that all their projects be investigated.

Dismissing Ethan's gentle protests about her refusing to meet Ean with a wave of her hand, Rose asked him to issue a statement to the press that Lee Constructions was very willing to cooperate with investigations and audits. 'But Ma . . .' persisted Ethan.

'Ethan, no! He brought this upon himself despite my desperate efforts to put him on the right track. What was he afraid of? You tell me. What was he afraid of? That he would not inherit anything? Or, that I would give everything to Simon or you? Who am I going to give all of this to?' she exploded, waving a hand around the room as she stood up abruptly. 'You are all that I have. And now one is dead. Who else is there to inherit all of this?' Rose was fuming. 'And was he hoping to get it all so that you will get nothing? Just explain this to me. What the bloody hell was he thinking?' she cried breathing heavily and her voice cracking slightly. The fact that her hands were shivering lightly was not lost on Ethan.

He stood up and reached out. 'Ma . . . ' he started but she shrugged off his hand.

'I'm tired of his constant need to get more and more and everything for himself and his need to show that he can do what he wants with the business, when he bloody works for me,' she cried stabbing a finger into her chest. 'I'm still the head of Lee Constructions, and as far as I'm concerned, Ean is no longer an employee of this company. His services are terminated with immediate effect. And you can tell him that when you see him. And you will inform the press of the same. I want it to be in the news tomorrow. You will take over his portfolio for now,' she snapped in Ethan's ashen face.

* * *

The Ean that Ethan met a few hours later was nothing like his usual self—self-assured and obnoxious. The Ean that sat before Ethan that evening was rattled, visibly so. Lee Constructions' lawyers had obtained permission for the brothers to meet where Ean was held. Ethan found it difficult to relate to the pale and frightened man in front of him. Gone was the smug certainty with which Ean always spoke. Instead, he mumbled softly and even incoherently. When he first saw Ethan and held his hands tightly, he reddened and his eyes moistened. And as Ethan dreaded, he asked for their mother. 'Where's Ma?' was his first question, his eyes searching Ethan's face.

'How are you? Have you eaten anything?' Ethan patted his brother's back gently.

Ean stared blankly back at Ethan and then looked past him. He then repeated his question while searching his brother's face, 'Where's Ma? Is she here?'

Ethan frowned a little with discomfiture and looked away before turning back to meet his twin's eyes. 'She's very concerned and worried. She's been working all night with our lawyers to help you. I had to force her to rest.'

Ean looked probingly at his brother, and said, 'She's furious, isn't she? She refused to come, right?'

Ethan looked away again before sighing and saying, 'Don't think about all that now. We need to get you out of this mess. She will be okay when you're out of this.'

Ean's response was a weak, short, hollow laugh. He then said, 'Do you think I'm going to get out of this? It was the only time . . . the permits were taking so long and the changes they wanted were so extensive, it would have cost us millions, I . . .' he continued softly.

'Ean, the building collapsed because the materials used were substandard, something that Lee Constructions has never ever done,' interjected Ethan matter-of-factly, looking directly at his brother. 'The man you paid off has been arrested, and he has confessed to everything, implicating you quite clearly. Honesty would be your best bet now.' Ean looked at his usually shy and nervous twin. Ethan's quiet confidence was now both reassuring and formidable. Ean was suddenly aware that he didn't feel any of the superiority he had once felt in his twin's presence.

After a grilling interrogation that lasted several days, Ean was extradited to Jakarta, where the trial was to take place. While awaiting trial, Ean had to spend several months in an Indonesian prison, and when he arrived in Jakarta, heavily escorted by law enforcement officials, there were protests and burning of effigies outside the airport. Relatives of the dead and injured demanded that Rose be brought to trial as well. Thankfully, Ean took full responsibility, denying that his mother and the company had any knowledge of his dealings with the official. Having failed in every attempt to coax his mother into coming to see Ean, Ethan shuttled between Jakarta and Singapore, and the strain of it was beginning to show on his person and his temperament. The last thing he wanted to deal with now was his brother's usual attempt to justify his failings or his mother's ego.

Ethan regarded his brother uncomfortably. They were separated by bars and a guard stood close. Ean looked alarmingly thin and worn. All of a sudden, he seemed much older than his twenty-eight years. 'Mother is never going to come, is she?' Ean asked, looking steadily at his twin. Ethan looked away uneasily. This was his brother's first question every time he came to see him, and he was running out of excuses. Rose wouldn't hear of it. But she was sparing no expense in paying the best lawyers in Indonesia and Singapore to defend her son. She had told Ethan to stay in Jakarta for as long as it took to be of support to his brother.

But when Ethan told her that Ean would appreciate a visit, her face was a mask again. 'No. I will be there for the trial. But someone needs to manage and clear the mess that he has made. We are losing deals. I need to revive the trust that he has destroyed. This is my company. I built it. I will rebuild it now. But I cannot forgive him.'

Ethan's patience was beginning to wear thin. 'Ma, yes, he was, as you say, avaricious, greedy and impatient, and all of those things but that does not negate the fact that he is family, your son. And yes it is your company, and yes you built it. But we have contributed to its growth too, at least in the last few years. This is not right. You have to come and see him. He will at least feel a little reassured,' Ethan retorted hotly.

Rose looked long and hard at her usually deferential son. She was both cynical and annoyed by the Ethan that stood up to her now. If he had done so before this mess, she would have welcomed it. But at this point, he was making it worse for Ean. She dug her heels in further. 'I don't need you to remind me that this man in prison in Jakarta for fraud, bribery, corruption, and the murder of several people is my son! I'm well aware of my relationship with him . . . painfully so,' she said flicking a bitter glance at Ethan. 'He is, after all, the sole cause of the destruction of my reputation. So how could I forget?' she asked icily. 'I'm sure you, in turn, are aware that it's my money that is buying the best legal advice in the country here and in Jakarta, so that he can come out of this as painlessly as possible even though he has caused so much damage,' she continued steadily, her steely eyes boring into Ethan. 'I don't need you to remind me of my responsibilities. I know what my responsibilities are, and I'm fulfilling them as best as I can, given the situation. I don't need to tell you this, but it is not in his best interests for me to see him now because I do not feel positively about him at all. If it weren't for the fact that he is, unfortunately, my son, I would happily let him go to hell. This is not the appropriate time for me to see him. I might just say hurtful things that will make him feel worse. Which is why I'm avoiding him. Right now, he needs legal help more than anything else. And I'm doing my best to give him that,' she said, her gaze never once shifting from Ethan, who was now looking down like a schoolboy. 'One more thing . . . Lee Constructions is *my* company. I started it, and it is my hard work that stands as its foundation. I don't deny that you and your brothers have contributed to it. But let me assure you that it would have been where it was before this whole mess, even without your help.'

* * *

The trial began six months after Ean was arrested, and Rose arrived in Jakarta with Ethan on the morning of the day it began. It was to be the first time she would see him since his arrest. A sense of foreboding filled her heart as soon as she stepped out of the airport into the waiting limousine. She had always liked Jakarta for its character and the warmth of its smiling people. She used to deal with the business in Jakarta before Ean had taken over, and the city had always made her feel at home immediately. But today, on the day of the trial, as the limousine weaved its way through traffic to the courthouse, she felt like an unwanted guest hunted by an unfamiliar hostility that froze her insides.

The statues of heroes that dotted the city everywhere seemed to stare down at her belligerently, questioning her intentions and

her deepest thoughts, so hidden even from her that she wasn't sure
what they were. Perhaps she should have visited Ean before this
day. Was this trial going to be the end of him? And was she to blame
for that? What were her real objectives in staying silent as he took
the blame for it all? Had they really been to do what was right,
or to save herself so that she could continue at the helm of Lee
Constructions? After all, she could have accepted responsibility
since she was the CEO. Accept the blame, even if she had known
nothing about the bribes and she would not have bribed anyone
ever, even if it meant a loss of business? She would have gone to
jail in his place for no fault of hers. But then again, she was past
her prime, while he still had his whole life ahead of him. What if
he went to jail? *A hypocrite! That's what you are, Rose! Nothing but
a power-hungry hypocrite*, screamed her conscience at her as she
sat perspiring in the air-conditioned car. Ethan, who sensed his
mother's tension, lightly squeezed her limp hand that lay on the
seat. She didn't turn to look at him. Her eyes were riveted on the
road ahead like she was looking for something unrevealed as yet.

If she was shaken by Ean's emaciated and pale self, she did not
show it. Instead, she requested Scott, who lived for the most part
in Jakarta and who knew people in high places, to have Ean moved
to a minimum-security cell, at least till the trial was over. When
Ean was led into the courtroom, the first person he saw was his
mother, and he felt a wave of relief and courage wash over him. But
his confidence was tragically ephemeral because when he tried to
smile weakly, he merely received a curt nod as a response. She was
far from forgiving him. But still, he was thankful for her presence.
He was sure that she wouldn't simply abandon him.

The courtroom was filled with people from the press, relatives
of the deceased and injured, and Rose and a few of her senior staff
in charge of communications. When she had stepped out of her
vehicle outside the courtroom, dressed in a black skirt suit, she
had been met with jeers and calls for her arrest. She had been
hurried indoors by Ethan and her staff, who did their best to

shield her from the heckling and the questions from the media. Lee Constructions' lawyers and Ean's defence lawyers in Jakarta worked hard to have him acquitted. If there hadn't been any deaths, this would have been a simpler case. But the relatives of the twenty dead demanded that Ean be handed the stiffest possible sentence, and so the eyes of the public were focused on the trial. The official who had confessed to taking the bribe had been imprisoned for two years and had lost his job. Despite the thousands of dollars spent on lawyers' fees by Rose and their best attempts, Ean was sentenced to five years' imprisonment, and Lee Constructions had to pay a compensation of twenty million dollars to the owners of the apartments. Every bit of colour abandoned Ean's face when the judge read out his sentence. He gripped the table until his knuckles turned white. The nightmare was now his reality.

As soon as the sentence was read out, there was both jeering and cheering in the courtroom. There were some who felt that the sentence was too light, while there were some others who felt that justice had been served. Rose, a little whiter than usual because she had spent the night praying that Ean would miraculously escape a jail sentence, watched impassively with Ethan and Scott, who had made it a point to attend every session, by her side. Those that turned to look at Rose with smug jubilance may or may not have heard the softest of gasps that escaped from her slightly open mouth when the sentence was read. They probably would have also missed the trembling hands that tightly clutched her purse. She had lost.

Rose continued to sit in the courtroom for a while after her son had been led away to serve his sentence. Her mind was darting from questions about Ean and his well-being to his future to the image of Lee Constructions and the compensation that they had to pay. But foremost on her mind was how Ean was going to survive five years in prison. She was so consumed with fear for his safety and health that she felt suffocated, and she began to breathe heavily. Ethan cast a worried look at his mother and placed a hand on her shoulder, 'Ma,' he said. 'We can leave now through the back as the press is waiting outside,' he said hesitantly. She reached up to his hand and clutched it in hers.

Ethan was a little taken aback by how icy they were. 'Ma, we can appeal. We will talk to the lawyers and see what else we can do,' he said gently.

Still gripping his hand tightly, she whispered, 'He won't survive this. He is too . . .' Her voice trailed off, unable to finish what she wanted to say. She sat staring at the front of the courtroom, her eyes wide with fear and her forehead wet with perspiration.

Scott took her hand in his and said, 'Rose, all is not lost. We'll figure it out. You have the best legal team. We'll work through this.'

'My son will not survive this, I know it! If I have to pay a bigger fine, I will. But I can't leave my son in a prison here. Ethan, can you have the lawyers arrange for me to see him?'

Ethan glanced at Scott before he responded. 'I'll do that, Ma. But for now, let's go back to the hotel. You need some rest. You haven't slept at—'

'How can I sleep in a hotel room when my son is on his way to spending five years in a prison cell?' she snapped back.

Ethan and Scott glanced at each other again, and Scott spoke. 'Rose, go back to the hotel for now. I will make some calls. I will do my best to get you a meeting with him tomorrow. Just go back and get some rest and wait for my call.' Scott made good on his promise, and by 9 a.m. the next day, Rose was sitting across from Ean in a visiting room.

If Ean was sorry about his mother's wan appearance, he felt sorrier for himself. That was Ean. His own well-being was always primary on his mind, and that was something that Rose knew. Despite the jail sentence that loomed ahead, Rose knew that what was predominantly on her son's mind was where he was going to be in relation to the company and her, and his inheritance. She knew that he was racked with worry that she would not forgive him and that she would disinherit him. Her worry was for his well-being and his health because he was her son. But she was not about to forgive him for what he had done as an employee of Lee Constructions, and there was no place in the business for him any more. Of that much, she was sure. So when they sat opposite each other, each one gauging the other's state of mind, they were also thinking of how best to ask what concerned them most, and how best to lay down the truth.

'How are you holding up?' asked Rose, doing her best to exude a calmness that she didn't quite feel. She hadn't slept well and spent the night vacillating between resignation and worry. Ean hesitated momentarily and said, 'I'm okay. What made you finally come?' he asked, barely concealing the malevolence that suddenly surged at the sight of his mother. The fear that had gripped him when he was arrested had given way to remorse and then desperation and entitlement. Initially when he had pleaded with Ethan, and even with his lawyers, to convince his mother to see him, he was convinced that the lawyers to whom his mother was paying huge amounts of money would somehow get him out of the mess. But as the days slipped by, he began to feel a little hopeless. Then, he felt a sudden awakening of that old confidence that he could wiggle out of any uncomfortable situation with his mother's money. However, as soon as his sentence was handed to him, the old resentment towards his mother returned. *She should have done more. She would have had it been her eldest son, or even if it had been the idiot son who has now stepped into his shoes.* It was her fault that he had resorted to what he had done, bribing officials to help him succeed so that she would see his worth, which she could otherwise never see. He had saved money for the company and finished the construction faster than Simon would have, and she still didn't appreciate him. She should, in fact, be appreciating him for taking the blame upon himself and bearing the cross so that the company could thrive. He was suddenly furious. She could never see his worth, and that was the whole problem. It was always Simon—and now Ethan.

'It was best that I didn't come before the trial. It would have done us both no good. I hired the best legal help I could get,' responded Rose, irritation creeping into her voice.

'Well, the best wasn't enough. I'm still here. And I will be here for the next five years,' shot back Ean, his eyes darting around the bare room and then settling on Rose as a malevolent stare.

Unfazed, she returned his gaze calmly and steadily. 'I did the best I could. Given the gravity of the issue, we need to be thankful that the sentence was not heavier.'

Ean stared at his mother, his anger mounting. 'You always have the answers, don't you? Always putting everyone in their place. What I did was for the company—'

'What you did was for yourself. Don't you dare say that you did it for Lee Constructions, which has never condoned dishonesty, and it never will because I don't condone it, and I'm Lee Constructions,' declared Rose, her eyes flashing with the fury that she had thus far suppressed. 'You are dishonest, and that's all there is to be said. You forget that Simon and I dealt with these same people for years before you, but it didn't as much as cross our minds to do this and that's the reason for Lee Constructions' success—our integrity and ethics. But you . . . you did not think twice because you were in a hurry, too much of a hurry to get to the top, to get everything, overnight! And that's what did you in and destroyed the good name that we took years to establish—the shortcuts, the arrogance, and the feeling that you will always be bailed out.'

Ean sat glaring at her. Everything that she had said that he had done, he had done for his role in the company. Now that role seemed to be slipping away from him. She had betrayed him, cheated him of what was rightfully his. 'That may be, but I did it for Lee Constru—'

Rose held up her hand and interjected, 'No matter how many times you repeat that you did it for the business, you are not going to convince me. In any case, save yourself the trouble of defending your actions with me. What I think does not matter. I'm here as your mother and I'm concerned about your well-being. You are my son, and nothing can ever change that, not even your actions,' she said flicking a glance at him. 'I did my best for you, and I will continue to do so for as long as I live but only outside of the company. You no longer have a role there. But as I said, I'm your mother and I know what's coursing through your mind right at this moment. You will receive your rightful inheritance. Just without my company,' said Rose Lee standing up, and thus signalling the end of their meeting. Ean looked up at her, more stunned than angry. Rose's ruthlessness as CEO of Lee Constructions coolly gazed back at him. Then she turned around to leave while he sat there staring angrily at her back.

* * *

Clearly, Rose and her problems did not matter a jot to bustling Jakarta because when she stepped out of the prison after meeting her son, the sun beat down on her brilliantly and made her squint. The blaring of the horns of traffic and the hustle and bustle of the city couldn't have cared less that the meaning of Rose's existence seemed to be eluding her more and more. She once had three sons. One had died. Another was lost to her now, forever. She was shaken, not just by the fact that Ean had gone to jail, but by the grievousness of his actions, his avarice, and the extent to which he was willing to go to fulfil his greed. She had not anticipated this, not for one moment. When she left Jakarta with Ethan on the same evening, mother and son barely spoke during the two-hour flight back.

When she got into her car at Changi, she barely acknowledged Maniam. She slid into the backseat and leant back resting her head on the headrest, so exhausted that she felt like she could stay there all night. Ethan sat in the front with Maniam. Their silence gave Maniam a clear picture of what would have happened in Indonesia as he sped through the night. When he finally dropped Rose off at the entrance of her apartment building, he caught a glimpse of her in the rear-view mirror. Thinking of his wife waiting with his dinner and his daughter studying in her room, and the calm in his little apartment, which Rose had helped him buy, a deep sadness filled him at the thought of how little his boss had.

The apartment was dark when Rose let herself in. A lone light shone down the hallway in Ming's room, and strains of old Cantonese songs, which, like Sylvia, Ming was fond of, floated down to the main sitting area. Disinclined to go to her room as she would typically have done, Rose slowly made her way to Ming's. Although she had made every effort to draw Ming into her life and had done everything in her power to do for Ming what she would have done for Sylvia, there was still a long bridge to be crossed. Mother and daughter continued to stand at opposite ends. Rose stood at the door and watched the old woman silently. Ming had not been blessed with Sylvia's good looks. And her harsh past probably played a role too, in adding more gloom to her face. She had small beady eyes beneath lids that drooped. Her once rounded face sagged at the jawline and her mouth drooped even when she was relaxed, as she was now, with her wrinkled hands worn by years of scrubbing and cleaning resting on her lap. Here too was a woman who had tried and lost.

For the first time since their meeting, Rose's heart went out to Ming. Even when she had discovered that Ming was her mother, Rose had accepted the fact without much ado or attachment. After all, this was the woman who had also sold her. What Rose had felt was a little pity for the lonely woman who did not have a soul in the world to look out for her. But right at this moment, when Rose realized that all that she had clung to, her business, her relationships, and her sons were all so distant from her, the old woman sitting on her bed listening to her old Cantonese songs, was a reflection of herself, Rose Lee, a lonely ageing woman. In that instant, all of Ming's follies of her youth seemed to disappear. Ming was her mother, and there was no denying that, and Ming had made it a point to tell her the truth boldly with no fear of rejection. She had come to terms with the idea that she would be rejected and had been prepared to go away, to walk her final stretch alone. She had wanted nothing and, in some ways, had been more courageous than Rose was now, with all her wealth.

'Mama,' said Rose softly. When she had not known who Ming was, Rose had called her Ming. After she had discovered the relationship, she had not used any term of address. 'Mama,' repeated Rose a little louder, and Ming opened her eyes and turned to look at her daughter. If she had heard Rose referring to her as 'Mama' and was surprised, there was nothing in her manner that revealed it. But she must have sensed her daughter's deep grief because she merely patted the space on the side of the bed next to her. All the grief of all her losses from the time when Stanley died seemed to suddenly descend on Rose and flow down her wan face as hot tears as she walked towards her mother. A gentle breeze wafted into the room, bringing with it the sounds of the late-night traffic and the scent of the sea not too far away. The night wore on, and Rose dissolved into loud sobs with her face in her hands as she sat with her mother, who stroked her hair gently with her roughened hands.

Chapter Fifteen

'Ms Rose, there is a call from an Evelyn Lee,' said Maryanne, a little hesitantly.

Rose frowned because the name rang a bell, and yet it didn't. 'Evelyn . . . from?' she asked a tad impatiently. She and Ethan were preparing to meet some potential clients.

'Umm . . . it's Mr Lee's daughter, Ms Rose. Umm . . . Mr Simon used to take her calls, but . . .'

Rose's frown deepened, but she responded shortly, 'Okay, connect her.'

'Hi . . . I'm Evelyn . . . Umm . . .' began the girlish voice.

'Yes, I know who you are,' interjected Rose without emotion. If she was impatient, her voice bore no hint of it. 'What can I do for you?'

There was a moment's silence before the girl spoke again.

'I . . . umm . . . called because I . . . umm wanted to meet with you,' she said. Rose was silent. The memory of her final conversation with Simon almost two years ago came flooding back. So much had happened since then that she had almost forgotten about Peter's other family. And then she remembered that Simon had mentioned that the girl's mother was dying then and, of course, the letter that the woman had written her. The impatience she had felt at the start of the call evaporated, and in its place was a semblance of shame. She should have gone to see the woman or at least tried to find out about her. She was probably dead now. Rose felt obliged to meet with the dead woman's daughter.

'Where are you, Evelyn?' asked Rose.

'I'm staying with a friend on Thomson Road. I promise I won't take up much of your time . . .'

Again Rose interrupted her. 'It's all right. I'm busy now. But I will send my driver down to get you in the evening, and you can come to the office. We can talk then.'

'Oh! That won't be necessary. I can take a bus or train down to the office,' said the girl.

Rose was silent for a fraction of a minute, and then she said, 'All right, I will see you here. Do you know where the office is?'

'Yes, I have been there once, when Simon . . .' and the girl trailed off.

If Rose was surprised, she didn't say anything. She hung up after the girl said that she would be at the office at five in the evening. Since her client meeting began almost immediately after the call, she did her best to shove the girl, the conversation, and the impending face-to-face encounter to the back of her mind.

* * *

Rose was still tied up when Maryanne informed her that Evelyn was waiting for her. She had Maryanne take her into her private suite, and it was almost an hour before Rose could meet Evelyn, Peter's daughter from 'that woman'. The girl was slim, actually 'a little thin', Rose thought to herself. She had long, straight hair that hung down to her waist and was fashionably dressed. The girl stood up, a little hurriedly, as soon as Rose entered the room. The first thing that struck Rose, and sort of stabbed her a little, albeit dully and momentarily, was the fact the girl looked a lot like Peter. She had his smile, which was his most attractive feature. But the feeling passed almost immediately, and she was able to look at Evelyn dispassionately.

As soon as Rose entered the room, she held out a hand that the girl limply took in hers. Their handshake was brief but when their eyes met, there was some warmth in Rose's and hope in the girl's.

'Hello, Evelyn. It's nice to meet you,' said Rose a smile playing lightly on her lips.

The girl nodded. 'Simon has told me a lot about you. So I feel like I know you quite well.'

Rose smiled but frowned a little as well and looked at Evelyn quizzically. 'It looks like you were in constant touch with my son.' The emphasis on 'my son' was not lost on Evelyn, and she smiled hesitantly.

'I did not know Simon for very long, unfortunately. He arranged for my education in the States, but it was my mother that he connected with at that time. I contacted him for the first time when my mother became very sick. He helped us a lot. We could not have managed without him. We're very thankful to him. My mother would always say that you raised an ideal son.'

While the speech was genuine and sincere, Rose couldn't help wondering about its preparedness. There was an awkward silence after this.

'Then, when we heard what happened, my mother wanted me to come for the funeral, but I was afraid of . . . ' she trailed off, and there was more silence. 'And then my mother died.' The girl fell silent and looked down. The girl looked lost and vulnerable as she sat with one hand clutching her handbag, and the other rolled into a tight fist.

Rose studied her for a brief minute and then asked gently, 'When did your . . . umm . . . mother . . . pass?'

The girl looked up to meet Rose's eyes and said, 'About a year ago . . . she had cancer. She seemed to be recovering for a while, and I really thought she would be okay. But, I guess . . . '

An uncomfortable silence hung heavily between the two women for what seemed like an eternity. The older woman looked away, for once a little tongue-tied. She no longer felt the disdain and anger she had once felt towards the girl's mother. If anything, she felt a little mortified by what she had felt, especially since Peter was just a memory that would have mattered little if she had not had two sons by him. She looked back at Evelyn sitting in front of her, looking down and biting her lower lip, and she saw a young woman, young enough to be her daughter. 'Did your . . . umm . . . mother have any siblings or relatives?'

The girl looked up and said, 'No, she didn't. She had a brother, but he died many years ago when I was still in school. We were pretty alone, especially after dad . . . ' She trailed off and looked down, knowing that Rose knew what she was going to say. But she had spoken the truth. Peter was all they had had. Rose smiled kindly. She felt liberated. This whole meeting with the girl was like a test, and she had passed. Peter and his betrayal of her no longer affected her.

'What can I do for you now?' asked Rose gently. The girl met Rose's calm gaze and replied, 'I need a job somewhere. I came back with a degree in business a year ago, just about when my mother passed. I worked for a short while in Johore Bahru, but the company was small and folded up. I have been looking for more than six months now. And I thought a hundred times before approaching you, but Simon once said that should I be in need, I could turn to him for help. I just need a recommend . . . uh . . . referral . . . some information . . . I don't know.' Rose looked at her for a few seconds before responding.

'And you felt that I would help you?'

The girl glanced at her briefly before saying, 'I realize it's a bit forward on my part, especially given our history. But I felt that I was not responsible for my father's actions and that you are too successful in your own right to be tied down by baggage left behind by a man who is no more.'

For a brief second or so, Rose looked quizzically at the girl, and then smiled. *Bold.*

'I'm not looking for a job here in your organization if that's what you're wondering. Anywhere else is fine.' Rose nodded before standing up, indicating that the meeting had ended. The girl stood up as well and looked a little nervous.

'I will get back to you in a day or two,' said Rose. 'Do you need a ride to some place?'

The girl shook her head. 'No. I just need a job.' Rose responded with a smile as she walked towards the door.

The end of the meeting left the two women frowning for very different reasons. As Rose shut the door behind Evelyn, she was trying to understand the reason for the visit. If this had happened earlier, soon after Peter's death, her reaction would have been predictable. 'The nerve of that twit!' she would have exploded. But now, while she was perplexed by the boldness of the younger woman, she was also appreciative of Evelyn's courage and drive. 'It could not have been easy,' she said to herself with a quiet laugh. 'I might have done that, at her age,' she said, shaking her head.

And it hadn't been easy for Evelyn. Her heart was beating so fast when she was riding the elevator to the ground floor that she thought it was going to burst out of her chest. If her mother had been around, she wouldn't have let her contact Rose. 'We were in the wrong,' Mable would say. 'We were taking what didn't belong to us.' As a child, Evelyn had accepted her mother's inclination to merely accept what she got. 'We shouldn't ask for more when he already gives us so much,' Mable had repeatedly consoled her daughter whenever she had complained that Peter did not stay with them or at least never stayed longer than a weekend

But as she became a teenager, she had questioned Mable's docility. The glimpse of the gold-coloured Mercedes that would come whizzing down the street every two weeks was what she longed for as a young child of five or six. Peter would come on Friday afternoon bearing gifts, and the whole of Saturday would be spent shopping and eating in nice places. Evelyn always remembered waking up with a heavy heart on Sunday morning, because Peter would leave around eight-thirty or nine in the morning, after promising her that he would come again the following week.

Her mother, who was eternally smiling benignly, would hold her hand as they stood waving goodbye to the man who drove away to his other family. Their plush but quiet house seemed extra desolate and dull after his departure, and they, Mable especially, would then spend the whole of the next two weeks in anticipation of his return.

Evelyn had loved her father dearly, but in her teens, she realized that her life was different from that of her friends. She had a father who didn't live with them all the time. Her mother was quite frank with her and informed her that she was old enough to know that her father had another family in Singapore. 'So who are we, Ma? And who are you to him?' she had asked curiously. Her mother didn't answer her question, choosing instead to say, 'I got more than I ever imagined in life. I was just a worker in his factory, and he noticed me and gave me all of this,' she would say gesturing with her hand around the big house. 'I could not have asked for more.'

Evelyn was filled with shame. She now knew enough to know that her mother was no more than a mistress. 'How can you be so proud of being a mistress?' she hissed at her mother, who promptly responded, 'You're not so old that I can't slap you, and you know I will.' She didn't dare to say anything to Peter when he visited, because her mother had threatened that he would stop coming. 'Then we will be left with nothing. We now have something at least. Don't ruin that. Don't take away the little that I have.' So Evelyn merely sulked and showed her resentment with her silence. No longer did she run out to the gate when she heard the car park in front of the house, and neither did she hang on to Peter's every word, as she used to when she was younger. She didn't jump at his offer of shopping and meals in nice restaurants. In fact, she excused herself from the outings by claiming she had homework to complete and chose to ignore her mother's glares. If Peter noticed, he didn't say anything. He merely bought her gifts that she refused to look at or even acknowledge. Then he died suddenly, and she was filled with remorse.

She felt responsible. 'Maybe he was distracted because he was thinking about the way I acted when he was here,' she kept telling herself, especially when she saw her mother cry so uncontrollably. Their life did seem hopeless when he was gone and more so when they went to his funeral. Just going for it had been demeaning. They would have never known if not for the fact that the manager of the factory, who knew Mable personally, had informed her, more out of pity than anything else. He hadn't been able to give her any details about the accident or the funeral. Evelyn and Mable had taken the bus to Singapore from Kuantan, and they had just found their way using the information in the newspapers. Evelyn remembered her mother's humiliation and tears of desperation, the anger, the glares and stares, and the whispers that had been all around them at the funeral. Her mother had sat through it all, asking for little else, other than to be allowed to sit by the body. One of the twins had rudely told her mother to get out and had had to be restrained by Simon, while Rose had treated them like they were invisible. Evelyn remembered the details of that day like it was just yesterday. And no one had even looked at them when they had left, a forlorn mistress and her daughter, by a man who had kept their existence a secret.

Evelyn had good thoughts about Simon because he had been fair. But he had not been overly generous, and the money that he had given them was running out because of Mable's medical bills. 'I don't have to do this,' he had told her mother calmly as he had handed them the final cheque, just before he had left for his European trip, from which he never came back. 'We, my mother, brothers, and I, are the ones hurt by all of this—embarrassed. My mother, in particular, was hurt for no reason at all. But she has raised me to do the right thing. For that reason, I feel you need some support. She is aware of the support I'm giving you. But since you are unwell, and Evelyn is still in school, I have been a little bit more generous. But I believe you will be gracious enough to not take this any further and make more claims. I'm happy to help Evelyn if she needs help but only if she really needs it.'

Mable had nodded gratefully, while Evelyn had watched. This was also the time when Mable had handed Simon a letter for Rose, and Evelyn was aware of the contents of the letter. It stung her that Mable had died without ever receiving a response. But she had died repeatedly telling Evelyn that she needed to stay away from the Lee family. 'Simon has done enough for us. You shouldn't expect anything more,' she had said, urging Evelyn to get herself a good job. But that was Mable, who had been raised in a village and whose docility and subservience were dictated by the fact that she had seen Peter as a godsend, a release from a fate that might have been the same as that of her mother, who had worked in a factory by day and as a prostitute by night. She had shuddered every time she had thought of how she could have ended up like her mother if not for Peter. So she had been more than willing to gratefully accept Simon's offer and withdraw with her daughter into oblivion.

But Evelyn was not Mable. She had long since stopped thinking that her mother had been right and that her father was a deity that descended into their home every fortnight. She had not asked to be born to a mistress. And, so, she was not willing to give up on what she perceived as her right to Lee Constructions, as Peter's daughter. 'Why should I?' she asked herself. 'If they have a right, I do too.' And that thought had goaded her to call Rose. The Evelyn that stepped out of the elevator after her meeting with Rose was calmer, even confident that Rose had believed that she had no interest in being a part of Lee Constructions. She hoped that if she didn't appear too eager, Rose would consider giving her a job in her own organization. She didn't want to put the older woman on guard by exposing her real agenda.

'She must think that I'm an old fool who can't see what she wants. The girl appears to be more astute than her mother,' said Rose to her friends Nalini and Penny, during their weekly dinner that week. 'But you know, it's not such a bad idea,' she laughed as she buttered a piece of bread. 'There is a void. There is no one to run Lee Constructions after me. Simon could have run it, but he didn't want to, and in any case, he is gone now. Ean would have been the best pick but he's obviously ... well ...' she trailed off with a wry smile tugging the corners of her mouth. 'Then there's Ethan ...' she began but was immediately lost for words and sighed.

'Give him a chance, Rose. Surely he will step up to the plate when you hand him the responsibility,' said Penny. Rose smiled gently, shaking her head, and then responded with resignation, 'He is a good son, and after Simon, he stepped up without missing a beat. I'm blessed to have him by my side. He proved to be great in a crisis, like a rock. But he is just not a businessman. I knew that a long time ago, which is why I thought Ean was best at the helm while Ethan supported him. Who would have imagined that it would turn out this way?' She then laughed drily and said, 'I will work for as long as I can since I started this, and then I might just sell the whole damn thing, and divide the proceeds between the two of them. That way, they are taken care of.'

'But why don't you wait for Ean to come back and take over?' Nalini interjected.

'And who is going to trust him? Even I won't. The business will die anyway,' Rose half snapped with a dry laugh. She placed the uneaten piece of buttered bread back on her plate.

* * *

After Ean's incarceration, and when she was forced to work as she used to before the string of tragedies that had come crashing down on her, the realization that Ean would have been best for the business—if not for the fact that he was so untrustworthy—stabbed her every day, especially when she sat down for discussions with Ethan. 'It's my fault. I should have realized that Ethan was not cut out for business early enough,' she said to Scott. 'I don't think I ever stopped to even think that he wouldn't want what I wanted for him. And, unlike Simon, he was not bold enough to tell me and now, I . . . ' She threw up her hands in frustration. The slot that she had put him in had been all wrong. Scott looked at her with sympathy in his eyes. He put his arm around her and drew her close to him. 'It will work out, Rose. Something somewhere will just work out,' he said gently. This was just two days before Evelyn had turned up in her office. And it was Ming who helped her see this young woman as the one who would help her work it all out.

'Sometimes you just need to forgive to achieve something greater. Your mother did that,' said Ming, dishing out the rice into her daughter's bowl. She was referring to Sylvia. Although Rose had accepted her as her mother, Ming still didn't speak of herself as Rose's mother. She always referred to Sylvia as Rose's mother. 'You're a smart woman since you have already figured out what this young lady really wants. Manage it well. As your mother managed me. I wanted to be close to you after all those years. She let me, but held the leash very tight. It was good of her to forgive me. And that is what I will remember till the end. I would not have had this time with you if she hadn't. Ultimately, you counted, for both of us. Your mother is probably at peace now that you are not left alone, and you have me, even if it may be for only a few more years. Likewise, what counts for you is that your business, what you worked hard for, is not lost, and that someone capable runs it after you. Maybe if you forgive a little, you will find that person in this girl. In any case, you can't take the company with you when you die. It doesn't matter if you have to give some to this girl to save something for your sons.'

Ming imparted this wisdom in her characteristic low and raspy voice, a result of years of smoking. Her years of hardship coupled with her experiences had filtered the emotions out, leaving just the wisdom, which she never shared unless asked for. But she got the point across by the time her daughter had finished eating. When Rose stood up after her dinner, she had a call to make. The only person she cared to convince now was Ethan, without hurting him. While she was duty-bound to ensure that Ean was taken care of, she was more concerned about Ethan and his well-being. The last thing Rose wanted to do was to hurt him.

Chapter Sixteen

The calm that surrounded mother and son was beguiling because, just about a mile away, evening traffic filled the expressway behind them. Rose and Ethan sat facing the sea, watching the sun sink into the horizon. She had just spoken to Ethan about her vision for the company and her plans to bring in Evelyn, and a quiet hung between them as each one withdrew into their thoughts. Rose felt a combination of relief and guilt. The relief was because there was a possibility of a solution to the dilemma that she was in, and the guilt came out of the fact that that solution was taking away from Ethan what he probably assumed was only his. Her need to groom someone who could stand by Ethan and manage the business when she retired, or, as she cynically told herself, ' . . . when I'm gone', was entirely practical.

She had lain awake for hours last night after Ming had spoken to her. ' . . . you can't take the company with you when you go.' These words of Ming struck a chord with Rose and drove her to take a decision on the subject. *Yes, I can't take the company with me. But at least I can leave my sons, one son at least, with a good memory of me. I do want to ensure that the business thrives for him and make up for the fact that I forced him into it.* Rose thought as the night slowly dipped into the cool of dawn. *I'm not sure what else he can do.* Guilt engulfed her because she had dragged her sons along in her quest to make the business the biggest and the best in the construction industry. One had resisted firmly but died before he could make his freedom count; another one had come along with her willingly and so greedily that he had landed in jail, and who knows maybe she had fuelled that greed. The last one had simply allowed himself to be dragged along because he didn't know what else to do—and she, his mother, had never stopped to ask. The least she could do for this son was to ensure that he didn't lose everything after her because of mismanagement or, worse, because his twin got the better of him.

Ethan's feelings were mixed, even confused. On the one hand, he felt exhilarated, free and like he could breathe again. In the past year, the burden of holding the fort, the burden of stepping into his brothers' shoes—shoes that were never really a good fit—had been unbearably stifling. Growing up, Ethan had been quiet, reserved, and always in Ean's shadow—always following, never leading. He couldn't remember a time when he had a distinct path for himself. They had both gone to business school because it had been Ean's decision. And then they had both gone into the business because that was Rose's decision. Of course that suited Ean because he saw it as his right, but Ethan had neither really relished the idea nor hated it. It was simply a reality he had accepted.

Initially, he had found the job difficult and tedious and his responsibilities huge, but he had managed with Simon's help. But even Simon had never asked him if he liked what he was doing. Perhaps it hadn't occurred to him. The point was that Ethan himself was not sure what else he wanted to do or could do. He felt lucky that he had a family business to support him. But it didn't drive him. It was just a job, and he turned up for it every morning and did what he had to do without ever feeling any excitement. He could never feel the euphoria that his mother, Ean, or even Simon felt when they struck a deal. He would pretend when they celebrated, pretend that he was excited, but he was bored and waiting to get away to his painting or music or just a quiet dinner at the quay. He could never understand the point of the chase and the joy when there was a killing.

On the other hand, he also felt like he had failed the test and disappointed his mother. She had not seen him as capable, and he felt ashamed and a little slighted. And then there was his loyalty towards Ean. At the end of the day, he was Ean's brother, his twin. He needed to watch out for him. It was the right thing to do. 'How do you know that she will be right for the company, Ma?' Ethan asked calmly without looking at his mother. Mother and son sat on a bench close to an embankment by the sea, watching the sunset. The calm that surrounded them was faintly interrupted by the sound of the traffic, which wasn't too far away.

'I don't. It's just hope, a gut feeling. I'm hoping that she can be groomed,' said Rose.

'And what happens when Ean comes out?' asked Ethan, his eyes still fixed on the horizon.

'What happens? Ean does not have anything—'

'Ma, Ean is your son, my brother. Yes, he made a mistake. But that cannot take away from the fact that he is one of us, whatever he may be.'

Rose was silent. When she spoke again, she was matter of fact. 'Ethan, for your own good, you need to understand that Ean cannot be good for the company. Yes, he is one of us, and therefore he will be taken care of. But believe me, he is bad for business. And he will think nothing of dragging you down with him,' she said shaking her head in the dark. Her exasperation was palpable. 'Listen. I'm heartened by your loyalty to your brother. But as your mother, both yours and Ean's, I think I know enough of both of you to remind you that Ean loves Ean most. I won't be around forever. So you need to watch out for yourself when I'm not there to protect you. You need someone strong who can manage the business because that is where he can hurt you. I don't think I was much of a mother to you. The least I can do before my time ends is to ensure that you get what is yours.'

The gentle sound of water caressing the embankment of rocks was clear in the stillness. When Ethan spoke again, his questions stared her in the face, demanding closure. 'And, you don't think I can handle all of this, do you?' he asked without emotion.

After the briefest of pauses, Rose replied, 'Do you think you can handle it? That's really more important. It doesn't matter what I ...'

'Ma ... did you ever have faith in me? Have I always been the son who has not met your expectations?' interjected Ethan quietly, like he had not heard her question.

Again, there was silence from Rose, but when she replied, there was sadness and defeat in her voice. 'It isn't that I don't think you can handle the business. It is more that I feel I made a mistake in pushing you into something that does not bring out the best in you. I was so consumed by what I wanted to achieve that I did not imagine that you might have wanted something else for yourself. I think you know what I mean to say. You are—'

'I know Ma. I know what's on your mind. All my life, I have just done what other people wanted me to do. I honestly have never thought about what I could really do. The family business saved my life,' he laughed dryly. He paused before he finally said with resignation and acceptance, 'It's all right, Ma. I trust that you have my best interests at heart. If you think this Evelyn can be groomed, I will go along with it. I always do anyway,' he said cynically and laughing a little.

Rose turned to look at her son, reached out, and picked up his hand that lay by his side. 'You've been a good son, Ethan. I absolutely could not have managed these last two years without you. You have a good heart, and that's important above all. My decision now is only to protect you and your interests.'

Ethan looked at his mother and smiled. 'But how do you feel, Ma, about this girl? Can you look beyond the fact that she is Baba's daughter from his mistress? It doesn't bother you any more?' Rose smiled in the dark. She had not told him about who Ming was, and she wasn't going to tell him or anyone. It wasn't important. As far as her two sons, and the rest of the world, were concerned, Sylvia was

Rose Lee's mother. The thought of Sylvia filled her with a warm, pleasant feeling of compassion and peace. 'My mother would have wanted me to forgive for my own good. And she was always right, in her own crazy way,' Rose said with a laugh.

Ethan and Rose stood up to make their way to the car. An uneasiness had settled in Ethan's heart. He knew there was no point in trying to change Rose's mind. The decision was made. His mother only shared her thoughts when she had made up her mind. Although he knew that she was doing it for him, there was a gnawing feeling in a corner of his heart that he couldn't ignore. But when she asked, 'So, you're okay?' he lied. 'It's fine, Ma,' Ethan replied without hesitation. There was nothing else to be said. As they got into his car, Rose turned to look at him and asked, 'So, are Linda and you heading towards a future together?'

If Ethan was surprised that his mother knew, he didn't show it. He merely chuckled half-heartedly and said, shrugging, 'Well, after today, I'm not sure she will want me any more. I have a niggling feeling that she is very much in love with Lee Constructions and not as much with me.'

Rose shook her head and said, 'That was something else I was afraid of.'

And, as Ethan had feared, Linda was furious when she heard, especially when she heard that he had accepted Rose's decision. 'What kind of a man are you?' she exploded, throwing to the winds her artfully developed cover of her real desires. 'Your mother has just told you that you are not good enough to head Lee Constructions, and so she is bringing in your father's mistress's daughter to be groomed? And you meekly accepted?' she said in an almost strangled and suppressed shriek. 'Do you have any . . .' she stopped herself when Ethan glanced at her with his eyebrows raised. A strange smile played on his lips.

'Go on . . . ask me. Do I have any what? Balls? Is that what you were going to ask?' he scoffed. Then he said evenly, 'My mother made the decision because she owns this business. She has a right to, and she doesn't have to explain her decision to you, or even to me actually, because we're employees. As employees, you and I either accept that decision or leave. I have accepted it. You are free to do as you wish.'

Linda stared at him, her eyes barely concealing the mounting fury she felt. All her hopes were dissolving into nothingness. 'What was her rationale for this decision that she has made?' she said, almost spitting out the word 'decision'. Her mocking tone and barely concealed contempt made Ethan narrow his eyes. His patience was draining, and he sensed that Linda was going to deride his mother next.

'As I have already said, she does not owe us an explanation. She still owns the business. You take it, or leave it,' he said shrugging.

'And what about us?' Linda persisted.

Ethan frowned at this. 'How does our relationship have anything to do with this? Are you telling me plainly that you were going out with me because I'm Rose Lee's son? Were you hoping to be the wife of the CEO of Lee Constructions someday soon? Or, better still, were you hoping to be the CEO yourself someday sooner perhaps?' he scoffed.

Linda walked right into the trap. 'You're not in my league by yourself, Ethan Lee! It's your connection to Lee Constructions that made you attractive.' The words were said in fury, and perhaps in haste, but they tumbled out unrestrained. If she regretted it, nothing in her manner at that moment suggested it. She sat fuming and unapologetic, while Ethan idly moved his food around his plate with his fork. Stonily silent, Ethan sat staring at the morsel he was pushing around. For a fleeting and uncomfortable second, Linda was taken aback by the inscrutability on his face that reminded her so much of Rose. She couldn't tell if he was angry or upset. He just sat there, across the table from her, looking down at the morsel like it needed all his attention. She had said what she had in haste, but now she felt like it was a good idea, a good ploy, really. A growing feeling of triumph began to make her feel deliciously thrilled. She was convinced that his silence had to do with his sudden apprehension that he was in real danger of losing her. She gloated secretly about how she had finally shoved him to a point when he had to muster enough courage to speak up to his mother. The thought that he would accept her leaving him without a hint of a fight did not even occur to her.

This time would be no different from those other times when she had threatened to end their relationship, and he had later apologized and placated her. Of this she was so sure that she was completely unprepared for what came as a response from Ethan. When he spoke, he spoke unflinchingly and without a shred of uncertainty, looking directly at her. His voice was hard and completely devoid of emotion. 'I strongly recommend that you resign and leave. Otherwise, I'm sure there will be an occasion when you can be asked to leave.' Linda stared at him for a few minutes. She had never seen this side of Ethan. It both surprised her and dismayed her to a point where she stared at him wide-eyed, her mouth open like a fish gasping for air. She had expected him to plead with her and cajole her into going back to his apartment with him for the evening, where they would try and plan a line of action to convince his mother to change her mind. She would then grant him the opportunity to make love to her and allow him to feel secure about them again. It had happened so many times, and this time shouldn't have been any different from all those other times. But it was.

He sat there like a rock, and if the earth had opened beneath Linda and swallowed her, there was nothing in his demeanour to show that he would have moved an inch to reach out to save her. Linda sat for a few minutes—angry, confused, and uncertain about what she should do next while he merely stared at his plate. She finally flung her fork down on her untouched plate with a clatter. She then stood up with as much pride as she could muster, grabbed her purse from the table, rummaged through it, and came up with a handful of dollars that she flung on the table. She then turned around to leave without a word. As she turned, she thought she saw Ethan smirk at the dollars that lay on the table. She could barely see through the tears that pooled in her eyes as she walked through the evening crowd that thronged the walkways.

Ethan sat for a while longer, nursing his glass of wine with clammy hands that shook slightly. He had expected the outcome of this evening but he had not expected the rawness, the unsaid truth that she felt nothing for him. He had always guessed at it, but somewhere within him he had been hopeful that there would be some attachment. Now, she had laid it bare; there was none. The only thing that had been attractive about him was his connection to Lee Constructions. He knew that he hadn't been the only one who had guessed the truth. Everyone who had seen them together would have wondered at their mismatch. He suddenly felt the loss of Simon more acutely than ever before. Simon would have slapped him on his back and said, 'Cheer up! You knew that all along. You're better off now.' Ethan left his unfinished glass of wine and dinner on the table and took a slow walk back to his apartment about a block away—a tall, lone figure with his hands in his pocket, on an evening that otherwise bustled with the after-work revellers.

The Storm Rages On

Chapter Seventeen

Evelyn settled into her cubicle a tad timidly. She didn't feel as much in control as she thought she was. When Rose had called her a week ago and asked her to come into the office for a 'little chat', she had smiled to herself. *It's working. She's falling for it. Now all I have to do is to play the game and bide my time.* In truth, she had no real plan. All she knew was that she felt entitled to work in and eventually have a stake in Lee Constructions, which had also belonged to her father. Part of this feeling of entitlement was also driven by her need to find a job quickly and the realization that much of the money that Simon had given her and her mother had gone for her mother's treatment and her own education. Now, the house that her father had bought her mother was all that she had as inheritance. It was her best friend, with whom she was staying in Singapore, who had mooted the whole idea of approaching Rose. 'You should take what's yours by right. He was your father too, and he would have helped build that business too,' Adele had said. And, soon, the germ of an idea that had been planted in Evelyn's mind had taken a life of its own, and she had sat down to plan her entry in a manner that she thought was extremely discreet. But Rose had read her like a book from the start, much to her embarrassment.

'I know you probably feel that you should have a stake in this business,' Rose had said with her gaze fixed on the young woman. 'You don't, by law. Everything about the business has always been in my name, and then my sons'. It was your father's idea when we first started. He felt I was his lucky charm. I thank God for that.' Rose chuckled when she said this. 'I think I was just plain lucky, given everything,' she said emphasizing the 'I' in a manner that made Evelyn flinch. 'I know that you have come here in the hope of somehow staking your claim. I could see that right from the beginning.' Evelyn felt a rush of colour and heat on the back of her neck. She opened her mouth to speak or protest, but before she could, Rose continued, 'I knew what your visit was about from the first time we met. It took a great deal of gumption on your part to do it though, and that's what I liked—the gumption. So, do you have a claim? No. But am I willing to give you a share? Yes, but you need to earn it fair and square. I would like you to work with my son and support him in the business. Of course, that will only be after you have worked here for at least a year, and you meet our expectations. Until that time, you will be an employee who can be asked to leave if you don't deliver.'

Evelyn was overwhelmed by differing emotions all at once, and so all she could do was move her mouth in an attempt to speak but fail miserably. The awkwardness was excruciating, especially since she was also overawed by this perfectly put-together woman in her off-white skirt suit, with diamonds sparkling in her ears speaking to her in such a measured manner that there was nothing Evelyn could say in her defence. Evelyn felt once again like the schoolgirl in the principal's room for forging her mother's signature on her report card. Those were the days when she had tried to distance herself from both her parents because they were the reason she was known as the child of a 'mistress'. But she felt pride in the fact that she had matured since then and was now a sophisticated young lady who had succeeded in getting a degree from the US. And now, this woman had, with a single stroke, stripped that pride away and laid bare the vulnerable girl that she really was.

'Are you listening to me, Evelyn?' said a voice that seemed to be coming from a distance. Evelyn snapped back into the present.

'Uh . . . yes . . . I mean no . . . I don't . . .' Evelyn stammered.

'Look, as I said, you seem like a driven young person and bold as well. And I admire that. The past does not bother me much now. So, I'm offering you a position in this company as my assistant. You will work with me, with my son Ethan, and with other senior staff. It will be stressful, but if you're a fast learner, you will do well for yourself. Who knows? You may be able to work your way to a share, although you don't have a birthright.'

Speechless and discomfited, Evelyn simply stared back at Rose for a few moments.

'I . . . uh . . . didn't expect this, but . . . yes . . . I'm grateful for the opportunity . . . I don't know what else to say.'

'Good, then we can think of when you can join us,' Rose said with a smile.

That was two weeks ago. Evelyn now sat in a cubicle next to Ethan, who for the most part did not speak to her directly, at least not yet. When Evelyn had come to the office for the first time for her little chat with Rose, he had deliberately kept Rose and Evelyn waiting before he joined them. And when he had finally joined his mother and Evelyn twenty minutes late, Rose had frowned but said nothing. He did not look directly at Evelyn and barely said anything. He merely nodded slightly when Rose directed a statement she was making at him. His indifference towards Evelyn was palpable.

Ethan had spent a sleepless night just before his meeting with Evelyn in the morning, tossing and turning, angry and bitter. For one, he had just been dumped by Linda. The knowledge that he meant nothing to her was deeply hurtful. That wound was raw. And then, on the morning after that, he had to meet the girl who was going to help him run a business that seemed to be consuming everything and everyone. Simon had run away from it and had died; Ean had lusted after it and had gone to jail; and now he, Ethan, was having to face all his shortcomings and flaws. He woke up with a headache. All the resignation that he had felt on the night

Rose had revealed her plans for Evelyn had now abandoned him. What he felt now was irrepressible resentment for everything and everyone that reminded him of his inadequacies, and his mother seemed to loom large at this point. For the first time, he dawdled about getting to work. What he lacked in aptitude, he had tried to make up for with diligence. But that was clearly not good enough. He felt that there was no reason for him to meet Evelyn. Everything was happening anyway, despite him and his contributions. 'Ma ensures that . . .' he said to himself bitterly as he dressed. 'Moving us all around the way she sees fits.'

The girl reminded him of his father, especially in the way she smiled. And that grated on his nerves. 'But she sits straight-backed and alert, just like Ma. Maybe it is something about the way you sit that determines whether or not you have the potential to manage a large business,' Ethan thought to himself as he sat silently, listening to his mother speak to Evelyn. His face was blank, and even though Rose kept glancing at him as if to get his approval or support, she didn't get any response. He didn't even look in her direction. He just sat there looking on as if the discussion had nothing to do with him. It annoyed her and gave her a little niggling feeling that disturbed her as she spoke with Evelyn. 'We talked about this, and he agreed. Why is he acting this way now?' she asked herself. He didn't know why it bothered him. The fact that she was his father's mistress's daughter? Perhaps. Or, that his mother saw more potential in this girl than she did in him. Or, was it merely that she looked like his father, and that reminded him of the embarrassment his family had felt during the funeral? He just didn't know, but he knew that her being in the office and being a part of the business was a reality that he had to come to terms with.

Evelyn had glanced at Ethan furtively a few times during the meeting. She remembered him from the funeral of her father. He had looked sullen then, but now, she could feel the frosty indifference and antipathy. Just as she decided that she wasn't sure if she liked him, she heard Rose declare, 'You will work closely with Ethan,' and her heart sank abruptly. Rose glanced at Ethan and said, 'Please involve her in all your work so that she learns everything about the office and the staff as quickly as possible.' Ethan merely returned his mother's glance without saying a word. At the end of the meeting, it was decided, or rather Rose decided, that Evelyn would sit in a cubicle next to Ethan's room for ease of interaction. But, at first, they would only communicate through Ethan's assistant, Irene.

Irene handed Evelyn a long list, about five pages long, of names and numbers of vendors for different types of building materials. Evelyn had to call every one of them and introduce herself as the new point of contact for all future business with Lee Constructions. Some of the names had asterisks against them. These were the ones that were suppliers for current projects. She had to check to ensure that they had delivered or were delivering on time. It was a long and tedious task but it had to be done, and, 'Mr Ethan felt that it was a good way for you to make a connection with our vendors,' smiled Irene, a kindly, cherubic middle-aged woman. It took Evelyn all day to complete the task. There were several similar long and tedious tasks that kept her busy for the rest of the week, during which time Ethan did not once speak with her or work directly with her.

When he finally chose to speak with her, it was at the end of the week, on Friday, around six in the evening. Irene called her and said, 'Mr Ethan would like to meet with you in his office.' When Evelyn entered his room, he barely looked up at her, preferring to keep his eyes fixed on whatever he was doing.

'So how's everything going?' he asked, while continuing to work on the papers in front of him.

'Hmm ... I'm getting used to the work ...'

'Getting used to the work? After one week? Just getting used to the work after one week?'

'Uh, no, what I meant was that I'm getting used to things. It'll take me a little bit of time . . .'

'Well, we hired you to start showing results quickly. This is not the place to take your time to learn the ropes,' he interjected with a laugh that sounded a little nervous to her. Evelyn's heart sank. Belligerence seemed to be in the air, and as the new member of staff, she could only listen and withdraw.

'I'll do my best,' she responded in a small voice.

'Don't disappoint my mother. She thinks very highly of you,' he replied, still focused on his papers.

'Uh . . . Ethan,' began Evelyn, and he looked up at her, his eyes narrowing. 'I mean, Mr Lee . . .'

'You can call me Ethan. Everyone does.'

'Ethan, I'm not sure we're starting off on the right footing here. I feel like you don't quite approve of my working here. I meant to say—'

'Is this the way you would speak with your employer?' he asked, and her heart sank even further. 'Do I approve of your hire? Well, my mother, whose company this is, chose to hire you, and she decides. There is nothing more to this. Are you wondering if I feel awkward about working with the daughter of my father's mistress?' Evelyn winced when he said this. He had pried the old wound open.

She stepped back from his desk, frowning, and making ready to leave. Ethan felt a sudden wave of shame at what had just tumbled out of his mouth. Meanness was not him, but defensiveness born out of a lack of confidence and self-worth certainly was.

'I'm sorry, I didn't mean to . . .' he began. Evelyn half smiled, and this time it was her turn to interject.

'There's no need to apologize. I'm the daughter of the mistress. But the mistress was a good woman who had a great deal of respect for your mother and admiration for Simon, your brother. She would always say that he was a model son and a blessing for any parent. She never desired what is yours. She was just thankful for what she got. She insisted that I never approach you for anything ever again, and had she been alive she would have been very disappointed in me. Yes, when I first met your mother, I felt entitled. But when I realized that she had read me like a book, I was overawed by her willingness to take a risk with me. I still cannot honestly say that I'm completely devoid of those feelings of entitlement, but here I'm telling you exactly what's on my mind, so that you can watch me and make sure that I don't take off with this entire business,' she said, with a slight toss of her head but a nervous chuckle. As she left the room, Evelyn was thankful that she had her back turned to Ethan and that there was no one in the office to notice her flushed face and quivering lips.

Evelyn avoided Ethan after that evening. She responded to his emails and answered his questions about work in an almost affected professional manner but was careful to avoid any other conversation with him. But Ethan's careless remark had inadvertently served a purpose. Later that evening, she would receive a call from Rose that would set the foundation of the pedestal on which the girl would place the woman in the years to come.

After his meeting with Evelyn, fatigue and mortification welled up in Ethan as he sat with his face buried in his hands. The one thing that irked him most about Ean was the carelessness with which he spoke with people, his arrogance. And now he had displayed those very traits. It had been a long day and the culmination of a long week. He opened a drawer to get his keys and wallet, and saw Linda's resignation letter lying in it. Her last day in the office was a week away. He had read and reread the letter. He had debated calling her all week. He considered it again, almost feeling like he owed her an apology for something. He just wasn't sure what it was. It took all his shredded pride and self-worth to stop himself from making that call.

After that evening, neither he nor Linda had made any attempt to connect. She was away quite a bit, clearing a backlog of vacation time. He felt a mixture of anger and embarrassment because she had been so clear about her reason for their relationship, and he felt like everyone in the office knew. But looking at her letter today,

Ethan felt the remnants of the fond feelings he had nurtured for her and toyed with the idea of calling her in the hope of salvaging something. But he didn't. He studied the letter for a while longer, before resolutely closing the drawer again, his keys and wallet in his hands. As he switched off the lights in his room, he called his mother. 'Ma, can I come over this evening? I need to speak with you,' he said. 'I will be there for dinner.'

Rose was always happy to see her sons in her apartment. They rarely visited 'because they get fed up with you in the office', Sylvia used to laugh. It was probably true Rose thought, but it didn't take away the hollowness that she felt from being so distant from her sons. The fact that Ethan, at least, was now close to her and understood her helped her feel a little less wistful. She hurried Ming and Lisa to include some of Ethan's favourites in the meal. It was just an evening meal at home, but it felt like a treat to her. The fact that he was silent throughout dinner didn't dampen her excitement at having him in her home. It felt like those times when the family lived together, somewhat at least. Most of the members from the dinner table then were now missing, but the presence of at least one person was something to be happy about.

'Have some of the fish. You like that,' she smiled, pushing the dish closer to his plate.

Ethan remained silent.

'Evelyn's hire still bothering you?' she finally asked, sighing, irritation creeping into her.

He glanced at her but, again, said nothing.

'Look. We talked about this, and you accepted it. I didn't hire her to take away from you. I hired her to protect your interests. I don't want to keep repeating or defending myself. And yes, I'm not going to mince my words. I don't think you can run this business by yourself while ensuring that you don't get the carpet pulled from under your feet. I felt it was best to get someone who was family—' Rose stopped when he flicked a glance at her but continued undaunted. 'Yes, she is family whether you like it or not. She's your father's daughter; accept it. It is better for you and me in the long run. Am I using her? Probably, but she's getting something out of this arrangement. I train her to support you, I gain her confidence, and I'll eventually give her a part of the business, and the whole thing is protected. She's a smart girl. She'll take care of it and, in that process, ensure that you're protected. Will she take it away from you? I don't think so, but that's my reading of her. I think she's a girl who has grown up with a chip on her shoulder about being the mistress's daughter, and so she is a little vulnerable, sensitive, maybe even feels that she was short-changed in some sense. But I think, given time and trust, she can be brought around. Just a gut feel.'

'How do you do it? How do you move people around to do exactly what you expect?' Ethan burst out, dropping his chopsticks with a clatter. 'How do you place them neatly in these slots that you create for them?'

Ming, who was clearing away some of the dishes, hesitated for a few minutes before continuing with what she was doing. Rose studied her son coolly before responding.

'Look, I'm not sure what it is you're unhappy about. The fact that I hired this girl or the fact that I hired your father's mistress's daughter. The reality is that I did what I thought was best for you. If you don't like it, change it. I'm waiting to step away from the business. If you can take charge, do it. But bear in mind, you're on your own. It would make me very happy to just hand over everything to you and walk away. Scott and I would like to live in the US for half the year, now that he, too, is thinking of retiring.'

Ethan didn't respond immediately, preferring instead to study his plate. He knew she had him there. As he pushed the plate away and stood up, his phone rang, startling both of them a little. He contemplated the unfamiliar number for a minute before answering it. The voice at the other end was a familiar one. It was Ean's. He was being released after two years for good behaviour and was arriving in the evening the next day. When he told this to Rose, she smiled wanly and said, 'Who knows if it really was good behaviour? Well, I'm happy to have my son back, but I guess now is when our troubles will begin.' Ethan merely looked at his mother and then looked at the message with the flight details that had been texted to him. He felt her disquiet.

Later that night, despite the apprehension that she felt about Ean's return, Rose called Evelyn. 'I didn't get a chance to ask you how things were going for you. How are you doing in the office and are you settling in?' she asked. The truth was that she had sensed tension between her son and the girl. She needed Evelyn to work out, and she wasn't going to let Ethan frighten her away. Evelyn maintained a pleasantness in her tone and didn't mention the conversation she had had with Ethan, but she avoided speaking about him, and Rose noticed it.

'I saw potential in you, and I hired you. I think you will be an excellent right hand for Ethan. I see you as someone who will support him and protect the business. Of course, there will be hiccups along the way, but I think you are smart enough to manage those. I knew that when you turned up in my office the first time. You came because you wanted to claim what you thought was also yours. As I said, you have no claim. But I'm offering you a generous slice of the business *if* you measure up, and by that I mean if you are a support to me and then to Ethan. Am I using you? Perhaps I am, but not for free. You get not just something out of this, you get quite a bit you are not entitled to. Now, you decide whether I should trust you.'

As she hung up, a faint and cynical smile played on Rose's lips. As ironic as it was, even if she had lost on many counts with her sons, something told her that she was right about this girl, the daughter of her husband's mistress. And perhaps she was right, because when Evelyn lay in bed that night, she thought of her mother. 'I think I will be okay, Mama,' she said in the darkness. 'I think I will have an ally in Ms Rose.' She lay awake thinking about her mother and Rose, and somewhere the two women blended into each other. And when she finally fell asleep, it was with a sigh of contentment.

Chapter Eighteen

Ethan nodded at his brother who waved from a distance. The broad smile of a thinner Ean quickly disappeared when he noticed reporters waiting for him. They seemed to have somehow got wind of his return. He shook his head determinedly when they threw him questions and started walking quickly towards his brother. The two ignored the reporters, whose presence had now begun attracting the attention of others at the airport. The brothers quickly walked past curious stares. It was when they were both safely inside Ethan's car that Ean sighed loudly with relief. 'Finally! I'm back!' he said, leaning back against the plush leather seat. He closed his eyes and said nothing for a few minutes, then opened them again and slapped his brother's arm, saying, 'So, how're you?'

He sounds like he's just returned from a vacation—this cynical thought crossed Ethan's mind. He threw his brother a sideways glance and, with a hint of a smile, said, 'More importantly, how're *you*? I'm sorry I couldn't come for two months. The workload has grown. I'm happy to see you back, although I'm surprised that—'

'I was released so soon?' interjected Ean laughing. 'Tell me the truth. Are you really happy that I was released so soon? Aren't you afraid that I will cause more trouble?' Ean laughed, nudging his brother in jest.

Ethan glanced at his brother again and shook his head. 'You sound like you're in good spirits. I'm glad the bad experience has not affected you. You look thinner though.'

'Oh! I'm okay. I was okay throughout the whole time. But I'm glad it's all over. Where are you taking me? I'm starving. I need to eat before we go back to the apartment.'

'Mother—'

'I'm not seeing the old dragon now. I'm not even sure that I want to see her,' retorted Ean.

'She is our mother. Give her some respect and don't call her names. And she's expecting you,' snapped Ethan.

'Are you going to start lecturing me now about what I should do? She is the mother who never came to see me these two years. She is the mother who threw me out of the business . . . the family business!'

'This is also the same mother who hired the best legal help you could have possibly gotten at that time. And this is the mother who has ensured that you don't want for anything even though you won't be working for the family business. Given what you did, I think she is a pretty good mother,' said Ethan without emotion. 'Given the fact that you damaged the reputation that took her years to build, and given the fact that you did everything that was anathema to her, I really think she is pretty kind.'

Ean chuckled cynically and looked at his twin, who had his eyes fixed on the road. 'Looks like you have become her favourite boy now that the other one is dead. Be careful! I'm not sure she is very lucky for her favourites,' he said harshly.

Ethan's eyes hardened. He turned to quickly glance at Ean and turned back to focus on the road. 'I will drop you back at the apartment,' he said. 'It's your apartment now, by the way. Mother wanted it that way. It's in your name.'

'So where are you living now?' asked Ean, unimpressed.

'Well, as of today, I'm moving into mother's apartment, and then I will figure it out. I just decided, right now. I think it will be good for us all, too, to give you some space.'

'Can we at least stop off at a restaurant? I need to eat,' said Ean sullenly.

'It's Aunty's day to come in to cook. I'm sure there will be something for you to eat at home. It's best for you to lie low for a couple of weeks if you don't wish to run into reporters.' He swung into Kreta Ayer Road and drove towards the apartment that he shared with Ean. As he drove back to Rose's apartment after dropping his brother off, he pondered about what he would give as an excuse for Ean.

* * *

'Where is he?' Rose said, looking past Ethan as soon as the elevator doors opened and he stepped into her living room. Ethan glanced at his mother and shook his head.

'He chose to go back to the apartment. It's better too. I think he needs a little time,' he said, settling on the couch slowly. Rose didn't respond for a few minutes.

'Are you hungry? Ming has prepared quite an elaborate dinner.'

Both ate in silence while lost in thoughts that neither felt inclined to share.

Ethan thought about what the days to come would be like. How were they as a family ever going to even be in the same room? Rose, on the other hand, thought about her son who had returned. Her sadness was profound, but she could not bring herself to speak about it to Ethan. She had an idea of what would have transpired between the brothers. She just couldn't believe that Ean's hatred was so deep. What had she done or not done that had nurtured it? It would have been extremely detrimental for her to have visited him in prison. They would have quarrelled each time, and, besides, she had to think of the business and the negative publicity it would have brought each time she visited. She was convinced that her reasons were sound. If she had sensed a change of heart in him, a less arrogant, a less entitled person, she would perhaps have visited as many times as it would have taken to make him happy. But she had seen none of that, and now she was afraid the imprisonment had rooted his distrust of her and Ethan. She worried afresh.

'Give it time,' said Scott when she spoke to him that night. 'I'm not sure it was right of you to not visit him in prison, but you did what you thought was best. He is angry because of it.'

'But what do you think would have been the outcome out of my seeing him?' she retorted, throwing up her hands in exasperation. 'Would he have changed? Would he have suddenly become an honest, less avaricious man? No! We would have fought every inch of the way. He would have been concerned about his inheritance, about his share of the business; he would have tried to get me to bend the rules to get him out quicker, and we would have got into a deeper mess. I know my son.'

Scott looked at her without responding but with compassion in his eyes. There was nothing he could say to make her feel better because he knew that Ean was going to hold his grudge against Rose—even if not forever, at least for a very long time. He was also very aware that the Rose that he now loved was a woman who distrusted more than she trusted, and who set up her defences expecting to be hurt.

'Should I try to call him?' she asked.

'No harm done,' he finally said. 'He's your son. He may forgive you. Just like you have. But be prepared to answer him if he asks to come back to the office and work for the business again.'

'I'll call him in the morning. I might even visit him. He can't ignore me if I visit him,' she said with resolve.

'Whatever you do, reach out to him as his mother and not as the head of Lee Constructions.'

Rose flicked a glance at him with a wry smile.

* * *

Rose arrived in the office earlier than usual. She had lain awake well into the wee hours of the morning thinking about what she

was going to say to Ean. Part of her wondered if she had acted in
the right way, and part of her was remorseful. 'Was I too harsh?'
she kept asking herself. But ultimately, she convinced herself
that that was the only way she could have communicated her
unhappiness to someone who did not think he had done anything
wrong, to someone who still felt entitled to his share. *His share!*
Rose scoffed. *Every bloody damn thing is about that! So I'll just give
him all the papers that clearly state his inheritance. Hopefully, that will
give him peace.* She picked up the phone and called him, and just
then, there was a soft knock on the door before it opened. She
knew who it was and so continued with her call. Aunty walked
in slowly, wheeling her little trolley with a lone cup of steaming
Teh-C in the middle. As she walked in, Rose noticed how much
more bent she had become. It was obvious that her arthritis was
worsening. Rose waited for Ean to respond, but the phone rang
for a while and then went dead like he had rejected her call. She
breathed a sigh, and then dialled again, frowning. Aunty gently
dusted the table and removed a cup that had been left there from
the evening before. Rose was about to speak with her when Ean
came on the line.

'Hello Ean, it's Ma—'

'I rejected your call when you called the first time. That should
have told you something. I prefer that you don't call.'

'Listen, Ean, son—'

A click sounded. Rose stared at the receiver in her hand before
she slowly replaced it, her heart sinking.

'Drink your tea before it gets cold,' said Aunty softly. 'You will
feel better.'

She began to slowly push her cart towards the door without
waiting for a response. Rose didn't say anything. She merely sat
back in her chair, embarrassed that Aunty might have guessed
what the response on the other side had been. The tea sat cooling
on the desk in front of her.

Chapter Nineteen

Rivulets of perspiration ran down Linda's back as she walked to the MRT station. She could have taken a cab home, and she typically would have, since it was a blazing afternoon, but she chose to take her time going home. She needed the time for some of the anger that burnt inside to be quelled. She hadn't bothered to see either Rose or Ethan before her departure. The week had been awkward, to say the least. She had avoided Ethan, preferring to communicate with his personal assistant, and Evelyn, whom she privately referred to as the 'new idiot'. While she wasn't overtly rude or unpleasant, it was obvious to Evelyn that Linda intensely disliked her. She was cold and matter-of-fact, sometimes even short when she handed her the work that needed to be completed. In the first week, she simply took a whole bunch of folders and files and dumped them on Evelyn's desk without a word, and when Evelyn had asked her about them, she merely smirked and said, 'Your boss should help you. I no longer work here,' ignoring Evelyn's wide-eyed perplexity.

Today was her last day. She had handed her keys and other office-related material to Maryanne, who had glanced at them and then looked at her with a mixture of compassion and curiosity. Although she disliked Linda, Maryanne's innate kindness always dominated. She looked like she wanted to say something, but instead, she merely nodded.

'Thank you, but are you sure you don't want to see Ms Rose?'

'No,' Linda had said emphatically, her tone bordering on tartness.

'And, what about Mr Ethan? Have you seen him? Shall I tell him?' persisted Maryanne, forgiving the attitude. Linda chuckled and shook her head obdurately. As she turned to walk back to her cubicle, she could feel Maryanne's eyes on her back and the pity that she knew was in them.

She had timed her exit from the office at lunchtime so that few people or, if she was lucky, no one would be around. She was not going to let anyone see her. She didn't want their concern or pity. As far as the rest of the office was concerned, she had chosen to resign. But, of course, those who had never warmed to her knew and tittered among themselves about the reasons, and those whose loyalty she had won because they were like-minded empathized with her. 'Not fair that this new girl is now working with Mr Ethan. But who knows how long that will last? Happy for you that you're leaving. With everything that is happening here, who knows how long this place will last.' Some suspected that her relationship with Ethan was deeper than what was obvious, while others speculated. All in all, she felt like she had been defeated. The tears came streaming down her face when the elevator doors closed, but they were tears of fury rather than sadness. Had she been a sorceress, Rose's head would have flown off her shoulders that afternoon, and Ethan would have spat blood. But she was just an angry and, in some sense, a scorned woman who was bent on somehow getting her own back on mother and son, and the resoluteness with which she trudged on her four-inch heels to the station seemed to state that with every step that she took.

In her race for a suitable plan to avenge her bruised ego, her mind was a jumble of thoughts about starting her own business, joining the competition, or just doing something to get back at Ethan. The virulence of her thoughts, goaded by her helplessness and combined with the heat of the afternoon, made her perspire even more, and so the cool of the air-conditioning inside the station was more than welcome. She hadn't realized that she was breathing quickly until she felt a tap on her shoulder, and a familiar voice behind her said, 'Hey! What's the hurry?' Frowning, she turned to face a smiling Ean. He had learnt to smile in jail, and it actually became him. In fact, it became him so much that he took her breath away and made her stare.

It was about a week after Ean had returned from Jakarta. Her eyes narrowed just a little when Linda realized that she was looking at Ean, and an eyebrow rose questioningly. She gave him a hesitant smile. 'Hello! I never—'

'—expected to see me again. Don't worry, it's really me, and I didn't escape from jail,' Ean said, with an affability that was new to Linda. She winced at the mention of jail. She couldn't imagine anyone laughing about an experience like that. Ean laughed.

'It's not such a bad word. I made a mistake, and so . . .' he shrugged.

Linda retained the hesitant smile.

'Are you all right? You look a little stressed. And are you going home now?' he asked with a smile.

The inconsequential questions and conversation were beginning to fray her nerves a little, and so she nodded slightly. 'Yes, I'm going home. I just resigned from Lee Constructions. I'm going home,' she said, with barely suppressed bitterness.

It was now Ean's turn to frown. He looked at her with a glint of something unfathomable in his eyes, and said, 'Why? Did the Dragon Lady get to you?'

Linda refrained from saying anything. Rose was his mother at the end of the day, and she wasn't sure that she could trust him. She smiled and nodded a goodbye before turning to leave.

'Hey, wait. If you don't have to go back to work, why don't you have coffee with me? Looks like you could do with some company.'

Frowning again, she surveyed his face. 'Don't worry. I was booted out, remember? I have nothing to do with Lee Constructions now. I'm quite safe,' he laughed.

After a brief pause for thought, Linda smiled and shrugged. 'I guess, I could do with some coffee now. Why not?'

And thus began a partnership that sat firmly on a foundation of hatred for Rose Lee.

Initially, Ean merely provided a shoulder for Linda to lean on, but as the days went by and they began to see more and more of each other, their relationship grew. To be fair, jail had softened Ean in some ways, specifically in his manner and attitude towards his love interests. He no longer saw himself as irresistible, and the main reason for that was that he was no longer a part of Lee Constructions. He was acutely aware of this. The other reason was that Singapore, being a small place, everyone who was anyone was well aware of his run-in with the law and his stay in jail. Many of his friends avoided him, fearful of the stigma, and those who still entertained him did so with a pinch of salt. Ean Lee quickly found out that his one-time popularity with women had evaporated. Therefore, Linda was a boon. She was beautiful, smart, ambitious, and shared his dislike for his mother. He knew that.

Another thing that gave him secret satisfaction was that Linda had thrown his twin's inadequacies in his face. He knew because she had told him while vowing revenge between tears of hurt and bursts of anger. He had listened expressionless, but inside, he had felt a slow spread of triumph. He had liked Ethan well enough while growing up and even in the recent past before his imprisonment, but it was more an affection born out of habit and because his twin had never posed any kind of threat. Ean had to be better, even if the competition was his twin. And if there was a chance that his competitor could be better in some way, Ean disliked him, even if it was his brother.

When Linda had chosen Ethan instead of him, he had felt a little slighted and surprised for a brief period but the feeling had passed as quickly as it had surfaced because he had a string of girlfriends anyway. But, now that Ethan irritated him because of his loyalty towards their mother and because he had replaced Simon in his mother's books, it gave Ean some satisfaction to know that Linda had dumped him. 'You'll always be just that, Mama's boy,' he said to himself with a smirk. Coffee that afternoon soon blossomed into dinner on other nights, followed by nightcaps ending with breakfast. But they were careful about being discovered, especially by mutual friends and ex-colleagues who had known about Linda and Ethan.

'It does sound a little odd that I'm sleeping with my brother's ex-girlfriend, but I'm the odd one in the Lee family anyway,' said Ean, wrapping his arms around Linda. For Linda, Ean was her second chance. At the end of the day, he was still a Lee. Family feuds could be forgotten given time, and besides, 'the old bitch', as she secretly called Rose, won't live forever, and Ethan was always easy to convince or to shove aside. So this new arrangement with Ean was beginning to look very rosy. The two of them were even talking about starting a little business together, with her name and his money. 'Who knows? We might grow as big!'

Signs of Abatement

Chapter Twenty

Too proud to accept charity, Aunty had requested Rose for more work because she was finding it difficult to make ends meet. This was a few years ago. It was then that the arrangement to work, on some afternoons, at the twins' and Simon's apartments was made. Rose had asked her if she would like to do some light housekeeping and cooking for her sons a few times a week. 'This will give you an additional salary,' Rose had said, and Aunty had readily agreed. The light housekeeping had dwindled because of Aunty's arthritis, but the cooking continued, although the men didn't always eat at home. Rose and her sons knew that the arrangement was only a means to help the old woman, while Aunty did the job diligently and happily because it gave her a little extra without a dent in her dignity.

After all, she had seen better days before her son and his wife had died in an accident. Aunty had been the daughter of a *sinseh* who had had a respectable business in the heart of Chinatown before she had married a bus driver with whom she had a son. Life had been reasonably generous, and she had no major cause for sadness. She had worked for the Singapore General Hospital for many years as a nursing assistant, before retiring to stay home to babysit her newborn granddaughter. Her son and daughter-in-law, who had worked as teachers and had lived a block away from her, would leave the baby with her every morning. Life meandered along idyllically for a few years in this blessed manner. And then the troubles that she had missed seeing for most of her life began, and the blessings gradually vanished.

Her husband of about forty years suddenly died of a heart attack at work. After the mourning period, her son invited her to stay with him and his family. He told her that she would be happier. What he did not tell her was that they needed someone in the house to watch over a growing child, and well . . . do some light cleaning and maybe even some cooking, if she could, while they were at work. They had all felt, including Aunty, that the rent from her apartment would be the income that she had lost after her husband's death. It all seemed like a happy arrangement, for a few months.

But her daughter-in-law, who had been attentive and respectful when there had been a distance, was now not quite the same. She resented the intrusion and showed it in subtle ways. Her son, who loved his mother, loved his wife more. So the happy arrangement slowly morphed into an uncomfortable one that continued for a year or two, and then, just when Aunty was seriously considering moving back to her own apartment, her son and his family met with an accident on a rainy night while they were returning from a day of shopping. The taxi they were in collided with a truck. The driver of the taxi, her son, and her daughter-in-law were killed, but her grandchild miraculously survived, though with serious injuries. All in one night, Aunty found herself to be the sole caregiver to a child who would need a great deal of care, which required money that she didn't have, for several years.

It would have been a lifetime of misery for the young girl if not for Auntie's fortuitous meeting with Rose Lee, who graciously and generously paid not only for physical therapy and surgeries but also for her education. The girl had a college degree and could now work in a deskbound job, and she was financially very independent— something Aunty was convinced she could not have achieved if not for Rose. So for Aunty, Rose was a beneficent goddess for whom she would do anything. She did not really need to work any more because her granddaughter could take care of both of them. But Aunty continued to work for Ms Rose, both at the office and in her sons' apartment, because it was now her way of giving back.

And so it was Aunty who first discovered Linda in Ean's apartment. She hadn't liked the young woman when she had worked in the office, and she didn't like her now. 'A rude and disrespectful young lady who hasn't been taught any manners,' was what she had felt then and what she felt now. She had discovered Linda in the apartment by accident. Since she had been given her own set of keys, Linda and Ean found themselves in a little bit of an awkward situation but only momentarily, because Ean quickly dismissed her as, '. . . just a cleaner. We don't need to be afraid of her. I'll pay her a little extra. Besides, she won't understand if we stick to English.' He laughed.

He was wrong. Aunty never spoke about the fact that she had had her elementary, and part of her secondary, schooling in a convent where she had learnt to communicate in English. Ean or Linda could not have known this because Aunty hardly spoke to anyone other than Rose in the office. Little did they know that she would have even continued with her high school education had her father had not died so soon. Aunty gathered from snippets of their conversation that Ean and Linda badmouthed Rose and that they were planning to start their own construction business. She could also see that their relationship was more than just a business partnership. *Shameless! Was with the brother and now with him. Only for the money. No shame!* But Aunty did not let her thoughts be known and went about her tasks with a quiet energy that could barely conceal the broiling fury that she felt, mainly because they were disrespectful to Rose. 'This son is not a good son. A son who does not show respect to his mother is not a good son,' she repeated to herself. 'I must tell Ms Rose.'

And she did, in her typical quiet, concise manner while serving her the usual cup of Teh-C. This was about three or four months after Ean and Linda had struck up a relationship and a day after

Aunty had discovered it. Rose was once again trying to speak with Ean on the phone. She had spoken about visiting Ean in person but Ethan had dissuaded her, saying that she would not be received respectfully. And she herself felt some trepidation about going to Ean's place. Perhaps it was fear that Ethan was right; perhaps it was ego because Ean had not visited her at all since his return. But she couldn't stop herself from at least calling him up, and she tried every week. But the reception was always the same cold rejection. Ean simply hung up as soon as he heard her voice. Rose chose to ignore Ean's reaction. It was her hope, maybe even belief, that if she kept trying he would respond positively one day, and on that day she would visit him.

One such day, as Rose was making one of her attempts to call Ean, Aunty walked into her room. In addition to Linda's frequent presence in Ean's apartment, she also informed Rose about the comings and goings of two or three men who looked like they were from some foreign country. 'Not *ang-moh*,' she said. 'They look like they are from some other country, maybe from the Middle East.' Aunty had not expected a response, and Rose didn't give her one. Aunty had told Rose without much ado, without stopping to make eye contact, speaking in her usual gruff, low tone as she went about dusting and then clearing the tray. She had always kept Rose's finger on what was going on in the office in this quiet and unobtrusive manner. Even Ean and Ethan had no idea just how powerful the diminutive old lady, who was scarcely seen outside the pantry, was. If Simon had had an inkling, he had never spoken about it.

Rose silently sipped her hot tea as she made up her mind. She couldn't wait any longer. She had to pay her son a visit before he got into a mess again. Linda's connection with Ean disturbed her. She had not had a good feeling right from the moment she had met Linda, and the girl had proven her right. But the information about the strange men from foreign countries alarmed her. She knew her son and his desire for money, and his willingness to embark on any foolhardy idea to get rich quick.

'Who are these men? What is he getting into now? I think I need to speak with him. I don't want him to go to jail again. I will pay him a visit in his apartment,' she said to Ethan. 'I don't think you should, Ma. At least, not alone. I would like to go with you.'

He kept insisting that she avoid the visit, and she appeared to accept what he said. After extracting an assurance that she wouldn't go, Ethan left on a business trip to Australia, and so he was not around to stop her. Because as usual, Rose, for the most part at least, did what Rose had decided to do. And she could not believe that a son of hers would humiliate her. So she had Maniam drive her to Ean's apartment.

The apartment had been a gift from Rose and Peter to the boys when they had graduated and started working for the company. Located in the middle of the city and close to Boat Quay, it was a large three-bedroom apartment—probably, a little too large and expensive for two young men who were rarely home. But they had asked, and she had given, because it assuaged her feelings of guilt about being busy building her business while they were growing up. It was a refurbished Peranakan house, much like Sylvia's. The only difference was that Sylvia used both floors, whereas the boys used the upstairs as their living quarters and leased the downstairs to a business. Since Ethan had moved out, it was only Ean who lived there now. Rose had given many such gifts to her sons, especially the twins, and they had quickly realized that all they had to do was ask and it was given.

As Maniam weaved through the late afternoon traffic, Rose sat watching the people and buildings whizz by. She realized that she had driven past the twins' apartment almost every other day but had never stopped to visit. She had never tried, and they had never invited her. Since she saw them every day at the office and the occasional family get-togethers, no one saw the need. 'Those family meetings hardly ever happen any more, and Ean would make it a point to miss them, particularly when Simon was there,' she mused wistfully. So when she arrived at the building, one of the many that she owned in the city, she was suddenly filled with apprehension. She hadn't called, and she hadn't heeded Ethan's advice.

'What if he is not home?' she asked herself as she walked up the wooden stairs slowly, feeling the strain on her back and her knees. She felt for the spare keys in her purse. Ean, in particular, had been so excited about the gift when she had given it to them that he had, very generously, handed her a set of keys with an almost comical flourish and told her, 'There is no need to call or let us know. It is your place as much as it is ours. Come whenever you please.' They had laughed about it then, but it helped her ignore her faint discomfiture about entering the apartment using the keys, since there was no response when she rang the doorbell. She had to see him, and that was foremost in her mind.

As she stepped into the apartment, she became aware of the stillness in the apartment, which was only disturbed by the sounds of traffic outside. Quite clearly, there was no one home. 'I will wait,' she said to herself stubbornly. 'He has to come back at some point.' She walked slowly through the living room to the huge windows, through which sunlight streamed in and lit up the whole place, spreading a cheerfulness that she could not feel. The apartment was divided into two parts. On the left of the front door was a large bright kitchen and dining area. The appliances and dining table were all top of the line. And on the right sat a large airy living room, tastefully filled with custom-made Italian furniture. A long hallway from the kitchen and dining area led to three large bedrooms. Rose made no attempt to walk down the hallway, preferring to sit gingerly for a minute on the edge of one of the Italian sofas, with the hope of catching her breath and calming her heart, which was beating hard. 'Those stairs . . .' She smiled faintly to herself.

She walked slowly to the refrigerator in the kitchen, her heels sounding sharp on the wood floor and helped herself to some cold water, brushing away a thin film of perspiration on her upper lip as she drank. Placing the glass on the dining table and looking around, the thought that she might have had been a little too indulgent and that she had played an integral role in Ean's ruin crossed her mind. 'But Simon and Ethan turned out fine. I think I was more generous with Simon.' She had given him a penthouse, with huge glass windows everywhere that provided a spectacular view of the entire city, right next to the office in the heart of the city. It was now Ethan's. He was just waiting for the painters to finish before he moved in. A sigh of regret escaped Rose as she glanced about her. She had paid dearly for her sons' affection, or the lack of it.

She turned to look at the door when she heard footsteps coming up the wooden stairs. While relief washed over her when she heard her son's voice, her nervousness heightened. The door opened, and she heard another voice outside, the slightly whiny and unmistakable voice of Linda, and her heart sank. So it was true, and this could only be bad. As Ean stepped in and saw Rose, the smile that was dancing on his face froze and the resentment that he felt showed instantly. He held the door, stopping Linda from entering, and quickly stepped outside. Rose heard whispers before he stepped back inside and shut the door. He ignored her and just went about putting his keys away and getting a drink for himself from the kitchen. Her eyes followed her son, but she remained silent, her heart thumping inside her—and it wasn't just because of her walk up the long flight of stairs. The time had come for her to face the truths that were bound to be thrown at her, truths that were going to stare her in the face for a long time to come.

Ean took a deep drink of water before placing the glass on the dining table with a thud that made Rose faintly flinch. She sat straight-backed on the edge of the sofa waiting expectantly for her son to say something. He was still ignoring his mother, but he could feel the anger surging within him.

'I suppose you didn't think it was necessary to call before you turned up, just as you didn't think it was necessary to visit when I was in prison.'

'I tried calling many times but you never pick up, and you were not accepting any of my invitations to come home,' said Rose, softly placating but mindful that she wasn't answering his last question.

'I would have imagined with your intelligence that would tell you something. I don't wish to see you just as you didn't wish to see me in jail. It's as simple as that. How hard is that for you to understand?' he said without looking at her. The hardness in his voice reminded her of how distant they had become. The child that she had borne seemed to be completely lost.

Since he continued to stand in the kitchen and refused to meet her eyes, she stood up and walked towards him.

'Son, listen. I did not visit you in jail, firstly, because I was ashamed of you . . . and me. I had failed to see what was really happening. Secondly, I was angry, furious with you for dragging all of us, me, Ethan and most of all the business through the mud because of your actions. Everything that I had worked so hard for was sullied because of your greed and impatience. And lastly, my visiting you would have become news. There would have been some reporter who would have discovered it and splashed it all over the news, making matters worse for the company—'

'So it's always the company. The company comes before your children, right?' Ean said, his booming voice exploding through the apartment.

'Well, it certainly seemed to come above everything for you. And you didn't even work very hard for it. So what do you think it would mean for me, who toiled for years to get it to where it is today? Everything was handed to you, including this place,' she said, waving a hand around the place. She had had enough, and her temper was beginning to fray. 'No one handed me anything. I had to claw my way to where I'm today. And do I care about it? You bet! Do I care about it more than I care about you? I'm not going to lie, sometimes, yes. If your actions are unreasonable and threaten the foundation of what I have built, yes I care about it more than I care about you. Are you happy now?' she declared, the anger reverberating in her voice.

He glanced at her when she said this, and the look in his eyes froze her inside and immediately made her regret what she had said.

'Look, son . . .' She reached out a hand like she was trying to touch his arm, but he moved back.

'Don't call me that any more,' he said icily through gritted teeth. 'I'm no longer interested in this farcical relationship that you and I share. I think it's time you left.'

She was silent for a minute before she said, 'I will. But before I leave, I just want to ask you, appeal to you, plead with you . . . whatever you would like to call it, to stop and think about how you can live your life in a better way now. I haven't denied you anything except a position in the company. You are free to do anything you like, and I'm happy to fund it, but please do it honestly now. You have your whole life ahead of you . . .'

Ean turned to look at his mother and calmly said, 'I asked you to leave. If you're going to give me a lecture on how you bought this place, well yes, you did. But you gave it to me, and it is mine. So leave.' And just as he said that, Aunty opened the door and entered the apartment. It was her afternoon to cook and clean. Mother and son had not heard her laboured footsteps as she came up the stairs.

As soon as she entered, she sensed the tension in the room. She glanced at both of them and mumbled in Hokkien that she would return later, but Ean immediately repeated that his mother was leaving and that she could go ahead with her chores. Rose's reddened face was not lost on Aunty, and she had heard Ean telling his mother to leave. She hesitated at the door. But Rose picked up her purse lying on the sofa and made towards the door. Aunty moved aside as Rose passed her but not before resting a hand on her shoulder, as if she needed the support. Just as Rose passed her, Aunty looked up and saw her biting her lower lip and the unshed tears in her eyes. Aunty stood for a few more minutes at the door, uncertain about going in as she heard Rose's footsteps descending slowly. She glanced at Ean, who was now seated where his mother had sat and was staring at his phone, his face still reflecting the hardness that he felt. He ignored the cleaner as she slowly made her way down to the bedrooms. She always started her cleaning there. Her mind was filled with one thought that seemed to come around repeatedly like baggage left on a carousel. 'Very bad son,' she repeated to herself. 'Only a bad son is so rude to his mother, who has given him everything.'

When Rose finally reached the car, she had to cling to the side of it for a minute, breathing heavily. Her ashen face made Maniam, who had seen her in the rear-view mirror, jump out of the car but she weakly waved him back and got into the car. She lay back with her head resting against the back of the cool leather seat throughout the journey, refusing Maniam's entreaties to see a doctor. Warm tears flowed from her closed eyes. She knew Maniam would be anxiously looking at her in the rear-view mirror hoping for some answers, and there was a small part of her that was embarrassed by the spectacle that she was making of herself in front of her staff. But she was past caring. What was there to care about now that everything seemed to be slipping away from her?

Chapter Twenty-One

Ethan and Evelyn had hardly spoken since the day he had insulted her mother, communicating only when necessary and, that too, through his personal assistant. Ethan avoided Evelyn because he was embarrassed. A month had gone by since their conversation. It was becoming increasingly difficult for Ethan to continue working with someone he just couldn't face. He didn't want to talk to his mother about it because she would tell him that it was his mess to clean up. Thankfully though, the opportunity for him to apologize presented itself one stormy evening. It was almost seven in the evening, and he was just about to leave the office when he noticed the lights in Evelyn's cubicle. He hesitated for a few minutes before he walked up and peered inside. Evelyn was still working. He tapped on the glass, and she looked up.

'It's late and everyone has left. I'm just leaving,' he said. She stood up but, as if to avoid eye contact, kept her eyes on the screen of her laptop.

'I'm waiting for the rain to stop or at least let up a little before I leave. It's a bit of a walk to the MRT station,' she said.

He hesitated again before saying, 'I can drop you if you like. It's not a problem. I don't think the rain will stop any time soon.'

'No that won't be necessary. I'll manage,' she said, still avoiding his eyes.

Ethan sighed before he spoke.

'You know, I'm extremely sorry about what I said the other day. I had no right. It was wrong. I cannot honestly say that I welcomed the idea of bringing you into the company. I didn't see the need. But over the years, I've learnt that my mother's judgement is quite spot on, and here too, she's clearly right. You're doing great. My own shortcomings and fears were acting up. I can't say that I've got over those fears completely, but I can promise not to blame you.'

From where she was, he cut a downcast and desolate figure, and she felt sorry and a strange kinship. They were in the same situation, just at opposite ends. She was all alone because she had no one and was trying to belong where she didn't. He, on the other hand, was alone because he didn't want to belong where he was, but he didn't know where else to go.

For the first time in a month, she met his gaze frankly and confidently. 'Look, I'll be honest too. When I came to meet your mother for the first time, I felt like I was owed. I felt I had to claim my right one way or another. I didn't know if I had a right but I sure was going to fight for it. But I wasn't raised that way. You were absolutely right. I'm the daughter of the mistress, and she ensured that I was aware of who I was. If your mother had turned me away, I would have probably just not come back. I honestly didn't have any plan or anything. You could say that I was just trying my luck in my own ridiculous way,' she said with a chuckle. 'I'm not out to take what is yours or your brother's. I just felt that I was a Lee too, and perhaps that counted for something.'

Ethan smiled. He felt a little sheepish. He couldn't find the scheming, conniving daughter of the mistress out to grab whatever she could from the sons of the wife in the young woman who stood in front of him. What he saw was a calm young lady with a lot of pride and self-respect. And she was right. She was a Lee too. What was the harm in her having a share of what belonged to the family? She would not be even remotely depriving him or his brother. He looked back at her and smiled kindly.

'I really would like to give you a ride home. That's the least I can do to show that I'm truly sorry.'

Smiling a tad shyly, she said, 'And I will take the ride to show you that I'm accepting the apology. Can you give me a few minutes to get my things together?'

Unlike his brother, Ean did not think there was enough to give to the daughter of the mistress. In fact, he found the idea of even giving her a job in the company 'ridiculous'! 'The old dragon is losing her mind! She is already getting too old for the job. Now she humiliates all of us by bringing this girl into the company,' he exploded when he heard from Linda. In the first few weeks of her hire, no one knew for sure what Evelyn's connection was to the family. There was much curiosity about the new hire, and why she was immediately given so much responsibility and had so much access to the boss. The staff were surprised that Evelyn attended meetings with Rose frequently, since most new hires in the company only met with their senior managers. The more curious ones, especially the ones closest to Linda, did their best to get the real story from Maryanne but their questions were met with a mere shake of the head and a smile.

Finally, about three months after her hire, when Rose was sure that Evelyn was going to work out and that she was going to stay, she made a brief statement to the staff. 'Evelyn is family, and she will be working closely with both Ethan and me towards a senior management position.' She didn't specify who exactly she was. The staff speculated but Ean knew immediately when Linda mentioned it to him, and his scorn and rage knew no bounds. He had secretly hoped that he would somehow find a way to get back into the fold. But now it was clear that he had been replaced. As much as he maintained a brave and defiant front, he was fearful of carrying on without his family to watch his back. Deep inside, he knew that his mother had done everything she could have possibly done to keep him out of jail. Perhaps, if she had not done what she had, he would have been tossed to the sharks and would have languished in jail for years. And despite everything, she had taken care of him financially. He still lived in the same way as he had when he worked for the company, wining and dining in the best restaurants, wearing the classiest clothes, and driving only the most luxurious cars. He just missed the stamp of approval that working for Lee Constructions had given him.

Ean didn't lack anything material but he was alone, and he wasn't sure he had it in him to walk his journey all by himself. He had even alienated Ethan, who had not called since the day he had picked him up from the airport. His old connections, whether they were friends or business contacts, seemed aloof. A part of the reason was the scandal, which he just couldn't shake off. The other reason, which he himself couldn't see, was his disagreeable personality, apparent even before the scandal. He was known to be brash and aggressive, unlike Ethan. Before the scandal, people put up with him because of his connection to Lee Constructions. The fact was that though Ethan had always been less popular, he was the more likeable between the two, and now that he was at the helm of Lee Constructions and closer to Rose, few had any use for Ean. Those who indulged him with their time for old times' sake wanted to keep it strictly social, not business. They had no interest in the business ideas that he was constantly proposing. He had recently started talking about a bunch of luxury condo hotels, complete with five-star facilities, that he wanted to build. 'Right here in Singapore. I have big guys from all over the world willing to jump in with me with cash!' he exclaimed. 'Owners of these apartments just rent them out to travellers or people who want the home experience when they are here for business or work. Huge bunch of possibilities there and a chance for fantastic returns on the investment,' he would say, his eyes dancing and his hands gesticulating wide sweeping movements as if to show the immenseness of the project and the flood of returns on the investment. But despite his best efforts at persuasion, none of his friends wanted to have anything to do with these projects that appeared to be full of hyperbole and shady to say the least.

They listened and nodded when he spoke and sniggered and gossiped about who the 'big foreigners' could be when he left the table.

'Who would be willing to give so much cash? Next time he's headed to jail for money laundering for sure,' they laughed.

Those who had known Peter were amazed by the resemblance. 'If not for his straight-laced wife, he may have done the same things. Even then, he managed to have a wife and child who would have remained secret if he had not died,' they said, shaking their heads.

'Must be in the blood.' And they were perhaps right. As Peter was fond of saying, Rose was perhaps the lucky charm that had enriched him in more ways than he had lived to tell. Unfortunately, Ean was not as lucky or as likeable as Peter. Despite his yen for being flamboyant and loud about his wealth, and his enthusiasm to get wealthy, Peter had one quality that had set him apart from Ean: he was generally a likeable man. Ean was as easy to dislike as Peter was to like. He hardly had any friends who genuinely cared, so it was easy for people who were looking for opportunities, to step into his life, temporarily.

He had Linda, of course, and it was nice to have her on his arm when he stepped out. People looked at them as they made an attractive pair. But he didn't trust her for one minute. Even when Ethan was going out with her, he had known that she was the kind of woman who would not settle for anything but the best. Ethan was her best bet for Lee Constructions. Now, Ean was glad he had her on his side because he needed someone like her to get back on his feet. But he also knew that if he didn't, if he didn't get back into the company, or come up with something even better, there was no way she was going to stay with him. And Ean didn't nurture any illusions about starting a construction company that was better than Lee Constructions. He had his mother's drive but not enough of it to start something from scratch. He had to do something quickly before the doors of Lee Constructions were forever closed to him. He had to think of something.

'He's suing me for unlawful and unfair removal from the company and the business,' said Rose tossing a letter to Ethan, who sat across the desk from her. Ethan picked up the letter, read it slowly, and then looked up at his mother, whose cool gaze was on him. She shook her head and sighed impatiently when he looked at her. 'Actually, I've no clue as to what I should do,' she said, throwing up her hands in exasperation. 'I don't want to file a civil suit against my own son for mismanagement and misappropriating funds and for abusing his position in the company when he had access to confidential information . . . I don't know, but I'm pretty sure our lawyers can think of a list. I could also disinherit him, take out a full-page ad in the papers for several days saying that he's nothing at all to do with Lee Constructions or the Lee family and that no one should have dealings with him assuming that he did. Yes, I'm pretty sure our lawyers can think of all sorts of things that I can do to destroy the twit. But he's my son. I want to rehabilitate him not ruin him, and I want him to start living his life,' she said, slapping her hand on the table in anger, her face red and flushed. Evelyn sat next to Ethan silently, watching a little uneasily. She felt guilty for a reason that she could not fathom. This was her first experience with a furious Rose. Her eyes darted nervously from mother to son. She wondered if she should excuse herself since this seemed to be an immediate family issue but was too nervous to say anything.

'You tell me, Ethan. You're probably closest to him. What can I do for him? What haven't I already done as a mother to convince him that I'm on his side and that I wish to make amends for the fact that I wasn't there when you two were growing up? I made a mistake. I thought I would build this whole damn thing for you, and yes, that was a mistake. Maybe the fact that I didn't see him when he was in jail was also misguided. Perhaps I was wrong. I don't know!' she cried gesticulating with a wave of her hand in the air. 'But I'm trying. I'm trying and doing my best, but he insists on going down a slippery path that can only end badly for him—' Her voice broke at this point.

'Ma, calm down. We will figure this out,' said Ethan. The harsh afternoon light that streamed through the glass settled on her face. Her immaculately styled hair, expertly done makeup, custom-made navy blue dress, and brilliantly dazzling sapphires nestling in a cluster of diamonds on her ears could do little to distract from the defeat that showed brutally on her face. Ethan's heart went out to her. He was about to say something when the door behind him opened. Rose looked past him at the door, and he turned as well. Both of them frowned at the intrusion but their frowns quickly disappeared when they realized that it was Aunty. No one else, not even Maryanne, would have dared to enter without warning. Rose and her son waited for her to finish, while Evelyn's eyes followed the old woman. Sensing that she had intruded into an unpleasant conversation, Aunty did her best to move as hurriedly as her arthritis would allow her. When she saw the old woman struggle, Rose quickly calmed down and gently told her in Hokkien to take her time and then resumed her conversation with Ethan in English.

'Ma, I will talk to him. I don't know if I will succeed, but I could try. I could try to knock some sense into him,' he said.

Rose shook her head in resignation as she listened. 'No, he's not going to change his mind. And I know what this is about. He has heard about Evelyn's hire. This is his way of fighting that.'

Ethan was silent for a moment before he spoke again. 'Ma, are you absolutely sure you don't want to just take him back into the company? Then all of this will just go away, and we can focus on getting back to work,' he said hesitantly.

His mother frowned at him and said, 'You do realize that everything will go away from you when I'm not around? He did what he did behind my back. How long do you think it will take him to pull the carpet from under your feet when I'm not there? And the next time, he won't hesitate to put you in prison in his place, and I may not be around to save you.'

Ethan didn't say anything because he knew his mother was right.

'I will get our lawyers to deal with this. I hope they can,' Rose said decidedly.

Her job in the office done for the day, Aunty walked to the bus stop. The hot late afternoon was slowing her down more than usual. But she was also preoccupied. *This kind of son is not worth having.* This was the thought that dominated her mind. *Poor Ms Rose has to deal with all this when it is time for her to rest and enjoy her hard work. First, that husband of hers hurt her, and now his son. And she lost Mr Simon, who was such a good son. This is all too much for her.* As she thought about 'Ms Rose's bad son', memories of conversations with her own son years ago haunted her. She still flinched when she was reminded of the harsh language he had used on the last day they had spoken just before he and her daughter-in-law had left for shopping. 'I will put you in a home if you can't adjust here. I cannot afford to support you in your home if you choose to move back there. The rent from that apartment can pay for your stay in the home.' She remembered the acute sadness she had felt that afternoon, thinking about her dead husband, who had never had a harsh word for her throughout their marriage. The rain that had started a little after her son and daughter-in-law left, had poured down in buckets all afternoon and evening that day.

And today, by the time her bus reached the bus stop, which was about a hundred metres away from home, it started to rain. As quickly as her arthritic fingers allowed her, Aunty opened her large black umbrella as she walked. The umbrella was so large that it completely blocked out the tiny woman, and if anyone had been watching from the apartments above, they would have only seen a black umbrella moving slowly like a large insect towards one of the blocks. They would not have seen the determined severity on her face and the pursed lips that made the faded pink line that was her mouth almost disappear. Glancing up at the darkened sky, Aunty was glad that her granddaughter was going to be late, and she could have the house to herself this afternoon as she was working in Ean's apartment in the afternoon tomorrow.

Chapter Twenty-Two

Ethan sipped his coffee slowly and looked out on to the street. The floor of the coffee shop that was on the covered terrace of a mall was splattered with the rain that fell with a steady rhythm not far from where he sat. The afternoon crowd of shoppers and office workers, caught completely by surprise, scurried around for cover while those blessed with foresight and prudence sauntered by with umbrellas of different hues, large and small. The traffic had slowed down, and soon, there was a line of buses, cars and motorcycles crawling along in the heavy and noisy shower.

Ethan watched the scene from where he sat, preoccupied with the constant sadness that dogged him and his mother since his father's death. Before that unfortunate event, their lives had been enviable by most standards. Now he felt like he and his mother were in a fishbowl swimming around while everyone around them watched expectantly to see what else could go wrong with their lives. He longed for the old days when he and Ean had worked together and did many, if not most, things together. Coming together for a coffee in the afternoon was almost a ritual in those days. He missed his twin. Even though they were so different in many ways, they could always share a laugh. Growing up, he would have never imagined that they could move so far away from each other to the point where he was disinclined to even have a conversation with his brother. In the past six months since Ean's return, the two had barely shared a few texts of one or, at the most, two words like, 'All good?', 'Yeah', 'Fine'. These days, he couldn't think of anything to say. And, even if he tried to force himself, he was afraid of where the conversation would go.

The rain was incessant and grew increasingly heavy. Perhaps it was the wrong day to meet his brother. Would he even bother to step out in this weather? But Ean had assured him that he would come. 'I need to show you how stupid you are to believe the old dragon. I will be there because it is just as important for me to see you.' But that was before the rain. Now, it was fifteen minutes past their appointed time. Ethan told himself that if his brother didn't turn up in the next fifteen minutes, he would leave. He didn't want to see him anyway. He was only doing it for his mother's sake. But Rose didn't know that Ethan had arranged to meet Ean. 'Don't waste your time. It's not going to be worth your while,' she had advised when he had told her. But Ethan had a faint hope that his brother had some remnants of familial affection left, for him, at least. He hoped that he could somehow convince him that he was destroying every shred of a chance that he had to get back into the fold. He was going to try and talk his brother out of this whole business of suing their mother and the company.

But when he thought of Ean and Linda, the bile rose in his mouth. He had heard. He had heard from his friends and their mutual friends, who had also mentioned that the two were now living together, flaunting their relationship, and even speaking of marriage. *This is after he has been out with us so many times*, he thought to himself resentfully. He was now over Linda, somewhat. Work kept him busy, and although he didn't get to go out very much, he managed to have a decent social life. He was seeing someone now. It was nothing serious, but he liked this girl. And she was an art teacher without any hidden designs on how she could get ahead in Lee Constructions. He liked that she hadn't even known who he was or how he was related to Rose Lee when they started going out. He liked that she enjoyed art exhibitions as much as he did. Linda had always been bored and would leave after ten minutes, asking him to go on alone. He was beginning to feel happiness again. But it offended him deeply that his brother, who had known that he liked Linda, could now sleep with her. He couldn't help the resentment creeping in when he caught sight of Ean running across the street in the rain towards the coffee shop. Ean smiled cheerfully at the sight of his brother sitting in a corner. Ethan, who was more used to a surly Ean, was pleasantly surprised, although grudgingly so. *Life is treating him better these days*, he mused mockingly. Ean came up and slapped Ethan on the back.

'Hello brother, how are you?' Ean said as he collapsed happily into the chair across the table. His clothes and his expensive loafers looked wet. 'Of all places to have coffee . . . the only parking I could find was two blocks away,' he said with a laugh.

'Didn't have a choice. Can't get too far away from the office at four o'clock in the afternoon,' Ethan shrugged with a half-smile.

Ean laughed in response. 'So the dragon lady's not sparing you, eh? Squeezing every ounce out when she can.'

Ethan frowned but stayed silent. He wasn't going to be goaded into taking a path that he didn't want to this afternoon. He had his own agenda. They ordered their coffees and made conversation about this and that, trivialities mostly. Ean spoke for the most part, and Ethan listened. He spoke about his plans to start a construction business of his own.

'We need something better than what we have now,' Ean said with a smirk. He was careful to leave Linda out when he spoke about what he wanted to do, and Ethan listened cynically, amazed at how he couldn't sense or see any guilt or remorse in his brother. *He doesn't have the decency to say anything to me, knowing what my relationship with her was.* As he spoke, Ean reminded Ethan of their father, loud and flamboyant, full of grandiose plans. He kept talking without regret or humility about what he had done or his having gone to prison. His self-assuredness astounded Ethan. If anything, he sounded like he had achieved great things and was going on to conquer the world. When he felt like he was going to explode with irritation, Ethan decided to speak. The rain had stopped, and the sun had come out brilliantly strong, flooding the island with light.

'Ean, about that letter from the lawyer that you sent Ma,' he began, interrupting Ean in mid-sentence.

Ean laughed. 'Why don't you say it? About the suit that I'm filing, you mean. I'm suing her for wrongful dismissal and also for wrongfully depriving me of my share of the business.' He looked smug and content. 'Finally, the woman is going to get her just dues. I will make sure she pays. Who knows? I might even drive her out of her own business!'

Ethan's eyes narrowed, as an intense distaste for the man in front him welled up in him. There he sat, selfish, mean, and completely self-absorbed, and memories of the years when Ean would set the rules and he was expected to follow now surfaced in a new, harsh light.

It had been Ean's idea to break the rules when they had cheated in college. And Ethan hadn't had much of a say because that's the way it had always been. Ean was physically the stronger of the two, and a secret fear had always niggled his younger twin, but that fear was indistinguishably and irrationally intertwined with a deep-rooted loyalty. Ethan could never tell the difference. It was only in the last few years that he had chosen to differ on many things. But even then, Ethan was always cautious about directly confronting his twin, which was why his heart was racing. But he had to do this for his mother. She did not deserve to have her name and reputation dragged through the mud any more. He was not going to have that at any cost.

'Look, I think you should withdraw the suit. There is no basis for it. You know that. You are just going to drag all of us, including yourself, through unnecessary media attention. This business that you're planning to start will not happen because you would have ruined it before you even started. Lee Constructions is the biggest and the best in the business. Everybody knows that. And if you take them on in a frivolous case like this, you know you're never going to win.' Ethan couldn't believe that he had spoken so much and so forcefully. 'I won't let you.'

If Ean was surprised by his usually malleable twin's steely and harsh tone, he didn't show it. But the fact that he stared silently for a few seconds before responding implied that he was taken aback. He had not expected Ethan, of all people, to display such resolve. The unflinching gaze certainly made him uncomfortable because when he finally spoke, he avoided making any eye contact, preferring instead to be looking into his coffee cup.

'I didn't expect this from you of all people, Ethan. What's gotten into you? Brainwashed thoroughly? The woman always knows how to get people to think like her—'

'The woman happens to be your mother. Have some respect. That would be your first step towards getting your life back in order. Think of other people for a change.'

Ean put his cup down and looked up at his brother with a tight smile. He didn't say anything but shook his head while keeping the smile. And then he said, 'So you have a new staff member who has taken Linda's place, I understand. And that new staff member is that woman's daughter. So what's all this about? Aren't you both ashamed? The whole industry must be talking about you. I'm not going to allow some girl that was born out of my father's affair to take my place in the business. The lawsuit is about safeguarding my interests and yours.' He reached forward and jabbed Ethan on the arm while repeating, 'and yours'. Then he said, 'You better know that. I'm taking care of you as well. If we are not careful, your mother will dish out what's ours to that girl. I cannot allow that.'

Ethan took a long hard look at Ean. 'Who are you to decide by yourself what is allowed and what is not? It's Ma's business, she built it—'

'Ma didn't build the company alone. Baba built it too.'

Ethan merely dismissed what Ean was saying with a wave of his hand and said, 'All the better then. If Baba built it too, then it is okay for his daughter to get a share of it, and the business is big enough for that.' Ethan shook his head, 'And I don't believe for a minute that you have my best interests at heart. The fact that you did what you did and the fact that you are now sleeping with the girl who used to be my girlfriend is proof of that.' The conversation was not quite going the way Ethan had envisioned it. The frosty edge in his tone when he spoke could barely mask his rising anger. He was agitated enough to want to leave before either one of them lost their tempers. Already, their slightly raised voices were attracting glances from other patrons. 'I came to tell you to withdraw the suit that you filed against Ma. You're not going to win this. You will do better if you just drop it and wait for Ma to get over the hurt. There might be a better chance for you to come back into the business. Right now, you're destroying any shred of opportunity that you might have.'

Ean shook his head defiantly and said, 'I'm not backing down. I don't want that girl working for the company, and I cannot accept her getting any share of what is ours. I will fight your mother because she cannot always have her way. She abandoned me, and now she is taking away what's mine.' Then, with a glint in his eyes, he said, 'By the way, Linda was never really right for you. The whole world could see that.' He had meant to hurt and he had succeeded. Ethan took a long sip of his coffee and put the cup down a little harder than he had intended to, gazing at his brother almost with pity. Smiling cynically, he stood up abruptly, indicating that the meeting was over for him. He was Rose Lee's son, and she was on his side, and she would go to any extent to protect him. There was no longer any reason for him to fear this man ranting in front of him.

'I will not stand by and watch you destroy Ma. This whole business is killing her. It started with you going to jail, and just when she is recovering from that, you throw this at her. I will

ensure that our lawyers do everything they can to have your case
thrown out of court, and maybe I will even make it such that you
don't get a penny. You don't deserve it. You don't deserve anything
from Ma,' he said resolutely. 'And, by the way, it became clear to
me that Linda was with me because I'm Rose Lee's son,' he said,
and then added drily, 'And that is the reason she is with you. I'm
sure you're smart enough to know that. But I wonder if she will
stick around if you end up being Rose Lee's son just in name, with
nothing to show for it.'

He started to walk away, but Ean grabbed his arm.

'Hey, we're not done here.'

Ethan pulled his arm away and continued to walk. Ean stood
up and moved towards his brother and attempted to grab his
shoulder, attracting the attention of the other patrons. And then
the strangest thing happened.

The police classified it as an accident.

Ean's shoes were wet, and that could have caused him to slip.
What the eyewitnesses saw was that he moved quickly towards
Ethan, who was walking away, and tried to grab his shoulder, and
it looked like he slipped and fell. They also saw him trying to grab
the table closest to him for support as he fell, but the table moved,
and he fell face down, hitting his head on the stone floor. Patrons
who had sat close to where it happened had heard the loud thud
of his head as it the floor. They had seen a horrified Ethan turn
around and call out, 'Ean!' They had seen Ethan turn his brother's
body over, and they had seen a nasty bruise on the fallen man's
head. They had seen that he was dead. It was a completely freak
accident that had left everyone in that coffee shop on that wet
afternoon stunned and with the memory of it etched in their
minds for years to come.

Horrified would be a mild word to describe what Ethan had
felt when he saw his brother lying on the floor. The meeting that
he had hoped would bring some reconciliation, or something good,
had gone terribly wrong. The minute he turned his brother over,

he knew. Ean was completely lifeless. The afternoon then became a confused blur of paramedics, police and crowds of people. By the time the body was removed, journalists had gotten wind of the accident, and it was news for the evening. *Rose Lee's prodigal son dead due to a freak accident.* There were pictures of Ean, Ethan, and Rose, and Ean's imprisonment and the reason for it was big news, all over again. It was, in essence, the worst day of Ethan's life.

Close to midnight that day, a few hours after his ordeal with paramedics, the police and the press, Ethan waited at the airport for his mother, who had gone to Sydney with Evelyn for a meeting. They had taken the first flight they could get as soon as they had heard. Ethan was aghast at the sight of his mother, who looked completely frazzled. A very anxious Evelyn was close behind her with her hand on her elbow. Rose's eyes sought him out and she hurried towards him. She could barely speak and looked like she had been crying. Ethan couldn't help thinking fleetingly that his mother had done more than her fair share of crying in the last few years, like she was making up for all those years when she hadn't. Ethan stretched out a hand towards his mother, and she grabbed it and held it tightly as she frantically searched his face for answers.

'What happened? Why were you seeing him? How could this happen?' she barely whispered. Ethan's pain was etched on his face. Evelyn now stood at a respectful distance.

'Let's go home first before we speak,' said Ethan gently.

Despite her fatigue, Rose was determined. 'I want to see my son first,' she said.

'Ma, he's uh . . . at the morgue, awaiting . . . um . . . autopsy,' said Ethan slowly. And as he feared, his statement brought on fresh tears. Rose covered her white and drawn face with her hands, shaking her head.

'How could this happen?' she whispered repeatedly. Ethan gently placed a hand on her shoulder, as if urging her to start walking toward the parking lot. As he walked with his mother, Evelyn following, the exhaustion from the day overwhelmed him, and he ran a hand over his eyes, which were now burning.

Chapter Twenty-Three

A head injury caused by an accidental fall was stated as the cause of death in the autopsy report. It was a rainy day, and eyewitnesses had seen Ean slip and hit his head. They had even heard it. What they could not have seen was that when Ean jumped up to run after his brother and grab him, his heart was beating so fast that he felt like it was going to explode. He couldn't breathe, and he felt like he was dying. Even Ethan could not see the look of utter perplexity in his brother's eyes as he fell, hitting his head hard against the table that he had tried to grab and then the stone floor. No one doubted that it was the fall that had caused his death. Maybe it was what caused his death . . . or maybe not.

Maybe it was Aunty's *Zhi Fu Zi*, or Aconite, which she used during the rainy season in particular because the moisture made her arthritis worse. She knew all about it because it was she who had measured and pounded the herbs and mushrooms and everything else that her father had prescribed for his traditional Chinese medicine practice. He had taught her what each herb was used for, and he had taught her well and taken pride in her knowledge and skill. She would have been good at the business, but it was her brother who had inherited it. That was just the way it was, since he was the son. But sadly, he had ruined it, and the respectable business that her father had built over forty years had been destroyed and finally closed. But her father had left her with the legacy that was still valuable—the in-depth knowledge of herbs and what they could do. Aunty knew exactly how much or how little she needed to be just right for her purpose, and she held on to the knowledge till she went to her grave, a couple of years after Ean died, peacefully in her sleep.

She certainly knew how to use those herbs. For example, she knew that while *Zhi Fu Zhi* was a remedy for her pains and numbness, it could also cause a heart attack, if used incorrectly. 'You need to be very careful with that,' her father used to say. 'If you don't prepare it well, or if you take too much, it can be poisonous and may even be fatal.' But Aunty was skilful and she knew how to use it, even if it was not exactly for her pains. Ms Rose was a good woman. She didn't deserve such a bad son, who gave her a bad name and so much sadness. Aunty carried a small amount of aconite in her bag every day anyway, just in case she had pains during the day. And she carried it with her to Ean's apartment. Just a little bit every day in the water was enough. 'No one will find out. And if they find out, Ms Rose will take care of my granddaughter. I don't have to worry,' she told herself resolutely, as she added a little bit more to the water on that rainy day. Ean always drank a lot of water since he was into fitness and health. And no one found out the truth anyway. It could have been the fall, or it could have been the herb.

But the one truth that stared Ethan and Rose in the face was that a calm had settled uneasily but surely in their lives after Ean's death. When he had been around, every day had the potential to be explosive in one way or the other. Either he was belligerent towards his brothers, or he was doubting his mother and her intentions, or he was thinking about how best he could get the bigger portion of the business for himself. 'What next from Ean?' was what it had come down to, especially after his release from prison. Dealing with the damage that he had caused had consumed the life and spirit of both Rose and Ethan, and given Rose in particular a continuous stream of sleepless nights. Her worry was mainly about what would become of him if he continued the way he was.

And now, all of a sudden, there was a stillness. It was like the universe had had enough and had removed the canker that was Ean.

Nevertheless, it shattered Rose, and no one, not even Scott, with whom she lived for the rest of her life after her retirement, could tell if she ever got over it. 'How could it happen?' was what Rose repeated first to Ethan and Scott for several months and then just to herself in her pensive moments. Her sorrow was more intense because she had also lost a son that she had never really got to know. Even though her relationship with Ean was almost completely demolished after his imprisonment, she had nurtured a hope that all would be well eventually, that they would be a family once again. 'Wishful thinking but maybe . . .' she would chuckle to Scott before Ean's death. Although somewhere in her heart she knew that she and Ean would never be completely at ease with each other, she kept the hope alive. But now he had died hating her. 'And, that's the end of that,' she said wryly.

'And, what did he get? What did I get?' she scoffed. 'I thought I was building the business, protecting it, fighting tooth and nail with one son so that the other one could get his share, and now this.' These days, mother and daughter always enjoyed a late-night Teh-C on the balcony of Rose's penthouse. Most of the time, Rose talked and Ming listened. But when Ming spoke, Rose learnt a little bit more about the family she never knew that she had and the stories that Sylvia never spoke about because she had been afraid that the truth about Rose's birth would come out in a careless moment.

Rose now had time to listen to the stories and mull over them because while Evelyn still had a very long way to go, she was much like Rose as a young woman, ambitious and hardworking. Unlike Ethan, she loved the business and enjoyed the chase for a deal. Although she worked under him, she very quickly proved that she could work independently without much supervision, especially because for a year or two after her retirement, Rose continued to work with Evelyn. It took a while for Ethan to become truly cordial with her but they learnt to accept each other, which was integral to Rose's peace of mind. In fact, they made a very good team because she made up for what he lacked, and that was drive and skill at negotiating, and he did what he was most comfortable doing, working in the office on routine work.

Most of all, Rose was at peace because the business thrived as usual, largely because the wheels had been well-oiled by her, and now they were in good hands too. It wasn't as if the odd family of three—mother, son, and daughter of husband's mistress—became a happy family celebrating special days together, with a still dour-faced but older Ming looking on with a contentment that did not show on her face. There was still a sadness that came from a sense of loss that hung over mother and son, but the peace that reigned eventually allowed happiness and good cheer to blossom.

Rose and Scott finally had a stable relationship that they enjoyed languorously. He either stayed with her in Singapore, or she stayed with him in Indonesia, where he maintained a home despite his retirement. They travelled together to the US during Christmas to be with his daughters. Ethan found his bliss in his art-teacher lady friend, who, like him, enjoyed quiet evenings painting or listening to classical music. She was so good for him that when he ran into Linda at a charity event, he was genuinely happy for her since she had married the son of a timber tycoon and was settled in Sabah, East Malaysia. She gushed and laughed, throwing her head back like she was posing for random snaps that appear in fashionable magazines while he was, as always, reticent and slightly self-conscious.

Evelyn was genuinely happy with this family that had strangely been her father's legacy to her. There were no pretences. She didn't love Rose like a mother or Ethan like a brother. And, they, in turn, didn't go out of their way to treat her like family. But in them, she had found good solid friends, who respected her ambition and drive and who invited her to their home for special occasions. They did not see her as Peter's mistress's daughter any more and that was more than enough for her to look to Rose as her inspiration and work towards building a bigger and better Lee Constructions.

Epilogue

A fashionable and well-dressed woman in her late sixties walked slowly to keep pace with a grim-faced older woman, who walked with the help of a cane, and together they carefully made their way to the Kuan Yin Temple on Waterloo Street. The two women made it a point to come whenever they could. The street was crowded with shoppers bustling about busily as the Lunar New Year was approaching. The large urn outside the temple was almost full with joss sticks. The smoke rings from these joss sticks curled up slowly, like they were carefully carrying the fervent hopes and wishes of the worshippers up to the heavens.

As the two women walked into the temple, the younger woman looked up at the benevolent goddess with reverence and devotion, her hands clutching her joss sticks. As she held her joss sticks up to the goddess in prayer, a bangle fashioned like a dragon with a jade ball in its mouth caught the sunlight and glinted. The bangle didn't seem to match the rest of her appearance, which was stylishly understated. Like her mother, who used to make this weekly pilgrimage to the same temple, the woman ensured that she always wore the bangle when she was in the presence of the benevolent goddess. But unlike her mother, whose fingers were almost all adorned with rings of gold and precious stones, this woman only wore the bangle and a pair of earrings.

The woman prayed fervently, as she habitually did, for the souls of her dead mother and her two dead sons, with her unsmiling companion by her side. But today, she had a special prayer. More than a prayer, it was an expression of gratitude. She was thankful for a young woman who had come into her life, first as an embarrassment and then as a necessity, but who was now a blessing, much like a daughter, a daughter she was so proud of that just the thought of her made her glow as she prayed. She was so happy that this young woman was going to be honoured this evening with a national achievement award for her accomplishments in business and her contributions to national charities. These were awards that the woman in prayer had herself achieved several times in the past. But the pride she felt now was greater than anything she had ever felt. This young lady was her protégé; she had moulded her. This young lady was her biggest achievement.

Once done with her prayers, she waited her turn for the *chim* bucket. The line was long because of the festive season, and everyone at the temple wanted to know what the New Year would bring for them. The woman was no different. She wanted to ensure that her son and her protégé lived long and prosperous lives. The benevolent goddess that she knew as Gun Yam, looked down at the woman with the gentle smile that was a constant on her lips. It seemed like she knew this woman from the time when another well-dressed woman would come faithfully every week to pray for the well-being of her Rose.

Acknowledgements

Chan Hsiao-yun for being a beta reader and her invaluable inputs on Cantonese culture, food and language

Catherine Cook for being a beta reader and her untiring help in editing

Dr Anitha Devi Pillai for her support and encouragement